FLIGHT OF DR,

WRATH OF THE KING

To Andy
The dragon slayer!
X

The crimson dragon

present day

The dragon raised his huge crimson head and turned slowly to regard the newcomers. His giant golden eyes shone in the relative darkness of the surrounding cave and his vision drifted in and out of focus as two humanoid creatures moved from the shadows to stand before him. He felt as though he recognised them, and his curiosity piqued.

He shifted his weight slightly and shrugged his left wing in frustration. A sudden jolt of pain shot up his side, causing him to grunt audibly. The growl echoed around the cave and the smaller of the two figures stepped back cautiously in response.

The dragon was heavily wounded and he reeked of burnt flesh. His scales, once magnificent, were now marred with deep fissures, which marked his once impenetrable hide. He was covered in dried blood, some of which was his own and some of his enemies. Scorch marks littered his entire body, like a fiery canvas of battle scars. The dragon was mainly a deep crimson colour with darker ridges that ran along his back, adorned with armoured spikes that continued to the tip of his tail, itself bristling with large, deadly barbs.

The dragon watched the newcomers with curiosity as they edged into the cave before him, his immense form casting an imposing presence within the cave's depths and his breathing laboured.

"Why did you save us?" The tallest of the two humanoids inquired as she moved from the shadows into a shaft of light. Her voice was soft and ethereal, a common trait of the Elves. Now that the dragon could clearly see the woman's features, he realised that she was indeed an Elf, perhaps from the Shattered Isles, an Elven stronghold located far to the east.

She appeared youthful, though Elves were known to have extremely long lifespans, and her shoulder length auburn hair was tied back behind her head making her long Elven ears stand out a little more than usual. She wore a mix of leather armour and Elven-crafted vine hide, and had a short sword strapped to her hip and a fine crafted bow upon her back. The Elf held herself well, clearly an able-bodied fighter but she also had a slight smell of the arcane about her, so the dragon guessed she had been trained in some kind of spellcraft, which was made more evident with the smell of herbs and essences that emanated from her backpack and hip pouch, both of which were adorned with runic symbols.

The second figure moved close to the Elf's side, and as the figure caught the light, the dragon's eyes widened. Standing next to her was a child. He had seen her before. The week before, to be exact, in the midst of a flaming village. The little girl eyed the dragon cautiously and hugged a small, tattered blanket closely to her chest. She was human, perhaps five years old, maybe a little more, and her black hair was matted to her head, simple ragged clothes hung from her skinny frame.

The memories of the day the dragon first set eyes on these two humanoids flashed back into his mind's eye.

The dragon had first sensed the fires from some distance away, the mixed taint of smoke and death struck his nostrils. It was a smell he knew all too well and he understood what a grim task he would face upon his arrival.

The screams pained him and his senses tingled as he landed at the village's outskirts, where a dozen or so human bodies littered the ground. They were twisted, burnt and ripped to shreds. He was all too aware of what he would face on that day, as the smell of charred bodies was strong.

The smoke was thick but he could sense the other dragons were here, their jeers and laughter could be heard close by as they went about their terrible work. It would not be long before he would be forced to face them.

Yet, amid the flames and the chaos, a faint whimper pierced through the cacophony, just enough for the dragon to investigate further, and it was there that he first set his eyes upon the small child who now stood before him in the cave.

The dragon had found the small child knelt over her dying mother and it was her cries that he had heard. Something in the mother's desperate gaze as she faced death, touched the dragon's heart. Without hesitation, he scooped the child into his massive claws, his intention to get her to safety, but just as he was about to launch himself to the skies a sharp pain seared into his long neck.

An elven arrow, sharpened by the steel of Lak' Lor had struck him and a second later another deflected off his scales.

He hugged the child close to his chest as he spotted his attacker, an Elven female. The very same as now stood before him within the cave. She leapt from a nearby blazing rooftop and landed before him, her bow drawn and ready to strike again. However the elf hesitated for just a brief moment, confusion etched across her face as she observed the dragon protecting the human child, and her eyes widened in surprise.

That brief pause between the dragon and the elf was just enough time for another large dragon to enter the fray. It was a breed known as a Lava Tooth, its mouth lined by searing hot teeth and lava-like saliva that dripped to the ground, scorching the earth and creating their own small fires. The beast snaked its way through the village street before glaring at the Elf with ravenous intent.

Almost immediately, the crimson dragon, still clutching the child to his chest, could sense the build up of inner fire within this newcomer as it prepared to breathe fire towards the Elf. He had no time to consider his move and blasted out a flame of his own into the side of the Lava Tooth before he swiftly passed the human child to the Elf.

"You must leave, NOW!" He bellowed, before turning his attention back to the shocked Lava Tooth. It was a look that swiftly became one of fury.

The two dragons were evenly matched in terms of size, but the Lava Tooths were known for their ferocious, and unrelenting fighting style.

"The traitor! He's here!" The Lava Tooth roared furiously, attempting to get the attention of his companions. It was ready to breath an attack at the dragon but instead lunged forward swiftly in an attempt to gain the advantage with its terrifyingly powerful bite. The move caught the dragon by surprise and all he could do was turn his neck from the attack in order to escape with his life. As he did so, searing hot lava brimmed teeth gripped him in his side and he yelled out in agony releasing a jet of flame into the sky.

The dragon rolled away and whipped his powerful tail into the Lava Tooth's side. As he did so, his spikes raked across the aggressor's scaled hide and it attempted to retaliate with its fire, but the dragon was already airborne, beating his powerful wings and blasting down hellfire from above.

Just as he gained the upper hand however, other dragons, who were now alerted to the new threat, had moved to aid the Lava Tooth. A jet of flame struck the dragon in his large side as two more Lava Tooths approached and he was quickly embroiled in an fierce aerial battle.

But the crimson dragon was outnumbered, and burning teeth and claws soon rained down relentlessly as he roared in pain with each and every blow.

That was the last that he recalled of that night. The next he was awake in this cave. The dragon was heavily wounded, but at least he was alive.

He stared blankly at the Elf before him now, his vision blurry from time to time and he struggled to stay conscious. Dragons had enhanced healing abilities that allowed them to regain their fight soon after battle, but it was an ability that came at a cost. Near total shutdown. A healing hibernation of sorts, placing their huge bodies into a magically infused recuperation.

The Elf sighed, seemingly deciding that she wouldn't hear from the dragon, and so she turned to leave the cave along with the young human child.

"I am not alone," the dragon managed to utter before she departed. The Elf turned immediately to regard him once again, a look of interest came across her.

"There are others, much like me," the Dragon continued. "They do not wish you harm."

The Elf paused before letting a slight smile cross her lips and she nodded in response. "We are grateful, this child and I, for your sacrifice in aiding us," she said. "Now rest, friend dragon, and heal."

With that the elf turned and left the cave, followed closely by the small human child who briefly glanced back to regard the dragon as she left.

He lowered his head to the floor and huffed, sending a cloud of dirt across the cave, and he closed his huge golden eyes. In just moments, he was back within a regenerative state. The huge wounds he had endured in his battle against the Lava Tooth riddled his body; scales were split and smeared in blood and black ash covered the entirety of his back. It would take just a few days of this regenerative state and most of the wounds would be gone.

The dragon's mind raced as he drifted in and out of consciousness and visions flashed before him. His mind remained turbulent, haunted by visions that eluded his understanding, and their timings were muddled and misaligned.

Another memory flooded his mind - an old man with a cold, heartless aura, who was dressed in long darkened robes. He oozed the smell of power. He approached and raised an ornate wand imbued with a purple gem that sparkled as he weaved a dark and arcane magic with impressive skills.

The dragon recoiled and shifted. His vision blurred and was replaced with a dark cell complete with huge steel gates and menacing-spiked walls along them. He looked around and noted that there were other creatures confined here. Some of which were in agony, their mouths gaping open and a smell of acrid smoke filled the room.

Several of the creatures were deformed, with limbs that were insufficient or boneless legs that were nothing more than loose muscle.

The dragon was small, perhaps just a hatchling that was fresh to the world and unable to comprehend the dangers that surrounded it.

A tall man, full of muscle and armed with a long and deadly looking spear, entered the cell and kicked several of the creatures aside, until he approached the dragon and spoke in an alien tongue. The dragon tried to pull away but was too small and weak and was dragged across the hard stone floor, out of the cell.

His mind raced once more, drifting out of focus until all he could see was darkness; a voice spoke to him. It was familiar, and filled him with anger. He willed to lash out and strike at the source.

"Let me set you free" it said over and over until the dragon roared in desperation. No sound came out, just a low and almost indistinguishable groan.

Then, there was nothing but flames that burst forth across his vision with such velocity. He tried to control it - he knew he was responsible but he couldn't stop. He heard the screams echoing across a large room until finally he fell exhausted to the floor.

The old man in the darkened robes appeared once again before him and smiled, but there was no warmth there, only ambition.

"We shall call that a success," he said and then he too was gone.

The dragon drifted onwards within his troubled mind. His regenerative state would take longer if he was unable to maintain it over a long period but the invasive visions continued to haunt him.

Maybe if he could just understand their meaning, he could piece together his past and understand how he arrived at that burning village to confront his fellow dragons.

Perhaps then he could return home, wherever that may be.

The Eastern Realms

Jarmunpek - present day

Thousands of years ago, the Eastern Realms were nothing but a brutal wasteland led by powerful barons of war. As the soldiers fell and the citadels burned the barons unwittingly weakened their clans, drained their resources and reduced their armies in a never ending cycle of war and destruction.

When the dragons rebelled seven hundred and fifty nine years ago, it was against the Allied Realms. This period was known as The Purge. Led by the mighty Voldestus Goldentail, a golden dragon with immeasurable power, they rose up to claim their freedom from the Bri-Tisa Warlocks who had created them and kept them captive. The Eastern Realms had little left to answer the dragons' wrath, and as a result, a land full of pride at their battle prowess fell swiftly against the might of Voldestus and the capital city of Jarmunpek came under dragon rule.

The human clans that survived the initial purge were unable to get past their differences. With centuries of backstabbing and political conflict to overcome, the result was almost pre-determined. They became nothing more than slaves and an occasional food source to the dragons that resided in the east.

But the dragons were not in harmony and Voldestus wanted complete rule over the horde and to utterly destroy the Allied Realms. This was not something that all of the new rulers could accept and many of Voldestus' supporters were removed from the realm one way or another.

There was a short, but unsustainable conflict between the two bands of dragons, and eventually a fractured peace broke out.

The eastern dragons reformed as an empire. Those who sought a separate existence away from the path of vengeance desired in the west, gathered under the protection and guidance of two elder dragons; Graxilius the warrior and Meduz-Larr the wise, and have remained this way for several hundred years.

A treaty of sorts was agreed by exchange of talon some years later, but the balance of power in the mighty east has been treacherous and some fear a war could be looming once again.

The Emperor and Empress laid claim to a large, heavily damaged palace within what remained of Jarmunpek. The Palace of the Five was once a resplendent beauty, and powerhouse of the Eastern Realms, but now it was nothing but a shattered ruin, barely hanging on by a thread. Its halls were thankfully large enough for a multitude of dragons to enter without issue and the surrounding lands were rich with vegetation and wildlife, providing ample food and resources.

The two rulers of the east sat atop two ornate golden thrones which had once belonged to the warlords Karlista and Boldarian of the Innerlowa clan. Graxilius and Meduz-Larr were relatively small for elder dragons, standing at around fifteen feet tall, with no wings. As they stood upright on their hind legs, they were described as being dragon-kin, however, both Graxilius and Meduz-Larr were powerful beings and not to be underestimated.

Emperor Graxilius watched through blazing blue eyes as a court scribe announced the arrival of a messenger. "Show them in," he said, his voice resonating around the palace as other dragons from amongst the empire's high court watched with interest.

The messenger was from a small, light green breed known as Grassrunners; swift dragons who could easily evade combat, thanks to their ability to fly higher than their larger cousins. It had a gnarled face that had seen better days and it grovelled before the Empress and Emperor to deliver its missive.

Graxilius leant forward on his throne. He was an impressive sight to behold with scales that resembled f brightly coloured gems and a large golden horn that sat proudly atop his brow. He was clothed in a large, delicately crafted purple cloak, and adorned with jewellery that included several large rings decorating his equally large claws.

Graxilius could, in one sense, be described as flamboyant, but he was also a keen and able warrior, with many victories behind him during his years as a servant to the Bri-Tisa Warlocks over seven hundred years ago, and during the brief war of dragons.

"Speak," he said calmly, as the Empress remained silent. She watched intently, her intelligent eyes boring deep into the very soul of the messenger.

The messenger raised its head and regarded the rulers who sat above him.

"King Voldestus Goldentail has repeated his request for you to send aid in the hunt for the Elf vermin and has made it known to many in his court of your refusal to comply," it said, garnering an immediate response from Empress Meduz-Larr.
"We made our position perfectly clear to your King!" Empress Meduz-Larr hissed as she stood from her own throne taking a step forward, her eyes burning with fused mana.

The Empress was an impressive dragon-kin to behold. She too was covered in ornate crystalline scales that shimmered a variety of colours, depending upon the light that struck them and the horns that lined the top of her head were almost crown-like in appearance.

Meduz-Larr was the first of the dragons to harness the ability of controlling mana, before the purge began, and had kept it a secret ever since. If her Warlock creators had known of such a powerful development, she would have been destroyed and her body discarded like a failed experiment.

The Bri-Tisa Warlocks, under the leadership of Grand Master Karl-Asvarian, spent years perfecting a dark sorcery that allowed them to take a drakling egg and fuse it with the arcane. Through this dark sorcery, the Darklings, a small and timid species of large lizards from the peaks of Mount Voltas, were transformed into a variation of powerful and often terrifying creatures the world would come to know as dragons.

The Grassrunner messenger paused thoughtfully before responding, it had clearly been given specific instructions and cautiously muttered "The Eastern Realms are sworn into an alliance with the King; it is unwise to ignore his request."

The messenger cowered as Meduz-Larr approached it, her eyes burning brightly with the power of her mana generation. The room fell silent as they awaited her response with baited breath. She glared for a moment longer, the mana still blazing clearly in her eyes and alighting her face with blue sparks of powerful magical energy which danced around her.

She was known to be more fiery than her husband and perhaps more of a match in battle. The dragons who were present in the court stood quietly as they watched the scene unfold before them.

The breeds present within the halls were a variation of sizes and colours, from the poisonous Blackfangs to Longtail Thunderclaws, but one thing was certain. All were fiercely loyal to the Emperor and Empress, having chosen their side many years ago, and would die in battle to defend them.

Meduz-Larr finally broke the silence. "We are indeed sworn into an alliance. However, the Elven peoples pose no further threat to us at this time. Nor do we wish to put our own sovereignty at risk by sending our armies to a foreign land to hunt for them."
"I assume that when Voldestus asks us to search for the Elves, he is referring to the rumours of Thalindor, the last Elven city?" Meduz-Larr added.
The messenger nodded. "You are correct. The king believes the lost city is somewhere within The Great Glade."

Graxilius laughed at this, as did many within the hall, for he, like many others, had heard the reports about the ancient and dense forest known to the dragons as The Great Glade. The glade was a powerful place indeed, and it would come alive to attack any dragons that even attempted to set foot there. It was a death sentence to approach it.

Meduz-Larr returned to her throne as she released the mana from her control. "You may inform Voldestus that we shall send a small unit of our hunters. They will not breach the glade but they shall approach. They will find your Elves and from there, I am sure your forces would be able to deal with any uprising."

The messenger was thankful for his life. He bowed his head low and then backed away from the throne before turning to leave, for a long journey to report his findings lay ahead.

Emperor Graxilius waited a moment, watching the Grassrunner retreat, before he turned to his wife and as their gaze locked his voice entered her head, a communication that the two dragons shared that allowed for a private conversation away from prying ears. "We must be cautious my dear; perhaps Voldestus is aware of our secret."

The Empress simply nodded, his concerns were certainly shared.

The seer's gate

Southern Marshlands - present day

Galen stood silently as the dragon-kin beside him continued their hushed discussion. He was nothing more than an elderly man, a human librarian, hailing from the fabled city of Feraxia, yet incredibly he had so far managed to pass himself off as a powerful wizard from the old realms to his captors.

Years after the purge, a dragon warband attacked Feraxia. There was a fierce siege that lasted for more than a month, with many casualties reported from the dragons. The city's defences were famed across the wider kingdom and they initially held out against the relentless onslaught from Voldestus' hordes.

Feraxia was protected by a huge defensive wall that towered over the inhabitants within the city and was more than thirty metres thick, but that wasn't the only protection.

Within the walls themselves and all along the battlements, gigantic golden statues stood, each depicting famous warriors from Feraxia's rich and ancient history. These imposing statues watched over the city, enchanted by powerful and ancient magics, and when the dragons began their siege of Feraxia, this ancient magic awoke the sleeping giants.

These mighty warriors killed many dragons during the ensuing conflict and caused real confusion amongst the dragon ranks.

However, even the city's great walls, its many defenders and the mighty statues were unable to hold out against the dragons once they were joined in battle by a fierce elder dragon named Lord Dragaar. He flattened the northern wall making way for thousands of dragon-kin to make their way into the city, slaying every living thing they encountered within.

During the resulting panic, Galen attempted to escape with a small group of citizens, but he became separated from the rest of the group. As he stumbled through the dark, he found himself within one of the city's many museums, its dusty tomes and blessed artefacts called to him from the shadows, and there, within the darkness, something incredible happened.

It was the blue light that attracted Galen first, but also a feeling that something was calling out to him from beyond. His curiosity piqued, and he investigated further. Within the room, on a pedestal surrounded by glass, was a crooked wooden staff, and at its tip, a curious blue gem that was the cause for the room's illumination.

Galen approached the staff cautiously, he pulled open the glass case, reached in, and retrieved the staff.

It was not long after that day that Galen was captured, but he retained the staff and noticed something surprising, for the dragons still had an overriding fear of human magic users following their creation at the hands of the Bri-Tisa Warlocks many hundreds of years ago. Although Galen was not magical in any way, the staff he carried was, and the dragons mistakenly took him to be a powerful wizard.

Galen had used his deep knowledge of history and a vast amount of misdirection to lie his way to survival, advising the dragons in many of their endeavours. He had, over time, become trusted and almost unquestionable in an incredible display of human guile and misdirection. If he stumbled, if they ever discovered he was completely lacking in any magical power, then he would surely be a dead man, but that day hadn't arrived and Galen happily went about his role, fully aware that each day may well be his last.

It had become known to the dragons that deep within the southern marshlands, a mysterious and dangerous portal of powerful energy hung suspended just a few metres in the air. King Voldestus ordered a team of researchers to the site, consisting of a number of smaller dragon-kin known as 'Wise Ones' and some of their human captives. Galen had been fortunate to be a part of this expedition.

Galen had spent the journey recalling all that he had learnt about portals and gateways over his years as a scholar, hopeful that he could use this knowledge to get through the ordeal in one piece. However, nothing could prepare him for what he witnessed when the group finally arrived at their destination.

Before him, suspended just a few metres in the air, was a huge circle of distorting light, that appeared to be shifting between dark red to pure black and then an assortment of vivid colours. Tendrils of mana rotated slowly around the edge of the circle, occasionally shooting out a few feet and burning anything that they touched. The circle hummed, hissed and crackled. It was a truly immense sight to behold as it lit up the surrounding marshland.

This anomaly was known to the dragons as the void. A mysterious portal that consumed any who entered it and occasionally gave birth to a wide array of mysterious creatures, who either died from suffocation shortly after appearing or were captured and taken for study by the Wise Ones.

Their assignment was to learn more about the void. Its purpose, if it had one, and how it came to be here. Perhaps it could be utilised in some way, to aid in the dragon's plans against the allied realms.

Galen raised an eyebrow as the Wise Ones approached. Despite them being small for dragons, they stood at least seven feet high, walked on their hind legs and were one of the wingless breeds. The Wise Ones dwarfed the old librarian as they approached. He tapped his staff on the ground once and they stopped, nervously glancing at each other, and eyed the old man with suspicion until one of them eventually spoke.

Galen knew this wise one as Karin, slightly shorter than the rest and as far as he could tell, a female of the species. She was mostly dark grey in colour, with startling green eyes that shone brightly under the darkness of the marshlands.

"Your kind created this void?" Karin asked, her voice was deep and her eyes searched Galen's for answers.

Galen gripped the ancient staff tightly. It was indeed a magical item, though he knew not how to wield it. He could feel it vibrate in his hand - sometimes a weak pulse and at others far greater, to the point that he sometimes struggled to hold it. The staff had in fact once belonged to a powerful and kind wizard named Polus Vindwaar, an honest man who used his powers to heal those that needed care while living a modest life. Upon the wizard's death, the staff was passed to the museum, where it had stayed until the day that Galen retrieved it.

Galen thought carefully about how to respond to the dragon's question. It was imperative that he keep his cover, so this would perhaps be his greatest challenge yet.

"I take it you refer to the great void?" he asked. "I have heard amongst the whispers that it is a gateway. No is the answer to your question. It was not created by humans, nor by elves, however, it is of significant danger."

Galen mustered his knowledgeable tone as best he could. A hard thing when lying through your teeth, but a skill he had fine tuned over the last few months. His heart was pounding and he sincerely hoped that the dragons did not notice.

"Then who?" Karin asked.
"Whom," Galen corrected. The dragons around him did not look amused. He cleared his throat awkwardly before continuing "The answers you seek are beyond the void. Whatever created this anomaly is there. Have your scouts returned?" He asked, to which Karin shook her head.
"Then patience is what is required here. The void shows no sign of closing and I do not detect any unusual signals, though I am hearing echoes of a voice from within," Galen concluded. He added the last comment on the fly and regretted it almost immediately, but luckily none of the dragons asked any further questions and just looked towards the void as it pulsated before them.

Galen paused a moment thoughtfully and then he took a step towards the portal, his staff outstretched before him. "Unless of course you wish me to close the void right now? It would be an easy task," he said testily. Karin shook her head, raising a claw anxiously. "No, the King has forbidden it!" she growled instructively.

She didn't really trust Galen, but she did value his knowledge and guidance. There was a certain aura to him that Karin found fascinating and almost familiar in some respects.

"What do you mean... voice?" She asked. Galen looked at her and shrugged, but within his head he was now cursing himself for complicating the illusion further.
"It could be a warning perhaps. I would need more time to study it," he said. "If you can spare them, I would also need some help from your slaves, Human hands are far more delicate than dragon claws."

Karin pondered for a moment. This seemed like a fair offer and she was keen to learn everything she could so as to please the great King upon her return. "Very well, you shall have your help with this task, but you must be cautious, for if the void were to close it would displease the King and I shall have you executed myself. Do you understand?"

Galen nodded but made a point of moving the end of his staff in Karin's direction. The blue gem atop the staff buzzed slightly. *Perfect timing*, Galen thought to himself. Karin noticed immediately and her eyes widened. Another Wise One stepped forward awkwardly with claws raised apologetically.

"We simply ask for caution, wizard. That is all," it said.

Galen acknowledged their concern and lowered his staff. He was about to speak when he realised it was vibrating wildly in his grasp. Looking down, he was surprised to see the gem emitting a series of sparks which were scattering across the floor around him.

Karin took a step forward, a look of surprise on her face, but she wasn't looking at Galen, she was instead looking past him, towards the void.

In the same moment, Galen registered an increasing hum from the void and he turned to witness it change colour violently between a deep red and a vibrant green and then blue, randomly phasing between the hues. The tendrils of mana that encircled the edge of the void began lashing out with a crack and a hiss as they struck at anything they could find. They seemed to be reaching for something, like hands clawing blindly at the darkness.

Galen's mouth fell open and he was sure he glimpsed some kind of city street within the clouded colours of the void, but as he took a step back, a tendril of mana lashed out at him and suddenly the marshlands surrounding him were gone, replaced by blinding light.

Karin and the Wise Ones looked on in shock. The void grew silent once more as it returned to its original form, but their human captive had completely vanished. As the other Wise Ones looked around in astonishment, the realisation of the moment slowly dawned on Karin.

The human had been under her charge, a great asset that she had lost. King Voldestus was not forgiving and he would have her executed for this failure. With haste, she stepped silently away from her companions and disappeared into the marshland, where she may yet have a chance to survive.

Audience with the queen

The Great Kingdom of Arlune - 765 years ago

The halls of the central palace bustled with activity as scribes, members of the council and those who had business within the palace went about their daily tasks. The palace stood proudly at the centre of the mighty city of Hylia. A bustling trade hub of the kingdom of Arlune and the centre of power for the Allied Realms.

The palaces' white stone walls reflected the overall sentiment within the kingdom. The summer had been exceptionally bountiful and times were prosperous for the people of Arlune, under Queen Catherine of Lothrington's rein.

During her eight-year rule, she had rebuilt many of the poorer sectors of the great capital city, something that her predecessors had promised, but failed to achieve and thus had secured much support amongst the working classes.

Overall, she had made a success of securing the kingdom's borders, with much of the hordelings pushed back to their lands in the steep and unforgiving mountains to the west and the Allied Realms, led by humans, elves and dwarf folk, driven as one towards a peaceful time for much of the known world.

This peace, however, was a fragile thing.

Rumours remained of a Shadeling army gathering beyond the Forgotten Lands, deep within the marshes of Moorvial. If these were true, the threat of an invasion was very real, for the Shadelings were determined and powerful opponents, each possessing the strength of at least three of the very best soldiers that the Allied Realms could muster.

They were primarily driven by a dark force, but they functioned as a hive mind, under the command of one superior Shadeling General, and as such, an army driven by this nature was a massive concern for those in power. Especially for the remote settlements located close to Moorvial.

In addition to this looming threat, the Shadelings had garnered support from bloodthirsty wastelanders, a mixture of various criminal elements, fractured races and fey folk who vied for nothing but revenge and the reclamation of what they viewed as their lands.

There were those amongst the council that believed it was time to use extraordinary measures to defend the Great Kingdom of Arlune. Amongst them were a mysterious yet overall respected conclave of Bri-Tisa Warlocks.

Their master, Karl-Asvarian, believed to be one of the most powerful mana-wielding humans to ever walk the world, had travelled to the central palace to address the council with a proposal he believed could secure the borders of Arlune once and for all.

Karl-Asvarian walked confidently through the hallways of the palace flanked by several tall, dark robed figures. His elderly form concealed his real abilities and his almost dishevelled appearance made him seem far more lowly than he actually was. Deep in thought, he almost missed the high-ranking official and several guards that had moved to block his path to the high council meeting ahead.

"Phillip, I believe?" Asvarian said with a smile as he came to a stop. The tall, blue robed man before him nodded almost cautiously as he welcomed the Warlocks, his pale green eyes glancing between them. "Grand Master Asvarian, we met at your previous visit to the courts. I had heard you would be attending today but I remain bemused as to why you are here?" He said.

His accent and well-spoken manner matched one of his position as a council guardian. The guards accompanying him were from the palace's own battalion, each wearing highly polished chainmail and the blue tabard adorned with the white twin hawks of Queen Catherine's family crest.

Asvarian laughed briefly, more of a scoff than anything else, as if he had already dismissed the men before him as nothing more than an annoyance. "It is, I am afraid, a visit of urgency. I must insist that I speak once again with the high council."
"Can you perhaps elaborate for me so that I may make the request for an audience on your behalf?" Phillip asked.
"You will recall," Asvarian began, as he paced a step or two in each direction before Phillip, "that I proposed a solution for our defences. One that would garnish our forces with the power to repel even the mightiest attack."
Phillip nodded, "Of course," he said cautiously.

Asvarian paused for a moment.

"As I recall, you were one of many people who were sceptical." Asvarian continued with a wry smirk and rise of an eyebrow.
Philip looked taken aback. "I did not believe it would be possible to create an army from drakling eggs. That there were many questions that needed to be answered, ethical and practical, before we proceeded with such a venture," Phillip responded.

Asvarian paused again as he considered his next words carefully, then he stepped close to Phillip.

"Well, we succeeded," he said at last.

His gaze fixed on Phillip. There was silence for a moment between the two men. Phillip looked somewhat awkward, until finally he looked back down the corridor to the council meeting that was taking place beyond two large polished oak doors, before he returned his gaze to Asvarian and the two cloaked figures beside him.

The warlocks often moved with raised hoods as many of them had, at some stage, sustained some kind of mana burn which disturbed some members of the public. Phillip had never really believed in the Bri-Tisa and like many others amongst the council, he didn't trust the Grand Master at all.

After a moment he responded "Wait here." He turned on his heel and headed to the double doors behind him. Two more guards opened the doors to the chamber as he approached and he disappeared from sight.

Asvarian began to pace once again, his hands clasped behind him as he returned to his thoughts. As a Bri-Tisa Warlock he had sworn an oath into service of the realm, operating from a great black tower to the north known as The Spire of The Wyvern. The warlocks were trusted with their magical independence as a reward for their service but were also watched closely by many within the kingdom, with some claiming the Bri-Tisa had their own agender. It was an uneasy arrangement that had been in place long before Queen Catherine's reign and one that was likely to stay in place long after.

A few more moments passed until eventually Phillip returned and ushered Asvarian and the accompanying warlocks to the council meeting hall.
"You have a small window to make your.." Phillip began.
"That's all I need." Asvarian interrupted as he strolled swiftly ahead of the nobleman.

The council meeting room was full of the land's lords and ladies, with the high council sitting on a raised platform, in an arc that spread the length of the room. The council consisted of officials from across the kingdom, carefully selected to maintain the voice of its people, from the western shores of Logram to the eastern mountains of Stonemile.

At this stage of the kingdom's vast history, the council gathering was the largest ever chaired, with over thirty kingdoms represented by their anointed officials. Below them, standing around the edges of the room were scribes and assistants, as well as lower level council members who were taking notes and providing information when requested. The entire room fell silent as Phillip, Karl-Asvarian and the Bri-Tisa Warlocks entered.

Asvarian took a moment to survey the members present, some of whom he would view as allies, however there were others who would be openly hostile towards the Bri-Tisa. Those that would oppose his ideas no matter how much they might benefit the kingdom.
"Well, Grand Master Warlock? To what do we owe the pleasure?" Asvarian recognised the voice immediately and the sound of it took him off guard. For it was Queen Catherine herself. It was highly unusual for her to sit on a council meeting in person and Asvarian feared her presence could complicate things.

He took a step towards the high council, his footsteps echoing on the polished floor of the chamber, and all eyes turned to him. He bowed his head low.
"My Queen, it is an honour to serve," Asvarian said calmly before raising his gaze to meet the council members above him.
"This is most unusual Master Asvarian, I have been informed by Phillip that the need is rather urgent," the voice was that of Lady Anglestierre, a stern woman, yet one who had voted for Asvarian's proposals previously as well as showing support for the Bri-Tisa in the past.
"It is indeed, I come with news of my success with our initial trials. The Conclave has successfully created, or bred, if that is the preferred term, an improved soldier. A loyal servant who, should the time come, would defend the realm with a veracity that our enemies have never before witnessed," He exclaimed proudly.

The room remained silent. Asvarian cleared his throat and continued.

"A fearsome warrior, one born from the egg of a drakling, who not only can combat with sword and shield, but with tooth, claw and fire! A combatant that will obey my every command!" he shouted, raising his hands triumphantly.

As he did so, the two hooded figures that had accompanied him into the chamber removed their hoods to loud gasps from within the halls.

The two figures, though humanoid in overall appearance, had the heads of draklings, but not like anyone had ever seen before. These two creatures were vicious, snarling beasts, with what appeared to be fire burning in their red eyes, and they were around six feet tall.

They appeared ready to devour anyone in the room at Asvarian's command.

"Monstrosities!" Someone called, along with "Save us all!" from another.

The crowds surrounding the room stepped back and pushed themselves against the walls and several members of the high council moved from their chairs. The Queen, however, remained calm but surprised, with several guards moving swiftly to her side.

Queen Catherine was a beautiful, middle-aged woman, with dark blonde hair and an aura of majesty about her. She was swift and intelligent, and was said to maintain a small amount of magical ability herself, though this was just a rumour spread amongst the populace. As the room filled with chatter, the Queen stared at Asvarian.

A few moments passed and she raised a hand in a command for silence.

"As far as I recall, Grand Master Asvarian, the council voted to stop all research into your constructs, yet here we stand today presented with two such creatures. Do you have a suitable explanation?" The Queen asked calmly as the crowd silenced around them.

Asvarian nodded.

"Your highness. Indeed the vote did not move in my favour, as we are all aware. However, these two specimens were already in progress and I have been extremely pleased with the results. I am present today to ask once again for the High Council's unwavering support. So that we may improve the Allied Realms defences against these new and very real threats," Asvarian said.

Queen Catherine considered his words for a moment, and then signalled to the council members around her to speak. One such member, Lord

Rosendein, a staunch supporter of the Warlock's research, stood and addressed the room.

"We meet here today under the shadow of a looming war. A war that, as we have been advised by our own military leaders, would result in significant losses. Master Asvarian has proven that his theory of using drakling eggs can result in us having an advantage that could protect the realms from the single largest threat that it has faced in any of our lifetimes. Yet we delay?!"

Lord Rosendein pointed to the two creatures who stood beside Asvarian. "Why? Because we fear his creation?" He bellowed, almost immediately another council member responded. This time it was Magi Gerjin, an elven member of the Mages Guild who stood to address the hall.

"If I may, Lord Rosendein, this kind of magical experimentation isn't new. There is a history of necromancy and many sorcerers of the past have tried and failed to create or control beasts of this type in the past. Where do you think the Lava Golems came from in Hyste Pass? Those abominations were the result of a terrible accident that wiped out its creators. The Mages Guild cannot in good conscience support this project," she said, before sitting back in her council chair and allowing others to have their say.

"In the meantime our enemies muster. As always this council is too slow to react and this time it will be our undoing; we MUST defend the realms!" Lord Rosendein bellowed again before sitting down himself, clearly flustered.

Asvarian watched in silence as the council members bickered amongst themselves for some time before Queen Catherine, who had been deep in thought as the High Council deliberated, arose from her throne, bringing the room to an immediate silence.

She slowly walked around the edge of the gathered council and down a set of stairs at the end of the platform before making her way, to Asvarian's surprise, towards the nearest of his creations.

Queen Catherine was dwarfed by the beast who stood emotionless before her while tiny tendrils of smoke arose from its snout. The Queen stood, carefully examining the creature for several minutes as the hall remained in silence.

"Can it breathe fire?" She finally asked.
Asvarian shook his head. "I am afraid not, my Queen, though we do expect to create creatures who can in the future, and we suspect that we can create creatures far larger than these specimens, and in fact are very close to such an achievement as we speak."

The queen slowly circled one of the creatures. "Do they have names?"

Asvarian shook his head once more. "They do not have individual names as they are merely test subjects, but we have named this group 'Queen's Guard'. Their purpose would be to protect your royal highness should the enemy breach the castle itself. They would remain close but out of sight until required."

He continued. "They are strong, swift and utterly loyal to the crown. They do not question orders and will never turn against us."
"And this variant of a drakling. Does it have a name yet?" The Queen asked.
"We thought 'dragon' felt both familiar and suitable," Asvarian replied.

Queen Catherine smiled and stepped away before walking back to her throne.

"I am sure we have much to discuss, grand master," she said as she turned and addressed the room. "The rumours of an amassing Shadeling army are sadly true."

Worried whispers immediately broke out amongst the crowded hall, and Queen Catherine raised her hand for silence.

"So it is with a heavy heart that I must prepare us for the very real threat of an invasion. This time from a force far more powerful than any we have faced in the history of these great and allied realms."

The Queen gestured towards Asvarian, "Grand Master Asvarian has provided us with a possible solution, to utilise drakling eggs, retrieved from the nests of a peaceful creature and to submit them to powerful magic, to create us a defence force that may withstand the upcoming threat," she paused and looked around the room before continuing.

"Grand Master Asvarian has previously advised us that this process does not cause any distress to the unborn creatures, that they are only taking a small number from the nests to start the process, and that all further dragon warriors will be offspring of these original creatures."

"They will not have the ability to breed amongst themselves by choice, so we would have full control of their numbers. Asvarian, I believe I am correct in stating this?"

Asvarian nodded. The Queen stopped a moment, seeming to think carefully before she said her next words.

"I am putting this to the vote once again, for the good of our realm on this dark day. I say aye, the Bri-Tisa are to continue their work."

The caller of the vote stepped forward with a parchment and a quill held in his hands. He proceeded to call out the High Council members' names one by one and they responded with their votes for or against the project's continuation.

Grand Master Asvarian listened intently, his confidence growing as the aye's outweighed the nay's. He made a mental note of those that showed support and those he may still have to be wary of in the future. For with this vote, and his dragon army to follow, he would become the most powerful man in the kingdom.

Eventually, he reasoned, he would not need to bend the knee to anyone ever again.

A scavenger's life

Hylia - present day

A young human male darted between the ancient ruins of Hylia. This city, once the centre of the Great Kingdom of Arlune now stood a scorched and desolate tomb. Where once the great leaders of all the Allied Realms came together to forge a path forward for the good of all, now lay nothing but dust and bone.

Arwin was nothing more than a young man trapped in a terrifying world, desperately attempting to survive each day as best he could. He was born into this world, as were his ancestors, and therefore knew nothing of life before the great purge, when the dDragons rose up against their masters and took the world for their own. A mighty and unforgiving force of nature pushing back against years of repression and control.

The young man was slight of build, filthy, with matted, shoulder length black hair, and he was dressed in nothing but rags that barely held together. His family were long gone, murdered by dragon-kin known only as 'Inquisitors'. Hunters, whose specific purpose was to locate survivors and either capture them for slavery or kill those who tried to fight back. Vicious creatures who were known to toy with their prey before delivering the final blow.

The forgotten streets of Hylia still provided the occasional food source or tool. A small short sword that Arwin had strapped to his back was one such find that he discovered laying amongst several corpses. Each time he attempted a scavenge run however, it became harder, pushing him further from his hideaway below the streets out into uncharted areas of this once grand city.

Hylia grew from a small riverside settlement, nestled against the mighty Tear of Duin river than ran all the way from Mount Voltaris to the Duin Sea, and as its citizens grew and the city prospered, it drew many within the safety of its walls, especially during the Western Wars when the Orc, Goblin and Brokka clans began raiding more than eight hundred years ago.

But the walls could never hold back the might of the dragon horde. Queen Catherine herself died here when the defences finally fell to Voldestus and his followers, though it was said that the dragons who were assigned to defend the late Queen never turned on her and instead perished alongside her as they fought back against the aggressors.

Arwin paused for a moment, peering silently from the darkness of an alleyway. Ahead of him he could see a large open area which he assumed used to be a market square, but was now littered with debris. He had never dared to cross this open space but beyond it, half destroyed was what appeared to be a city hall, or perhaps a temple. It was hard to tell, and his desperation was such that he felt he needed to push into the area and perhaps find something of use.

A light wind blew across the open space, causing a dust cloud to form just above the surface and the badly damaged buildings around the young man rattled and groaned in response. Arwin was about to move on when a huge screech echoed around the empty city followed by the unmistakable sound of large wings beating against the air. He froze completely still, heart beating fiercely within his chest.

A moment later a shadow fell over the market square, Arwin glanced up to see a huge grey dragon, its hide sparked violently with some kind of electricity and its huge claws reached out for the ground as it lowered itself into the square. With an almighty thud it finally landed, throwing up a huge dust cloud all around.

Arwin tried his best not to cough, keeping himself hidden in the shadows. This wasn't his first dragon encounter but he had never seen one this large before.

The dragon turned its great head and at that moment Arwin spotted the horse it had clenched in its jaws. Gigantic teeth had ripped through the creature's hide and it lay limp, blood oozing from the open wounds.

The dragon dropped the horse to the hard stone floor, glanced around for a moment and then proceeded to feast on its prey as Arwin held his breath in check, shaking from head to foot.

The dragon's entire back, which was riddled with sharp spikes, expelled bursts of random electrical discharge into the air around it and the power within hummed and reverberated across the open space.

A few minutes passed. The Dragon would occasionally pause to listen to its surroundings. It didn't appear to feast on its catch so much as was simply toying with it, perhaps saving it for a later meal. Eventually, it struggled back to its feet and leapt into the air, beating its wings and launching itself skyward once more.

Arwin stayed where he was until he could no longer hear the dragon and silence once more descended across the area, but he couldn't take his eyes off of the remains of the horse. He could feed himself for weeks on just this alone. It was a huge risk, but perhaps he could carry a small amount at a time back to his hideaway in the old city sewers. It was a risk he decided he needed to make.

Arwin crept slowly from the alleyway, eyes darting around the area, carefully watching for any signs of movement. He made his way across the open space, finally arriving at the horse's remains. It was a fresh kill, and the meat would be good.

Arwin knelt beside the horse's remains, removed his sword from the back strap and began cutting away pieces of meat before placing them in a small leather satchel that he had by his side. It wouldn't carry much but he could make several runs back to his sanctuary.

He had taken his mind off of the surroundings and was startled when he heard the sound of a bow string being pulled from right behind him. He spun to find a large, tough looking man dressed in a dark cloak with the hood thrown back, holding a drawn bow aimed at Arwin's face. Beside the large man was a female Hill Dwarf in a similar cloak, armed with what appeared to be a wooden chair leg that she waved at Arwin in a threatening manner.

"That's ours," the big man growled. His face was scarred from what appeared to be burns and his brown hair was kept short. Arwin froze, unsure how to respond to the new threat.
The dwarf female stepped forward, eyeing Arwin closely. "He's just a boy," she said.
Arwin had never been this close to a dwarf before. She had thick blonde hair that was wildly doing its own thing, but under all that hair was an attractive face, and she was stocky, certainly giving off the impression that she could handle herself in a brawl.

Dwarves had always been known to be effective in a fight, their thick, sturdy skin led to the famous saying amongst humans, "clump a dwarf and get clumped harder".

Arwin moved slowly, keeping his hands in view. "I just found it, please, I'm hungry."

The big man shook his head.

"Don't matter, it's still ours. Hands off," he grumbled. Arwin slowly lowered a piece of horse flesh he had in his hands and then crawled back from the big man, who still had his bow primed.

The big man lowered his bow and shrugged.

"That was easier than I thought," he said, his voice suddenly having a far more friendly tone to it. The dwarf, meanwhile, sighed, and reached out a hand to Arwin in the process.
"Take no notice of Barn, he's just takin' the piss." she said with a smile.
"I'm Heg, well my mates call me Heg anyway but.." she stopped mid sentence, "do you hear somethin'?"

Arwin listened, alert and ready to bolt. Several guttural sounds came from the far side of the courtyard just beyond the church. Without a moment's hesitation, Arwin leapt to his feet and began sprinting from the market square as fast as he could, Barn and Heg following swiftly behind.

It wasn't long and they were back in the shadow of the side alley just in time as three large creatures emerged from the far side of the market square. Arwin recognised them immediately as inquisitors, the same creatures that killed his family and village members.

These creatures once served the Great Kingdom of Arlune and were terrifying to behold. As one of the Bri-Tisa Warlock's early creations, the inquisitors were unable to completely control their inner flame, the origin of many dragons' fire breathing ability. Instead the flames escaped around the snout, appeared in the eyes and ignited much of their head.

They wore specially forged plate armour, carried huge spears often adorned with the heads of their prey and were known as dragon-kin due to their bipedal stature and lack of wings.

The three figures stood communicating with one another in their unique guttural tone, their flames lighting the far side of the open space in an eerie red glow. It wasn't long until they noticed the horse carcass that now lay in a pool of blood at the centre of the market and they started to walk towards it.

"Move.. Quick, they'll smell us," Barn whispered as he made his way through the back of the alleyway and the others followed close behind, weaving between close knit streets full of rubble and decay, sometimes having to scrabble over the top of fallen stone and charred wooden beams.

They ducked through the streets as fast as they could, hearts pounding. Situations could change at a seconds notice out in the open, some dragons could move far quicker than even the most nimble Elf.

Barn ducked into a semi-intact building with the others close behind. Once they were all inside, he turned and shut the door, bolting it swiftly.

Arwin glanced around as they passed through the structure. It appeared to be an old workplace, with parchments littering the floor and several benches with rusted tools and tattered clothes scattered across them. It had clearly been a busy place in its time. A large hole in the roof let in the sun, which was the only real source of light in here.

"Wait." Heg whispered as she disappeared behind one of the benches before reappearing with a rather large metal hammer. She grinned and signalled to keep moving.
"Nice Heg. That an upgrade?" Barn whispered as they neared an entrance towards the rear of the workshop.
"Course it is!" Heg replied

Barn peered outside and they listened for a moment. When he was certain the coast was clear he turned back to the others.

"We'll head back to Fort Valian. You comin'?" Heg asked, looking at Arwin who paused to consider his options.

He had never heard of Fort Valian and hadn't been in contact with any humanoids for some time. But the inquisitors' raised voices behind them grew closer, forcing his decision - he would be discovered if he tried to stay in the city any longer.

"I'll come," he replied. Heg nodded with a smile and led on away from the ruined city centre and towards the outskirts of Hylia.

A damaged mind

Mount Voltaris - present day

Shadowy forms surged through red mist, the sound of a battle rattled all around. The dragon stood watching the scene play out below him, he towered over the humanoid creatures fighting amongst themselves. A brutal display of carnal reflex, the terrible voraciousness of warfare played out in every detail.

Beyond the battle, a tower loomed amongst the smoke filled skies. The dragon recognised this place. The sight of it filled him with an overbearing sense of fear, of which he became instantly ashamed. Where was he?

He turned slowly, it seemed difficult to move, as if something was holding him back. As he glanced upwards he could see the skies flash with fire along with brief glimpses of electric energy flashing across the scene.

He heard a roar of agony, as a large form dropped from the sky as if in slow motion. A dragon, its wing shattered and smoke billowing from a wound in its side, was spiralling towards the earth. He watched until it finally hit the ground with an almighty thud, throwing up clouds of dust all around the site of impact.

He tried to walk but could not. He looked down at himself but all he could see was his immense flame like nothing he had witnessed before. What was this?

And then, in a moment, it was gone.

The cave around the dragon seemed cold and empty. Before him on the floor was a deer carcass. The elf had been visiting, leaving food for the dragon in the brief times that he was awake. They had spoken occasionally. Her name was Nialandra. Though she preferred Nia, and the human child had no name and would not speak, though she seemed to be attached to the elf, unwilling to leave her side.

Nialandra often talked about the world around them during her visits. She asked questions, and wanted to know of the other dragons who fought back against the King.

The dragon was unable to answer. It was as if a piece of his past had been erased, but he knew that there were others out there fighting back against the reign of the King.

Ah yes, King Voldestus, as he was known. The golden dragon. His face appeared in the dragon's troubled mind. A gigantic creature, perhaps the largest of all the elder dragons; the select few who obtained greater power and incredible abilities that their younger brothers and sisters had not.

Voldestus was pure gold in colour, with a heavily armoured hide that some said was impenetrable. Despite this, the Steelhide Dwarves, slaves to the King, forged him a chest plate armour of black Darian steel, an incredibly rare material that only they could master.

The King's heart was cold and his searing black eyes were fueled with his darkened inner flame, that was so powerful that you could smell it in the air from miles away. The King wanted nothing but to burn the world utterly. To destroy the Allied Realms and drive its people to ruin.

The dragon struggled to recall more, but as he drifted in and out of his healing cycle, his mind refused to release the information.

He shifted his weight and decided to attempt to stand once again. With a low groan that echoed down the passage of the cave, he managed to struggle to his feet and glanced at his side. Where a week ago there was a huge gaping wound, surrounded by burnt flesh, it was now almost healed.

The cave where he had been resting was a large space, disappearing deep into the darkness of the mountain. A small shaft of light in front of him allowed some luminance into the area and it appeared that could be an exit.

The dragon took a tentative step forwards, followed by another, his huge bulk slowly but surely moving around the cave wall ahead, until he could see a wide opening with what appeared to be afternoon daylight beyond.

As he moved on, his vision blurred and for a moment he could see nothing but darkness. Just seconds later it cleared once again. He took a moment to pause and look around the cave entrance where he discovered a cleared campfire and some items that perhaps Nialandra had left behind on her previous visit.

The dragon moved forwards tentatively, until his head reached the edge of the cave, revealing the view beyond and what a view it was; lavish green woodland ran throughout the canyon below the mountain, trailing into the distance as far as the eye could see. The dragon recognised this forest as the 'Great Glade', an enchanted place as ancient as the world itself.

The sun was indeed retreating just beyond the treeline, small orange coloured specks of light flickering through the trees as the last of the daylight faded from sight.

Mount Voltaris towered above the Great Glade, and was once a home for all draklings, a sanctuary for the small, peaceful beings of the old world. A distant home that the dragon had never known but he would have, if he had hatched within his natural habitat alongside his brothers and sisters.

Instead his egg was snatched by a hunting pack on the payroll of the Bri-Tisa Warlocks, taken from the mountain and placed into a laboratory where a dark and twisted magical essence was infused into the structure of his egg, forging the unborn drakling within into something totally unnatural and constructed with one purpose in mind.

To kill, by command.

The dragon's mind was full of clouds, a piece of memory here, a flash of a face there. These confusing pieces of a larger puzzle were possibly tied to his fierce clash against the dragons that resulted in him secluding himself within this very cave.

His mind would heal, eventually, but he was also fearful of what these memories might reveal about him once they came together. Was he responsible for innocent deaths before that day in the flaming village?

Was he a danger to the elf and child who had shown him kindness?

As his thoughts wandered, the sun finally vanished completely beyond the treeline and night fell over the land once more. The dragon searched his thoughts, revisiting the scene of battle within his mind, focusing mainly on the large tower. It was an imposing structure, oozing the taste of mana from within.

He recognised that taste, foul and tainted. Like a mutated version of pure mana, the magical energies that his kind were so familiar with.

The tower itself was dark, uneven and distorted in appearance, spiralling upwards and disappearing out of sight above the clouds. A monstrous creation from a time long forgotten.

The dragon remembered this place, and suddenly the realisation hit him that it was known as the Spire of the Wyvern. This was where he had been created.

It was a place that filled him with a sense of fear, sadness and anger all at the same time. It was a place of torture, of extremes of mistreatment brought about by the warlocks' misguided experimentation.

What he needed to know was if this was a memory or simply a nightmare, one of many that plagued his thoughts. Was there a battle upon this place and if so, what role did he play in it?

Was this the beginning of the uprising against the warlocks? The time known as the purge?

His thoughts shifted back to the tower once again, and he found himself asking if it survived the uprising and battles that followed.

It was at that very moment that a loud noise broke his concentration. A flash of light filled the cave and Nialandra appeared before him. The child stood beside her gripping her leg tightly. Both of them looked startled to see the dragon awake and standing by the cave entrance, but not as startled as he felt at this sudden appearance before him.

"How did you do that?" he asked, his voice echoing across the valley. Nia put a finger to her lips to signal for quiet and pulled a small metal sphere from the discarded backpack by the fire.
"Do you not remember these? We call them echo orbs. If you have two of these you can transport between them with the correct command phrase," she said, before placing the orb in her pack and setting it down next to the fire. Then she knelt and began lighting the fire with a spark stone.

"Keep your voice low, for you may attract unwanted visitors," Nia instructed in a gentle whisper, the child beside her nestled in as close as she could get while eying the dragon cautiously.

"I have been deep in thought," the dragon said quietly. "More feelings, partial memories. A tower I recall. It was known as the Spire of the Wyvern." Nia nodded and looked at the dragon for a moment, deep in thought.
"The tower is said to have been destroyed during the purge, but that was before my time here. Is the tower where you were created?" She asked.
"Yes," the dragon sighed. "Perhaps if I can find the ruins it will aid me with my memory."
"Perhaps I can ask the Ancients what they recall," Nia suggested. The dragon looked puzzled.
"What is an Ancient?" he asked.
"Dragons are not the only creatures blessed with a long life. Elves can live for thousands of years during times of peace. Those who have

gained great powers and knowledge are declared as Ancients among our people" Nia replied. "There are other races with such gifts as well, or there were before the dragons destroyed so many innocent creatures."

Nia turned to face the Dragon, studying his huge face carefully.

"You mentioned there are others like you, those who wish to stand up to the King. To bring peace back to the world, is this true?"
The dragon nodded slowly. "Indeed it is, though I fear many of them have already been silenced, and I must admit that I am unable to trust my recollection until I am fully healed. I am concerned that I might be a danger to yourself and the child."

Nia sat for a moment, deep in thought, before speaking once more.

"Do not fear, I can sense your true purpose. Your heart is pure. Perhaps, when you are fully healed we can try to locate these dragons together, bring them to safety within the Great Glade."
The dragon considered her words for a moment, "All they would bring is flame and ruin. I would not wish your people any harm."

The dragon did not understand the elf's motives but he sensed that she meant to do good. Perhaps together they could save those dragons that sought peace and with their help, protect those who had suffered at the hands of King Voldestus and his armies.

"Perhaps your Ancients can help me piece together my past, so that I may find those that wish to end Voldestus," he suggested.

The elf regarded the dragon for a moment, a glimmer of hope in her eyes.

"The Ancients are the oldest and wisest of our kind" she said. "They possess ancient knowledge and memories that have been passed down thousands of years, through many generations. They wield the most powerful of our magics and have witnessed the rise and fall of kingdoms, the ebb and flow of magic and the struggle against tyrants like Voldestus."

Nia paused for a moment, gathering her thoughts before continuing.

"They reside deep within the heart of the Great Glade, hidden from prying eyes and protected by powerful enchantments. The dragons are unable to reach them there. Though they have tried, they have failed."

The dragon listened intently, his golden eyes focused on Nia as she spoke. The prospect of seeking guidance from the Ancients intrigued him immensely. Perhaps there was hope after all.

"But gaining an audience with the Ancients is not an easy task," Nia cautioned. "They are selective with those they choose to meet and are understandably wary of your kind. They value a pure heart however, and they can sense the intentions of those who seek their counsel."

The dragon nodded, understanding the importance of approaching the Ancients with respect. He knew that he had much to prove, not only to the Ancients but to himself. The memories and flashes that haunted his mind may hold the key to his purpose in this world.

Nia looked at the dragon, her gaze filled with determination. "Once you are fully healed, we shall embark on the journey to reach the heart of the Great Glade. I will guide you and vouch for your intentions, but the path shall be treacherous. If the dragons become aware of your presence here they will stop at nothing to see you destroyed."

The dragon nodded solemnly, his massive form radiating a newfound sense of determination. "I understand, I am ready to face my fate and will do all I can to prevail against the tyrant king."

As the fire crackled and cast its shadows across the cave walls, the dragon and elf formed an unspoken bond.

A voice in the dark

Fort Valian - present day

The past week had been an incredible experience for Arwin, following his arrival at the underground city of Fort Valian. The city itself was located a few days' travel from the ruins of Hylia, and was nestled within a deep ravine that split the land. This place had been one of mystery for hundreds of years before the purge. It was once the home to a wise and ancient species known as "Valian", that mysteriously vanished from the world shortly before the times of warlocks and dragons.

Little is known about the valian, but their impressive city populated the very walls of the ravine, constructed into the rocky surface by skilled artisans and mana-wielding craftsmen known as founders. Fort Valian ran deep into the gorge, and was home to thousands of valian before they disappeared.

After this time, looters would occasionally venture to the city in search of valuable artefacts that they could sell on the black market, but it was a dangerous place. An earthquake had hit the area some years ago and much of the city had been damaged or destroyed and the surrounding caves were riddled with various critters that lurked within the shadows and even a small but deadly goblin camp in the lower levels, so many of these opportunists never returned.

The valian were a petite, subterranean species, technologically advanced and capable of casting powerful spells thanks to their unique approach to controlling mana. They preferred their own company to mingling with the surface dwellers and were a secretive race. The human scholars that now resided within Fort Valian believed that they survived mostly off of the various deep-dwelling critters, cave moss and mushrooms that grew here.

They were, according to the various statues and mosaics that littered the city, part ethereal and highly magical in nature, though in a way that mages of the current age seemed unable to recognise.

The valian recorded a fair amount of their history within a huge library located in the heart of the city, but much of this was destroyed by the earthquake many years ago and it was now unreachable. What little was left was now in the hands of a small pocket of survivors, using the city as their refuge and naming it Fort Valian.

What became of the valian was a mystery to this day. The city was seemingly abandoned before the earthquake hit. Perhaps they had exhausted the resources here or were forced to leave, but they were an incredible race nonetheless.

Much of the city appeared to once be powered by strange magical gems that had unfortunately lost their abilities many moons ago, leaving much of the function of the city dormant.

Either way, Fort Valian had proven itself to be a suitable hideaway and would remain so as long as the dragon overlords were unaware of its existence. It had certainly made an impression on the young Arwin.

Heg and Barn had stayed reasonably close over the last week. The three companions slept together in the lower quarter of the city centre and had been instrumental in helping to construct a more suitable living area for the growing populace.

Part of the construction involved moving huge slabs of stone from a collapsed section of the city to the new location. It was tiring work but Arwin was eating better than he had in his entire life and for the first time, he felt like he had a purpose. It was rewarding work and he had made two great friends in the process.

Heg and Barn were fun to be around, with a dry sense of humour and a lot of conversation as the days progressed. Arwin had discovered that they had been working as scavengers, moving through the shadows on the surface world to gather whatever they could, while also looking for those of the Allied Realms that might be out there surviving alone.

In addition, Heg was a very capable blacksmith, and she had been instrumental in constructing suitable tools for the survivors, with Barn helping.

They had gained a lot of local knowledge during their journeys and had told Arwin of several of their discoveries, including tales of a village hidden beneath a powerful concealment spell just a few weeks' travel from Fort Valian. It was fascinating to hear and Arwin had pleaded with them to allow him to join the next scavenger run, but Barn seemed reluctant to increase their risk of discovery by adding an extra member to the party.

He was a kind giant of a man and also a damn good shot with a bow and arrow. Barn had originally travelled from a small survivor camp a few days south of Fort Valian, looking for food. The camp had struggled to survive and according to Heg, Barn had suffered the burn scars to his face while trying to rescue his wife from a band of Orc raiders who stumbled on the camp a few winters back.

Orcs were barbaric creatures, larger and stronger than humans, which made them formidable opponents. They were also desperate to survive, just like every other race across the world of Neefi, so there were no negotiations when you were unlucky enough to stumble upon them.

Barn's wife had survived that attack but later died of disease, along with other members of the group. Barn was later discovered by another scavenger party from Fort Valian and as a result, he brought the remaining members of his group to the city where they had lived ever since.

The survivors within Fort Valian were led by a military unit under the old queen's banner and the orders of a skilled human soldier named General Ivass Dervish. He was a seasoned veteran who grew up in Fort Valian and swore an oath to protect it at all costs when he was just fourteen years old.

The people trusted Dervish, and thanks to him they had stayed safe since he took command just over five years ago. He was military through and through and that was how he ran the city. Everyone was part of the finely oiled machine, working to improve their home and continuing to grow. It was a balancing act and those within Fort Valian were under strict regulations about revealing themselves on the surface world, to keep its existence a secret.

Arwin had also met new friends within the city itself, in particular a sweet young girl named Joselle, from the Indictni Tribes, who had shown a keen interest in the young man. This had caused much amusement to Heg and Barn, who had spent the last few days teasing their young companion on his new found love.

"She, erm, comin' over for dinner and cuddles tonight?" Barn asked as he cooked some questionable meat over their makeshift fire. Around them the city had grown quiet with many settled down for the night. The companions' current home was basically a makeshift tent, some blankets, and a fire at the edge of a wide city street that lay in ruin thanks to the quake.

Heg and Barn seemed to prefer to camp a little away from the main area of the city, partly due to the added defensive advantage but mainly because they preferred their own company.

"Aaarwin?!" Barn called mockingly.

Arwin kept his eyes closed, laying on his back with his hands behind his head. Suddenly he felt a poke in his side and grimaced.
"What!?" He snapped grumpily and Barn and Heg chuckled together.
Barn laughed as he asked "Is Jojo coming for dinner?"
Followed closely by Heg, "and cuddles."

Arwin sighed loudly and sat up. "Her name is Joselle and no, she's got to practise for her librarian test."

Joselle was hard at work training for her upcoming role as a librarian, once the great library deeper within the ruins of the city was cleared and made safe for public use. She was fascinated by the valian, and wanted nothing more than to pass her knowledge on to others.

Heg gave Arwin a wry smile. "Ah ok, maybe Jojo will come tomorrow."
Arwin gave a loud sigh, "Joselle."
"Jojo," Barn replied immediately.
Arwin let himself laugh, "Whatever, ya old git!"

Arwin lay back down as Heg and Barn started a conversation between themselves, and let his thoughts wander. He thought about the city, and what it may have looked like many years ago in this very street. Who lived here and what happened to them, as well as thoughts about General Dervish whom he had seen from a distance but never spoken with in person. Heg and Barn had met with him a number of times over the last week to discuss locations for further scavenger runs and other matters that perhaps Arwin wasn't yet to learn of.

Slowly, as the minutes passed, Arwin drifted deeper towards sleep, he felt his body drifting peacefully as the sounds of the fire and the chatter faded away.

"Arwin!" A feminine voice called, and a momentary flash of an alien face appeared in his mind, while small dark eyes drove into his very soul.

Arwin sat up instantly. "What?!"
He opened his eyes only to see Heg and Barn looking at him completely bewildered and still sitting together by the fire.

Heg looked surprised. "You OK?"

Arwin paused to catch his breath, sighed heavily and attempted a smile. "Must have been a nightmare," he said quietly.

Heg shrugged and continued her conversation with Barn as Arwin sat, puzzled. It didn't feel like a dream. He couldn't put his finger on it but it felt like something else. Real somehow.

He took a few minutes to gather himself and then got to his feet and strolled away from the camp out into the cool darkness of the empty city. Above him loomed huge pillars that disappeared out of view above, sending a chill down his spine. There were certain areas of this place that felt daunting, lifeless and sad.

Arwin strolled on, quietly contemplating the voice and alien face in his dream. She looked like one of the statues here, like a valian. Slim features, large cheekbone structure, large ears that wrapped around behind the head almost like a bat and small dark eyes.

Heg's laughter broke through the silence as the conversation continued from the fireplace. Arwin shrugged off the dream and turned to return to the others, but as he did so he caught a glimpse of something standing watching him from the end of the street.

With a chill, Arwin turned back slowly, hoping his eyes were playing tricks on him.

A ghostly form, casting an eerie blue light across the surrounding area stood completely still.

Arwin froze in fear, not daring to move. From this distance it was hard to figure out the details of the apparition but it seemed to be the valian from his dream. A female, cloaked and very thin, two deep set black eyes and large batlike ears that rose up behind her.

Then, just as suddenly as it had appeared, it was gone, without a sound.

Arwin stood for a moment, his eyes fixed on the empty darkness ahead while his heart pounded in his chest and his hands shook from the fear. What had he just witnessed? Was he losing his mind?

He pulled himself together and broke into a fast walk back to the campfire, checking over his shoulder constantly to see if he was being followed.

Barn watched him as he returned from the darkness. "Kid, you ok?"

Arwin's face was pale as he walked to the fire and sat down next to Barn so that he was facing outwards towards the dark street where he had seen the apparition. He shook his head.

After a long moment of awkward silence, he said. "I.. think I just saw a ghost."

There was a pause around the fire as Arwin's words hung in the air and his companions exchanged glances. Heg leaned forward, her voice laced with curiosity.

"A ghost? Are you sure Arwin?"

Arwin nodded, his eyes still wide with fear.

"I know how it sounds, but I saw her. She looked like one of the valian, just like in my dream," he said.
Barn lowered his voice. "Dream? You saw her in a dream? Did this ghost say anything?"
Arwin shook his head. "No, she didn't say a word, she just stood there. Watching me. Then she just vanished."

Heg pondered his words for a moment. "The valian spirits could still linger in this place."
Arwin's mind raced with questions as he continued to watch the darkness beyond the fire. "Why would a valian spirit appear to me? What does she want?"
Barn placed a comforting hand on Arwin's shoulder. "We can't say for certain kid, but if you saw this spirit, we need to warn Dervish, maybe get the clerics involved."
Heg nodded in agreement. "We need to be cautious. If there are ancient spirits in this city, they may not be friendly, but for now we keep this between us. We don't want any panic or suspicion directed towards Arwin. He's the newcomer here, you know what the others can be like."

Arwin felt a surge of gratitude for his companions' support and as they settled back around the campfire, their conversations became more serious. They discussed the possible significance of this spirit's arrival and the deep history buried amongst the ruins of the city.

The bloodborne

Tower of The Wyvern - 764 years ago

Talon Bloodborne stood silently as the final preparations were made. He was not born with this name, it was bestowed upon him by the Bri-Tisa Warlocks following what they called his re-birth.

Talon once lived near the northern marshes in a small village called Lower Venix, but at the age of just five he was taken by slavers and eventually sold on to the warlocks. This was just the start of his ordeal, as Talon and many other small children; a mixture of orphans, slaves and discarded youths, some as young as a year old, were taken to a new life within the imposing Spire of the Wyvern.

The spire itself was one of six ancient arcane towers known as the Pillars of Twilight. These towers that littered the known world were gigantic constructions of incredible ingenuity that were built long before records began, and some believed by the Gods themselves before they eventually abandoned the world altogether.

The Spire of the Wyvern had been known by many names over the thousands of years that it stood. Previously it was simply named the Black Tower, a twin of The White Tower which still stood to the north. However, when the Black Tower became occupied by the Bri-Tisa, under the leadership of Grand Master Karl-Asvarian, it was given its current name and the darkness that now enshrouded this hellish place had never been stronger.

Talon was now a bloodborne, as were the other children who had survived the ordeals placed upon them by the warlocks here. Magical experimentation that pushed their growth to new levels, imbued them with powers beyond those of a mortal being and most importantly gave them the ability to command a dragon without question.

This 'tether' as the warlocks had named it was key to controlling the dragon horde that they had created and now numbered more than three hundred incredible beasts of varying strengths and abilities.

The years had been harsh and the combat training that the bloodborne were forced to endure was like no other, but the results were a new breed of fighter, whose tether would be an irreplaceable asset in controlling the dragons as their numbers grew.

Talon had been instructed in what to expect from the dragon that he would be charged with mastering. He had been told of the fury of a dragon and its want for destruction. That the evil that resides within these immense creatures was never to be trusted, no matter the appearance.

In fact a large portion of the training bestowed upon bloodborne was drumming into them the importance of using their tethers to ensure a dragon never thought for itself.

Dragons were simply a tool to get a job done. Nothing more, nothing less, and today would be the day that Talon finally would meet the dragon he had been assigned to and step up the ranks of bloodborne to join the others amongst the skies.

Battle Master Vandire was a dull man, whose only real experience was from a previous career as a senior soldier of the Queen's Guard. He was stocky, unfit and arrogant. However, he did know his dragons, and he had been specific with his instructions to Talon over several months of drill training.

Talon was to mount the dragon, gain the tether link and then command it to lay down before dismounting for further instruction. Any further dragon control was forbidden until later training sessions.

This initial test was to ensure that the tether was strong. That Talon and his assigned dragon were compatible and only when Vandire was absolutely certain there would be no issues with the pairing, would Talon be signed off to take flight. This would be the first test of many on the road to finally being given the freedom to ride the dragon into battle.

Talon now stood patiently but anxiously, as a full set of blackened armour was placed upon him by two squires. The armour was finely crafted and imposing to witness, with an array of deliberately fear-inducing beastlike references in its exquisite design.

The metal used for bloodborne armour was black Darian steel, mined by Steelhide Dwarves and famed for its imbuement properties and incredible strength. Each piece of the armour was enchanted by skilled warlocks, who would ensure that the steel was able to repel dragon flame and keep its wearer safe.

Finally there was the full plate helm, which had a different design for each and every bloodborne. Talon's resembled a snarling reptilian face with fierce fangs, and this was placed carefully upon his head.

Once all was ready, Vandire stepped closer.

"This helm shall guard you from the flames. This armour shall strike fear into your enemies," he said.

"You are never to reveal your true face to others outside of the Spire of the Wyvern. To do so would breach our code and without the code we are nothing," he said before turning and instructing two guardsmen to open the large metal gate that stood between them and the dragon beyond.

Talon stood calmly as the gate slowly opened and light poured into the room from beyond. For there, standing in the middle of a large open pen was an incredible sight to behold.

The dragon was immense, far larger than others that Talon had witnessed during his years within the Spire and he had never seen anything like this one before. It was completely covered in flames, engulfed by a fiery fury that burnt its surroundings and made it appear as if the dragon were embraced by the hells themselves.

Talon was speechless, standing in the gateway, unsure how to proceed. Surely he couldn't ride this creature? He glanced back at Vandire who impatiently gestured for him to move towards the flaming dragon.

The entire pen was aglow thanks to the light generated by the incredible creature that stood at its centre and the sound of burning flames was immense.

"Do not question, only command!" the battle master shouted from Talon's side as if he read his mind. "Walk to the beast and command it to bow. Take control of its mind!"

Talon walked forward. The ground below his feet was scorched and the Dragon turned to watch him calmly with two huge golden eyes. He expected the heat to be unbearable but his enchanted armour negated the effects perfectly.

When he got to a comfortable distance Talon stopped for a moment. He and the dragon regard each other with curiosity. Talon couldn't be certain, but in that moment, he experienced a connection.

"Command the beast! Demand obedience!" Vandire yelled from behind Talon, but he ignored the instruction. If Talon was going to do this, he was going to follow his gut instincts.

Talon bowed his head low and knelt before the dragon, and almost immediately he could hear Vandire shouting in frustration at the act, clearly unhappy with Talon's approach. Thankfully the sounds of the flames drowned out most of the complaining that was being aimed his way.

The dragon watched with increased curiosity. Talon looked up at it but remained kneeling. It deserved his respect, he felt. The creature before him was a beautiful, majestic and extremely powerful being, and he was nothing in comparison. It was as if years of training had just evaporated from the moment Talon set eyes upon the dragon that now towered over him.

A few awkward moments passed. Eventually the dragon brought its head low to the ground, and within the flames on its neck was a large saddle, partly made from the same black metal as Talon's armour.

Talon stood and placed one hand on the saddle, briefly turned to witness the surprise on Vandire's face, and then mounted the dragon as the flames surrounded him in their fiery embrace.

The dragon stood once again and Talon felt himself rise up until Vandire and the other warlocks were just small figures below them. Vandire issued commands to the guards around him, who ran over to unsecure the chains which held the dragon to the earth.

"Do you have control?" He shouted.
"Do you?" Talon answered cheekily and Vandire started to gesture for him to dismount by frantically waving his hands about and shouting as he grew more and more frustrated with the brazen acts of the bloodborne.

Talon took a deep breath. He had trained for years for this moment. When he and his dragon mount would finally take to the skies. He focused his mind and found an almost immediate connection to the dragon, who understood and responded.

Talon's heart raced as with an almighty push, he and the dragon leapt upwards into the air, leaving the pen behind them, and circled away from the dragonhold, around the immense and imposing Spire of the Wyvern, as Talon peered through the multiple openings of the tower. Each room was lit by an array of torches and magical implements where the warlocks continued their dark work within.

The higher he and the dragon got, however, the less imposing the tower felt, and the pair soared gracefully across the surrounding marshland.

"Hold tight little one," Talon was shocked to hear the dragon say and together they swooped over the landscape below, passing fields and farmhands who looked up in awe and then out across the immense

Fetland Lake, where small fishing vessels were dotted around and the tiny village of Fetland sat upon its banks.

The world was beautiful from up here, away from the troubled landscape in which the Spire of the Wyvern stood. To Talon, the colours were astonishing, with trees and fields of green rolling away into the distance as far as the eye could see while the sun's brilliant light sparkled off of the lake waters directly below and the dragon's flaming body reflected back at them.

"It's incredible," Talon said out loud.
"Indeed, it is," the dragon replied.

As the land rushed by below, Talon realised that in the midst of the excitement of this first flight with the dragon he had forgotten his training. The training which instructed him that the dragons were to be controlled through the tether. He had not expected from his teachings that the dragons would speak to him in the common tongue, and instead would be a troublesome and untrustworthy creature to command.

This was not the experience he had felt so far with his dragon mount.

"Do you have a name?" Talon asked and as the dragon looked back at him, Talon felt a tinge of appreciation.
"My name is Surexx, and you are?" Surexx said.
"They call me Talon Bloodborne."
Surexx paused for a moment, then he asked, "May I call you Talon?"
"Of course," the young bloodborne replied as they broke through the cloud cover and cruised across the sky.

Talon was speechless at the view as wispy cloud vapour whipped up around them and the sun nearly blinded him with its brilliance. Then to Talon's surprise, Surexx began to turn back in the opposite direction.

"We must return to the dragonhold or my punishment will be severe," Surexx said.
"They will not punish you, for now we are as one. Fly Surexx, spread your wings and fly a little longer," Talon replied, Surexx glanced back at

his rider once again and Talon detected confusion and perhaps appreciation through their tether.

The pair spent many hours exploring the surrounding landscape and marvelling at the mixture of settlements that they passed over. The tiny people below must have been shocked to see the flaming dragon pass them by and Talon wondered how they would greet them in person.

As the dragon and bloodborne spent more time together they spoke in brief but meaningful ways, discovering more about one another as best as they could and Talon felt comfortable with Surexx. He had learnt a great deal about the hierarchy of the dragon brood and was impressed to hear that other dragons were also able to communicate in the common tongue as well as embracing their own language that had been named Draconic.

After some time, they finally made the decision to return to the dragonhold. There was silence between the pair but they were able to sense one anothers appreciation for the time that they had spent, and as Surexx landed back within the pen he sensed a small amount of foreboding from Talon at the welcome that awaited them. Sure enough, Vandire's stern face told Talon everything that he needed to know. He dismounted and almost immediately several guards passed him by along with a warlock who began to weave his dark magic.

"Foolish!" Vandire squawked as Talon approached, "I was clear in my instruction! You did not bow. I was clear in my instruction! You did not command and I was clear in my instruction! Yet you still took flight!"

Several guards appeared by Talon's side and they grabbed his arms as several others pointed their spears at him.

Talon was surprised at just how animated Vandire was, and he tried a few times to get a word in but the rampant scolding continued unabated. As Vandire continued his rant, Talon glanced back at Surexx, whose chains had been secured and was now barely able to raise his head from the ground.

"Surexx doesn't need those chains," he said and Vandire paused mid-rant and glared angrily at Talon.
"You are nothing, but a pawn in a much larger game! Learn your place, I should have you executed on the spot for this ignorance!" Vandire yelled "We clearly failed when we created you. You shall stay grounded. Another bloodborne can be tethered to this dragon."

At that moment an imposing figure stepped from beside Vandire. It was an old man, with short grey hair and a scruffy beard, dressed in long brown robes.

"I disagree" the man said calmly.
Vandire looked flustered, "Grand Master Asvarian, my apologies," he stammered as he bowed his head.
Asvarian ignored the gesture and continued in the same calm voice. "Did this bloodborne not take flight? Fully control one of our largest dragons through a lengthy period and then land with ease?"

Talon watched the exchange in silence as Asvarian approached the young bloodborne and slowly circled him.

"An impressive display of tether control. Allow this one to ride tomorrow, I want that dragon battle tested," he said, and then he departed just as quickly as he had arrived.

Verdine watched Asvarian as he strolled out of the dragon pen and stepped forward to eye Talon closely. "Get back to your bunk," he said through gritted teeth. Then he spun on his heel and stormed away.

Talon turned to look once more at Surexx who still watched him with his large golden eyes.

"Make sure Surexx is well fed, or you'll have me to answer to," Talon instructed the guards who glanced at one another in shock. Then he turned and made his way out of the pen with a new confidence in his step.

As he strolled from the pen back out into the drawing night, Talon recalled this incredible day and allowed himself to be escorted by the guards.

The reclusive dragon

present day

      Galen continued to walk the barren wastelands where he had found himself some days ago. The skies above were troubled and full of anguish, rolling across the heavens like a stormy sea might smash upon the rocks. He had walked on and on without rest nor sustenance and yet, he had not found himself hungry, nor thirsty or indeed exhausted.

This place. This hellish, empty shell of a world, was like nothing that the old scholar had witnessed in his long years.

The landscape around him was nothing more than a flat, desolate world, lifeless and devoid of any discerning features. It was terrifying and daunting in equal measure and as each day dawned, Galen gripped his staff tightly and pushed onward, seemingly making no ground in his search for clues as to his current whereabouts.

Surely this was not real? Perhaps when the void reached out and struck him, he perished and this was merely a world between life and death, where he would have been judged. But the gods left the world long ago and perhaps this was all there was now beyond the world of the living.

As the monotonous days rolled on, Galen's thoughts returned to the moment the void took him. To that feeling he had within his body, that grip he felt as the tendrils of energy reached out and touched his skin. That burst of pain as the marshes around him vanished from sight to be immediately replaced with this place.

Whatever this place was.

He thought about the other prisoners he had left behind, at the whim of the dragons who no longer had to fear Galen's response if they mistreated them.

He stopped walking. *"What's the point?"* he thought hopelessly. Eventually he dropped to his knees as the clouds above rolled on and flashes of lightning crackled across the darkness.

"You are not alone," a deep voice boomed through the world around Galen and he looked up, clearly shocked. He listened intently, heart beating in his chest. Did he imagine that?

The wind blew lightly across the landscape, distant thunder echoed across the angry skies, but the voice remained silent.

"Are.. are you there?" Galen whispered, his eyes searching the landscape for anything that might give him hope.

"I am," the voice said.
"I'm not imagining it?" Galen asked with a gulp of fear, and there was laughter in response, loud but friendly.
"No little one, you are not imagining it," the voice said.
"Who.. who are you?" Galen asked cautiously.
"My name is Alacatus, but I am also known as the Seer," the voice replied.

Galen recalled that he had heard tales of a dragon elder who was known as the Seer from before the great purge, a dragon of immense power, kindness and incredible abilities.

The writings told of a dragon who could see things, outcomes and events, that no other man nor beast could see. However, it vanished during the purge, never to be seen again and was believed dead. Could this be that very dragon and if so why was it here, wherever here was?

"You are a dragon?" Galen asked warily.

There was a sudden beating of wings. Mighty gusts of air blew across the landscape and a dragon landed before him, bigger than Galen had ever witnessed. The creature was utterly remarkable, with a striking mix of greens, golds and reds across his immense frame and just one single, huge eye in the centre of its head that looked down to regard him.

"You are astute, little one. I am indeed a Dragon, but you have nothing to fear from me," it said. Galen was in awe at the majestic beast that towered above him, but he was also shaking like a leaf, and tried his best to calm his nerves.
As he did so the dragon leant down. "You are confused, and I shall explain, but first I have questions of my own little one. May I ask you?"

Galen nodded in response, but he was sure that he didn't really have a choice.

"That staff that you carry. It is known as the Staff of Vanis. It was once carried by a dear friend of mine, many moons ago. A human named Polus Vindwaar. How did you come by it?"

Galen looked at the staff that he held in his hands, its blue gem tip glowing silently. He explained to Alacatus that he had found the staff while retreating from the dragon siege on the city of Feraxia and that Polus Vindwaar had passed away many years beforehand.

Galen watched as the great one-eyed dragon before him listened and noted his sadness as the story progressed. "I am sorry for my brethren's assault on your kind. They have brought much death and pain to the world."

Galen nodded once again and sensed that Alacatus was being sincere.

"However I am pleased that the staff has found a new master, and a worthy one at that," Alacatus concluded with a smile.
Galen raised his hands apologetically. "Oh, no I'm afraid I am no sorcerer," he said. "I don't have a magical bone in my body"
Alacatus laughed once more. "Ah but you are, little one. Yes you most certainly are. You just didn't know it!"

Galen pointed out that he had never cast nor weaved a spell in his entire life and had never felt anything like what he imagined a magic user might feel, but the dragon continued regardless.

"The gem within this staff would not be glowing as it is now if you had no magical ability," Alacatus explained, "and it would not have brought you to me."

Galen was clearly still confused. "But you see I.."

The dragon ignored Galen and continued regardless. "You have always nurtured the ability to weave mana, you just weren't aware of it. You were without guidance and this gem, it works very differently to magical energies native to the world of Neefi."

"For the gem within this staff moves from master to master, of which it has had many, and each time it takes a small piece of its last master with it, enhancing its power, knowledge and personality. It really is quite a remarkable device," Alacatus explained.

Galen was now completely lost. The gem had a.. personality?

"Polus Vindwaar was a rather incredible man. When he happened across the gem it was part of a broken and rather garish wand, at least that's how he described it to me."

Galen had stopped trying to interrupt altogether and just listened to Alacatus boom on.

"The original wand was damaged beyond repair, but Polus retrieved the gem and toiled day and night to construct that marvellous staff, and then of course he learnt how to master the unique methods of drawing power from the gem," the dragon paused and it raised its one eyebrow, "What's your name again?"
"Galen Dinn, I just.." Galen started, but Alacatus continued.
"Yes Galen. A scholar from Ferakis. Beautiful city. Shame about its fate," Alacatus said and appeared to then be lost in thought, its one great eye

darting about as if viewing a million things all at once. Somehow distant, but still present at the same time.

Galen took the opportunity to speak. "Where are we exactly?"
The dragon's eye settled back on Galen. "Ah, of course, you must be confused. You are within mind."
There was a pause, Galen glanced around at the desolate world. "Your..mind?"
Alacatas nodded. "This is a place of my own creation. I exiled myself here. For I shall never walk the grasslands again."

As Alacatas responded Galen detected a touch of melancholy to his voice. "You are unable to return to the world?" he asked.

The dragon blinked once, sighed, and then answered. "I am able, but I shall not. For we dragons do not deserve to live in your world, it is not ours to rule. It is not ours to take," Alacatus paused and then continued. "We were mountain dwellers, us dragons. It was a wonderful place. Were it not for the warlocks, that would have been my choice of home, so peaceful and full of natural beauty."

Galen felt sorry for Alacatus and sensed a real sincerity in his hatred for his own kind. Perhaps with time Alacatus would see fit to return once more to the world he left behind. It was this thought that gave Galen an idea.
"You could come back to the world with me, surely one of your immense power and influence could stop the dragon king and bring peace?"

Alacatus' head dropped, it's one eye staring at the ground. "He is no king of mine. No.. no I do not have such power, and would be destroyed by Voldestus."
Alacatus paused for a moment, then continued. "Though there was one that might have bested him."

This was curious, Galen felt a renewed sense of hope. "Who would that be?"

Alacatus sighed. "He was known as Surexx The Kind, a Fire Hive like no other and the brood brother of Voldestus. He attempted to stop the purge before it began but he was sadly defeated."

Alacatus seemed to stop suddenly and then leant down close to Galen, it was so sudden that Galen jumped out of his skin. "Ah yes! We must teach you, little one!"

Alacatus chuckled to himself and before Galen could react, the barren wastelands around them were gone, replaced by a confusing mass of every colour in the rainbow, twisting and swirling around him in beautiful and complex patterns.

Moments passed and then finally Galen fell awkwardly to a cold marble floor, as various gasps erupted around him. He looked up and as his eyes focused he could see that he was now standing in the middle of a very large chamber, lined by huge support columns on either side.

Above him the ceiling arched over the room, but was shimmering with a strange purple gas while the ornate pillars and various adornments that lined the hall shimmered or flickered with a wide array of magical energies. The room was breathtaking, but as Galen looked around the scene, he saw no sign of Alacatus.

It took him a moment to realise that there were several people in the chamber with him, from various races, and all wearing white wizard robes lined by gold. They looked highly amused at this newcomers arrival, some holding up their wands or staffs in case Galen was a threat.

Galen wasn't really sure what to say, until a tall, dark skinned sorcerer made his way towards him with his hands tucked into his sleeves.

He was middle aged and had a dark red tattoo that ran across one side of his face, marking him as a mage who followed the path of firelight, if Galen recalled correctly.

"Curious." the man said calmly. Galen just blinked in bewilderment. "I am High Mage Plagar Narlstrom of the Tower of Light, with whom do we have the pleasure this afternoon?"

Galen's confusion was evident for all who witnessed his arrival, he thought the mages from the Tower of Light had been eradicated many years ago. "I.. am Galen Dinn, I'm afraid I'm as confused as you," he said with an apologetic smile.

"You were transported here by accident? That would be an incredible feat," Plagar said.
Galen shook his head."No, I...Well you see, a dragon transported me here."

The mention of a dragon in Galen's sudden appearance in the chamber set Plagar immediately on guard, and there were some concerned responses from the surrounding mages.

"Which dragon?" Plagar asked, with some urgency to his voice.

Galen tried to reassure the mage. "A friendly one, I can assure you. Alacatus, an elder dragon in a self-imposed exile. He said I needed training and the next moment I found myself here."

Plagar appeared to relax once again at the mention of Alacatus, and an amused look spread across his face. "You have met with the Seer? This is unheard of, most peculiar indeed."
The blue gem atop Galen's staff gleamed brightly for a moment, attracting Plagar's attention, and his eyes widened.
"The Staff of Vanis!" He exclaimed, clearly recognising the magical item immediately.

Galen had drawn quite the crowd, some looking on with awe and astonishment and a few still with suspicion. Plagar decided it was best to move elsewhere and he gestured to Galen to follow him through the chamber.

"Come Galen Dinn, we have much to discuss."

"Where are we?" Galen asked as they walked side by side.
Plager smiled and looked at Galen. "This is the Tower of Light."

Galen was utterly astonished once more. He had heard and read so much about the famous Tower of Light, which had stood for thousands of years, through generation after generation of mage's and their incredible magical abilities. Abilities that had defended kingdoms, supported kings and queens and forged the very history of the land itself.

He had believed that it no longer stood. "The Tower of Light was rumoured to have been destroyed by the dragons during the purge, yet it still stands?"

"Indeed it does," Plagar answered with a smile, " it is hidden from the world and shall remain so until we are ready."

Galen stopped suddenly. "Ready for what?"

Plagar stopped walking and turned towards Galen with a confident smile. "For war, Galen Dinn. For war."

The battle of Ruyan's Ridge

The great kingdom of Arlune - 763 years ago

      The dragonhold was used as both a holding area for those dragons deemed worthy enough of service to the Allied Realms and a training ground where the bloodborne could hone their skills to perfection.

The trials, which often pitted the dragon riders against one another in brutal competition, were often a spectacle for both the bloodborne and the Bri-Tisa warlocks who operated in the Spire of the Wyvern.

It was yet another day of hard training and Talon stood at the centre of the arena, surrounded by the other bloodborne and several warlocks who spectated with keen interest. He was exhausted, having fought hard for the entire day, relentlessly being put to the test over and over against the other bloodborne in a knockout tournament, through which he had successfully seen off a large portion of the pack.

However, his next opponent had him concerned, for Relaya was the bloodborne tethered to Voldestus, and she was relentless in her pursuit of perfection and as cold and calculating as they come. Both had battled through the tournament without reprise but where Talon now looked exhausted, Relaya appeared relatively fresh. Her breathing was steady and she held her sword and shield without any sign that her stamina was dropping.

If Talon could best Relaya in combat, he would proceed into the last five bloodborne in the tournament. He placed himself deep in stance, ready with his choice of twin practice blades. These weapons were quick and deadly, so they were perfect for Talon's selected fighting style.

Talon would not be the first to strike. He needed to save as much energy as he could for the battles ahead, should he beat Relaya here and now.

So he waited, as his opponent moved forwards inch by inch, the purple glow of her eyes lighting up the eye slit in her dragon helm making her appear all the more formidable.

Talon stooped low, adopting the 'rat who dances' battle stance, a method taught to him by one of the many swordmasters employed by the warlocks. The stance would allow him to rise and drop swiftly between stabs of his blades, and perhaps give him a swift victory point.

The rules of the tournament were simple. A body strike would result in one victory point,while a head strike meant two points. The first to three would be declared the winner and move on to the next round

Strikes were only counted from weapons. So fist blows, head butts and kicks were allowed but would not score any points.

One of the battlemasters acted as the official. He stood by the side of the arena area with two red flags which he used to announce the victory points each opponent had gained from a successful strike.

Talon could sense Relaya move before she actually did, a slight tense of her lower left leg was the tell that he needed and sure enough she pounced forward, twisting her sword across the top of her shield as she did so.

Talon spun to his right and pushed with his legs, so that he launched at speed behind Relaya's shield, where he was sure he could land the first blow. Sure enough, he slid past the attacking bloodborne, raising his left arm as he did so. The stab rattled along the underside of Solent's shield arm and the official raised a red flag to signify a point for Talon.

Relaya was furious with the swift loss of a point and glared at Talon in frustration as they returned to their starting positions, but this time Relaya launched swiftly back into action, landing several blows across talons raised guard before she shoved him backwards with the shield. Talon slammed into the watching crowd who cheered and pushed him back into the circle. He tried to duck low again, but Relaya slammed her sword across his helm and the referee raised a flag in each hand.

She had dealt a heavy blow and now just needed one point to pass through and knock Talon from the tournament.

"I can read you like a book" Relaya mocked.

Talon tried to stay calm, but he had a history of mistakes in these matches and he refused to repeat them. They lined up once again, and Relaya was swift to push forward with her shield raised before her. Talon backed off as the pressure mounted, and he made to lunge with his left blade, a move he would later regret, as Relaya parried with her sword, forcing Talon's stance to open up.

A swift kick sent Talon backwards and he barely managed to keep his feet on the ground. Relaya then came at him once again, but Talon attacked with his right blade, a faint sweeping motion that forced his opponent to lower her shield. Talon seized the moment by following up with a swift rotation around the outside Relaya's lowered guard. He quickly reversed his left blade and stabbed backwards striking Relaya in her side and she yelped as the hardened wood struck her ribs.

The referee raised a flag.

"The combatants have two points each," he announced. "The next point is for victory."

The bloodborne crowd began to thump their fists upon their chest plates, eagerly awaiting the final round.

"If you can read me so well, how did I land a blow?" Talon said as he settled once again into a stance.

This infuriated Relaya. She leapt forward with a series of angry attacks at Talon, who parried each of them as his opponent pushed on. To his surprise, Relaya suddenly took one quick step back and then threw her shield at him. He didn't have time to move and the shield slammed into his shoulder, knocking him slightly off balance and turning his body away from the combat.

Before he could react, Relaya had already lunged forward, and the blade from her sword glanced off of a lucky parry from Talon, but he missed the left hook that followed and her plate mail glove smashed into the side of Talon's helm, dazing him.

As the two bloodborne battled on, the crowd cheered in thunderous response as Relaya's relentless attacks began to wear down her stamina. Just as Talon was about to strike, a bell sounded across the arena, signalling a sudden and unexpected end of the session.

The confused bloodborne stopped fighting and Battle Master Vandire approached them.

"You are both urgently required on the field of battle! Mount your dragons!" He shouted, and Relaya and Talon exchanged a glance, retrieved their weapons, and made their way to the preparation area.

As they approached, Vandire was already there waiting for them beside a table upon which sat a detailed battle map. Surexx and Voldestus stood nearby, their chains still fastened.
"The combined armies of the Allied Realms are about to engage the shadelings, perhaps for the final time. Listen up!" Vandire pointed to the map, upon which was drawn a lengthy ridge line with a divet in the middle.

"This is Ruyan's Ridge. The shadelings have been forced into this area and are being funnelled into this opening," Vandire pointed to the divet. "They work as a hive mind, and each of them is connected directly to the general. We understand that this general is within the force heading to Ruyan's Ridge, so we have a unique opportunity to end this war here and now. Your assignment is to kill the general. You kill him, the rest of the shadelings have no way to communicate with one another and will be easy to destroy. Understood?"

Both Talon and Relaya nodded their understanding.

"One more thing. The shadelings are venomous. If you expose your dragons to them, they will most likely die. Wait for the signal which will highlight your target, and then attack with haste. It is imperative that we end this invasion today."

Talon and Relaya snapped a salute and collected their belongings, mounted their respective dragons and took to the skies.

Meanwhile, the rains pelted down across Ruyan's Ridge, a stretch of land that lay in a strategically important location just north of Nuume, it was one of the most influential trade hubs this side of the kingdom. If the shadelings managed to breach Ruyan's Ridge, they would have almost unimpeded access to Nuume itself.

The past few months had brought a terrible wave of losses for the Allied Realms, as the shadelings pushed forward with more unity than expected. Entire armies decimated in the darkness as poor vision and a lack of overall strength resulted in heavy losses.

However, the armies of the Allied Realms had managed to use their losses to their advantage, luring the shadelings forward into a carefully orchestrated trap. The hope was that here, along Ruyan's Ridge, the armies could make a stand and turn the tide in what had become known as The War of Shadow.

The Allied Realms had gathered just days before the expected arrival of the shadeling horde, and positioned themselves along the largest section of Ruyan's Ridge in strategic strongholds, backed by spearmen of The Queen's 16th Battalion, elves from the Red Hills and Sun Magi from the eastern realm, who had erected a large magical barrier around the area as they prepared for the onslaught.

The barrier's glow cast welcome light across the rain soaked ridge, where lines of archers stood watching the dark pass below for any signs of movement. The allied scouts had reported the shadelings making progress in this direction, and it was expected that the enemy would reach this position any moment now.

Amongst the ten thousand allied units, were various teams each assigned a specific task. One such team had just three members, specifically chosen for their skill sets: Alias Kane, Lo Vin'li and Krea Darkmire. This team was assigned the name of the wardens and their task was the most important of all. They moved through the right flank of the allied forces with haste towards their first objective.

Alias Kane was a warrior through and through, a mass of muscle and near unmatched skill with a great axe. His experience in battle was paramount to leading this team to success. He was a middle aged man, with short black hair and a carefully trimmed beard lined with streaks of grey. He was perhaps getting close to retirement, but he would never admit defeat in battle nor against aching bones.

Lo Vin'li was a young but highly skilled elven beastrider from the dark woods of Bast'lor, her bow strung with the might of the Bast'lor vision givers. She was also amongst the best archers of her people. Lastly, Krea Darkmire, a dark haired, grey eyed Bri-Tisa warlock, whose power wielding the weave was perfect for the task ahead. Though she was scarred terribly from years of the abuse of her magic, she was a dedicated follower of the ways of the Bri-Tisa.

These skilled fighters were known as the wardens, and their task today would be paramount to the success of ending the war.

Alias led them towards their destination, where a shallow cave entrance sat on the eastern side of the ridge. It was here that the wardens stopped and made their preparations for the task ahead.

"When the bastards attack we make our way down, show no mercy for neither enemy nor friend" Alias instructed as the heavy rains pelted his silver and gold plate armour which glistened in the darkness thanks to its magical imbuement. The armour had belonged within his family for generations, passing from father to son along the bloodlines as each warrior from the house of Kane took up the mantle and continued the fight.

The order "Show no mercy for neither enemy nor friend" was a well known phrase for combatants such as these. It meant that should one of the three be overcome by enemies, the mission was to continue regardless.

"Once we reach the objective, I will need cover to complete the ritual," Krea said. She was an accomplished warlock, as denoted by her black cloak and clean shaven, tattooed head. She pulled her hood up to give some respite from the rain before continuing. "Lo, if I fall you must complete the ritual exactly as you have been instructed."

Lo nodded in acknowledgment. She was already reaching out with her senses to track the shadeling movements, vision walking between critter and crow until she reached her limit, but all she found was empty pathways and muddy fields that extended out into the north.

"No sign yet, surely the enemy should be upon us by now," she announced, her eyes glowed a deep green, signalling to those around her that she was deep within a vision walk.

Elsewhere, along the main ridgeline, hundreds of archers grew uneasy as they stared down into the dark valley below, rain pelting them as the cold night set in. Occasionally a sun mage would launch a sun flare from his or her staff into the sky providing brief light for the forces but these moments were short lived as the mages attempted to save themselves for the battle ahead.

They would need their mana reserves, as the mages would provide a significant defence against the sharpened claws of the shadelings. One strike would be enough venom to kill even the largest bear.

When the attack finally arrived, it was swift and brutal, taking the defenders by surprise.

The archers across the ridge were peering into darkness one moment. A second later, as a sun flare launched across the scene, a mass of shadowy forms were spotted climbing the ridge with alarming speed.

The shadelings had used dark magic to cloak their approach to perfection.

"Release!" Came the calls and archers swiftly responded to the danger, firing volley upon volley of flaming arrows into the climbing mass of claw, tooth and tentacle, while the sun mages reacted with blinding sun fury to weaken the attackers as they attempted to breach the defences.

As the cries for war went up across the battlefield, the wardens leapt to their mission, Alias leading them down into the darkness of the tunnels below, while floods of water from the heavy rainfall above ran down into the depths creating a muddy and difficult terrain.

Krea spoke an incantation and a faint but welcome light helped the unit as they weaved their way down into a complex maze of underground tunnels. The echoes of battle above slowly faded away to reveal the terrifying sound of the shadelings approach, through a series of possible entrances at the bottom of the tunnels.

The allied armies had laid traps at those entrances in an attempt to slow the shadelings if they discovered them. The wardens could only hope that those very traps would give them the time they needed to reach their target.

Lo primed her bow as she dropped nimbly to a tunnel below and almost immediately released a series of enchanted arrows in quick succession, resulting in ear-curdling screams from further down the corridor.
"They are on us!" she yelled as Krea and Alias joined her.
"Keep moving!" Alias ordered and the wardens continued.

A large black shape moved swiftly from the darkness ahead with almost impossible speed, mounting the tunnel wall, while narrowly avoiding one of Lo's arrows. With unnerving swiftness, it leapt forwards into the light, whipping out a barbed tentacle which deflected off a hastily created forcefield. Alias did not delay, he stepped forward, swinging his mighty axe down, cleaving the tentacle in two pieces, but it left him open to attack and the shadeling relentlessly clawed at Alias's open guard, but his armour thankfully deflected.

However, the attacks were enough to send him flying backwards past the other two wardens as Lo released a series of enchanted shots into the shadeling beast and it finally dropped to the ground, dead.

However, there was no time to rest as Alias got back to his feet. More shadelings were approaching through the tunnels and the wardens pushed down into the darkness with as much haste as they could muster.

Meanwhile on the surface, a huge explosion split the front row of archers, and a barrage of rocky debris slammed down onto the battlefield causing more casualties amongst the defenders. A second later a massive black and silver creature scurried over the ridge and let out a victorious screech as its allies followed through the gap in the defences.

The giant beast was similar in appearance to a beetle but with eight long legs that were covered with spikes and a ridged head with an enormous mouth full of sharp teeth. Like the shadelings, it had two long tentacles lined with barbed spikes that whipped out at any approaching enemies. Those that were struck either died from the impact or staggered away only to succumb to the venom seconds later.

A shadeling stood astride the large beetle as its tentacles whipped out at any soldiers who dared approach. The rider spent a second searching the battlefield until its gaze rested on some of the sun mages, who were still encased within their protective shield as they launched barrage after barrage of spells into the fray and protected as many soldiers as they were able to.

One of the mages thrust his staff into the ground. A powerful sun spell burst forth across the earth. There was a loud rumble and the ground beneath the beetle exploded upwards in a flash of blinding light. It staggered to the side and some spearmen took the opportunity to move in, attempting to strike at the creature's legs and underbelly, but they were soon overcome as the shadelings surged through the gap to join the fight on top of the ridge.

The beetle screeched and charged forward as arrows and spears deflected off of its armoured hide. One unlucky spearman who had been struck by a tentacle was soon crushed beneath its long legs as others attempted to protect him.

The mages strengthened the shield around them as the creature came into range, angrily thrusting its tentacles at the barrier in an attempt to breach it and kill the mages within. The barrier vibrated, flashing and crackling as the blows rained down upon it and the mages had no choice but to concentrate all of their energy on holding the shield up until help could arrive, but none came.

With one last flash the shield exploded and the mages fell to their knees clearly exhausted from their efforts. The beetle reared back and let loose an almighty screech of triumph.

Deep below the ridge, the wardens battled on. They had slain many shadelings until finally reaching the exit to the caves, but the sight that befell them was shocking beyond belief. Before them was a sea of shadelings, some completely stationary as the general focused its efforts elsewhere, while others were joining the surge towards the ridge.

This army was far larger than any that the shadelings had previously mustered and it was impossible to see how the defenders on the ridge could overcome this immense force.

"There!" Lo shouted. She had spotted the general with her keen elven eyesight and was pointing to the centre of the horde where a shadeling stood twice the size of the others around it. Instead of the usual two tentacles, this creature had six and each of them glowed with a sinister magical energy.

The wardens did not hesitate in their preparations. Krea knelt beside Lo, reached into her cloak and pulled out a single purple gem. She nodded to Alias, and began her incantation.

Several of the nearby shadelings spotted the wardens and began to move to intercept them, covering ground at a terrifying speed. Alias moved swiftly to defend his companions and Lo let loose a series of enchanted arrows at their foes but as the shadelings fell, more of them filled their space and the companions would soon be overwhelmed.

The shadeling general turned to face them, its red eyes glowing with hatred as it commanded its troops to attack with a snarl.

Alias slammed his axe into the chest of the nearest shadeling and a bright flame burst forth, splitting the warrior in two with a sickening crunch. Black ooze spilled out across the battlefield, but Alias was not finished, slicing the approaching shadelings with great speed as Lo's arrows brought down a few more of them.

Despite their best efforts, the wardens were hopelessly outnumbered and eventually Alias's blows became slower and weaker. Desperation taking over he took one last glance back at his companions.

"Show no mercy!" he yelled. Lo just managed to bring down a shadeling who was about to strike him, but a second and third landed their blows, splitting his armour, and he yelled in agony.

Just a second later, he was gone, lost amidst a sea of black creatures, barbed tentacles whipping through the air amongst a red mist.

"Now!" Krea shouted as a large mass of purple energy rose up in front of Lo, who retrieved one arrow from her quiver and aimed carefully before releasing.

The arrow flew straight through the purple mass, enchanted as it did so and launched across the battlefield, soaring above the mass of shadelings before slamming into the ground directly in front of the general.

"It is done," Lo said quietly before she and Krea were overwhelmed by the shadelings that surrounded them. Their screams were lost amongst the throng of clattering feet and slicing tentacles.

A moment passed, the Shadeling General eyeing the glowing arrow embedded in the ground near him with suspicion and then, an almighty roar, louder than the combined sound of the battle itself rang out across the landscape, causing every shadeling, human, dwarf and elf to stop in their tracks and look upwards.

The general just had time to glance to the skies as it was suddenly engulfed in searing hot golden flames. A second later, the most enormous dragon dropped from the skies.

Voldestus beat his mighty golden wings, before landing with such force that it resonated across the entire battlefield and threw dust into the air, clouding everything.

Relaya barked a command and Voldestus' massive mouth immediately scooped up the shadeling general and swallowed it whole. The great golden dragon turned and began to decimate the surrounding army that had still not reacted, bursting out golden flame that incinerated any in his way.

The shadelings spread in terror at this new threat and the sudden loss of their general sent panic through their ranks. The communication was severed, and each shadeling attempted to rally an attack, but it was an immense task given the size of the beast that towered over them. Relaya, meanwhile, unleashed arrows which struck down more of the Shadelings.

Voldestus blasted out a furious barrage of flame which engulfed the combatants and set the surrounding battlefield alight. Shadelings scattered into the darkness in all directions.

Meanwhile on the ridge above, a searing blast of fire ripped through the shadeling horde, engulfing them in devastating flames as Surexx arrived, ridden by Talon.

They swooped down to defend the allied armies who felt a renewed invigoration at the arrival of the dragons. As they landed, Surexx let loose a long burst of fire that created a protective wall before the surrounding soldiers.

Talon spotted the large beetle moving in to attack and used his tether to pull Surexx away from danger. Surexx lurched to the right as a large barbed tentacle snapped past him and he turned to face the new aggressor.

The dragon roared before blasting a bolt of hot lava from his nostrils and then reached out with flaming claws. He scooped the beetle and its rider up like nothing more than a snack and launched them across the battlefield with an ear shattering roar before setting to work on any other shadelings he could find, either engulfing them in flames or ripping them in two with his fiery claws.

The allied troops were gobsmacked, standing in total shock as the two elder dragons obliterated the enemy army, turning the tide of battle in their favour as they did so, shrugging off any attempts the enemy forces made to retaliate.

Once the allied troops got over their shock, they pushed forward once more, delivering the final blow to the shadelings who now fought in absolute chaos, completely unable to communicate with one another.

The shadeling army scattered back down the ridge but the dragons pursued them into the darkness as the elven archers rained arrows into their backs.

The two dragons would become well known to the citizens of the kingdom and the battle of Ruyan's Ridge would be etched into the history books. Surexx and Voldestus would be revered for their powers and the safety they and their kin brought to the world.

The mighty golden dragon Voldestus, whose golden flame would bring freedom and prosperity back to a kingdom in fear of destruction. And his brother, known as Surexx the Kind, whose flame would protect the people and whose kindness would become legend sung in the taverns across the kingdom and beyond.

The Battle of Ruyan's Ridge was deemed a huge success and opened the way for the Bri-Tisa warlocks to continue their work, but Queen Catherine was not aware of the dark magic that was wielded within the Spire of the Wyvern, or of the atrocities that had been performed in the process of bringing her dragon army to action.

A greater danger loomed for the Allied Realms, and it was one of their own making.

An unexpected meeting

The Great Glade - present day

The dragon skulked moodily alongside Nialandra and the young human child as they made their way deeper into the Great Glade, making his displeasure clear with an occasional snort, sending small plumes of smoke puffing from his nostril, and each time, the child chuckled in amusement.

Nia smirked, "Stop complaining, dragon."
The dragon stopped walking. "Why do you not call me by my name?" he asked.
"Because you have never told me your name" Nia replied matter of factly.
The dragon paused thoughtfully, "I.. do not recall my name."

Nia turned to face the large dragon who appeared confused, and she noted a tinge of sadness in his expression that took her by surprise. She stepped forward and placed a hand on his claw, the young child copying her as she did so. "I believe a good name is Drakarim."

The dragon mulled the word over in his head, he recognised it immediately as a draconic term meaning 'free'.
"I like this name" he said before he paused once again. "What about this little one?"

Drakarim gazed down at the child who still stood with her hand on his claw. She had grown more comfortable with him over time, but still had not spoken a word since her rescue from the village.

"I feel she will tell us her name when she is ready," Nia said as she smiled at the little girl beside her.

They continued on their way through the Great Glade, travelling slowly as Drakarim was forced to weave between the massive trees that towered above them. The glade was famed for its Nedai trees, as they were known to the elves who lived there. They were ancient and imposing trees, providing home to thousands of woodland creatures. Drakarim's huge body would occasionally cause a crunch as it caught the edge of one of them and a flurry of leaves would fall from above.

The crimson dragon's poor mood returned and he began to huff once more as he struggled on.

"Why must we walk when we can fly?"
Nia had already explained this once but she did so again with the utmost patience. "Because you risk being spotted if the enemy has agents here. This way the glade conceals you beneath the leaves and we move freely."
"And slowly," Drakarim huffed, causing the little girl to giggle once again, this time Nia joined in.
Drakarim stopped again and he thought for a moment before he broke into a smile. "I shall call you Giggles."

The three companions laughed as they continued to wind their way slowly through the immense forest. This area was just the outskirts of the Great Glade, which had been home to a myriad of beings for hundreds of thousands of years.

The elves that called it their home had travelled here around four thousand years ago, when their own lands were said to be ravaged by a war between gods. The war ended but the lands were forever cursed with decay and the gods themselves faded from existence.

Elves were in tune with nature and the environment around them. They used these senses to attune perfectly with any latent sources of mana and to reach out into the wilderness and find information that the best human scouts could only dream of.

They were also fierce fighters, swift and accurate with both sword and bow but lithe, able to avoid danger when needed. Their attunement with the environment blessed them with an ability to move freely without making sound, and as such those few elves who found themselves living within a city or town were often lured into the life of a rogue, joining the thieves guild and earning coins.

Those elves who followed a less honest path were known as f'airen to their kind and would have been banished from ever seeing their homeland again, but this law had recently been rescinded due to so many elves finding themselves stuck in impossible situations and unable to travel back to their homeland.

Elves lived a long life, and could reach a thousand years old or more, if rumour was to be believed. Their vast knowledge and years of expertise in their respective fields made them a treasure to their people. They were well treated and many elven leaders from the times before the purge were powerful beings often gifted with the arts of spellcasting. As such, they were deemed a huge threat to the dragon king.

The king had ordered many hunts against elven survivors following the purge and any small settlements that were discovered were utterly destroyed, with no prisoners taken. However, many elves had so far survived, travelling as far away from these lands as they could, never to be seen again.

The three companions travelled deeper into the glade as early evening set in.

Nia stopped and began to gather firewood, but Drakarim's gaze was drawn to the orange sky above. "I smell something foul."
"Down!" Nia called and Drakarim tucked himself as low as possible to the ground.
"I can smell them. Orcs," he whispered.
"It can't be, the glade would surely have attacked them," Nia said as she retrieved her bow from her back and notched an arrow.

As Nia moved off to investigate, Drakarim whispered "Be careful, dark magic walks with them."

Nia glanced back at Drakerim and whispered, "I'm always careful," before winking and disappearing amongst the bushes without a sound.

Nia opened her senses, using her soulwalker abilities to connect with the living essence of the surrounding glade. Sure enough, just up ahead, there was a partially concealed ancient shrine, and orcs were nearby, perhaps exploring it. She made her way closer and could hear them talking in a language she couldn't understand.

She decided to move closer, carefully darting from shadow to shadow in order to get a better idea of the numbers of orcs. Nia's elven abilities meant that she was able to blend in with the surrounding undergrowth and remain undetected, where a human would likely be discovered. She was able to accurately count the size of the force outside the ruins, and disturbingly, it was larger than any that she had witnessed before.

There were multiple clans present, clans that would usually be battling against one another, but appeared to be working as a team. To the right, a group of Tallis Purebloods, who primarily wore red leather, coloured by the blood of their fallen enemies. In the clearing were several Shade Berserkers starting a campfire, over which they were about to cook some dubious looking meats.

As Nia watched, a new group of orcs stepped from the entrance to the ruins. These wore black and grey garb, and their hair was styled into a mohawk or shaved. Perhaps they were members of the Grondy or Bugmucks but it wasn't clear.

Nia was just about to return to Drakarim to report her findings when a large shadow fell across the area accompanied by the sound of beating wings.

"Oh no!" she cursed as Drakarim landed in the centre of the clearing.

He immediately scooped up one of the orcs in his mouth and tossed it into the air, as you might a small stone. As the orc tumbled to its death, the others scattered for cover in panic. Some of them nervously fired arrows at Drakarim but they simply bounced off or shattered on impact against his thick, crimson hide. As Drakarim turned to engulf more of the Orcs in flames, Nia noticed he was grinning. If she didn't know Drakarim, she would think he was having fun.

As Drakarim spun around, Nia noticed the sound of a child laughing, and was dismayed to see Giggles riding Drakarim as if he was a pony. Nia could not allow any harm to come to Giggles, so she burst from her cover and unleashed several arrows at the nearest orcs and attacked them at will. Any orcs that emerged from the entrance to the ruins were slain almost immediately, and just to be sure, Drakarim ignited the entrance in a torrent of red fire.

Eventually the clearing fell silent. Orcs lay around the area, their bodies charred and burning in the evening light.

Nia stormed towards Drakarim, who seemed very pleased with himself.
"What in the hells were you thinking?!"
"It was Giggles' idea" he responded nonchalantly, not taking Nia seriously.
"Giggles could have died if an arrow had hit her!" Nia screamed angrily and finally the severity of the situation dawned upon Drakarim.
He stood awkwardly for a long moment and glanced at the small child he had come to care for.
"My apologies, you are correct. I will take more care in future," he said with his head bowed low.

Nia frowned. She wanted to chastise the dragon, but she had more pressing matters to attend to. She walked over to one of the broken orc bodies and turned it over.

"What are you searching for?" Drakarim asked.
"I have no idea, but somehow these orcs got into the glade unscathed. We need to know how."

The orc before her was a warrior for sure. It had all the hallmarks of a Silver Fang Elite, known to roam the far side of mount Voltaris. Her eyes were drawn to a small charm that hung around its neck.

"That's.. odd," Nia said.
"What is it?" Drakarim asked. Nia snatched the charm, which was made of ancient Nedai and bore a strange symbol that Nia could not match to any runes that she knew of.
"This is elvish woodcraft," she said as she turned the charm over in her hand.
"This one over here holds the same charm," Drakarim said as he examined another corpse.

Nia moved from body to body, each had the same symbol upon their person. Eventually she sighed and stood up. "We need to reach Thalindor swiftly, something is afoot."
"Agreed," Drakarim said, and they immediately left the clearing, making their way towards the elven city.

It was now imperative that Nia reached the city of Thalindor to inform the elven council of her latest findings. She was not sure what kind of a welcome they would receive as they came closer to the barrier wall, but she pushed these concerns to the back of her mind as she and her companions made their way slowly into the darkening forest.

Knowledge is power

Tower of Light - present day

Far from the Great Glade, across the Northern Pass, the Gaping Ocean and the snowy wastes of Direfold, there stood a mighty and proud tower of purist white. It's magnificence once a beacon to all who sought knowledge in the magical arts, now hidden away from dragon eyes.

The Tower of Light was home to all who harboured the gift of the weave and within its great halls those who were taught were preparing for the downfall of the dragon king and all who supported his cause.

The tower had served the old world through unbiased engagement with those who ruled the various kingdoms, always keeping its applications open to any who wished to learn and enhance their magical capabilities.

There were, of course, other ways to expand your knowledge of magic, perhaps through druidical circles, following the life of a cleric or as a warlock amongst many others.

The tower was fabled for its skilled mages and meticulous approach to the learnings involved, combined with full and unimpeded access to over a million magical tomes and artefacts that many could only dream of acquiring.

When the purge began over seven hundred years ago, the mages of the Tower of Light knew that it would be a target. That Voldestus would seek the mages out and attempt to destroy the tower. At the time, the grand mage had activated an artefact that had been hidden within its walls and kept a secret through generations of grand mages, transporting the tower a great distance away and concealing it within a magical force field where it has remained ever since.

Travel to the tower was heavily restricted. Controlled by the mages and communication with this remote outpost was difficult, yet the resilient mages had found ways to keep relevant with the world and remained confident in their attempts to turn the tide on the dragons and their king.

The current grand mage was named Lorias Kwin, whose magical ability and knowledge of the arcane had been paramount to keeping the Tower of Light hidden from the world. Her leadership earned her immediate respect following her rise to the rank of grand mage when her predecessor died some years ago.

Lorias was a direct descendent of a proud line of mages, many of whom had been a grand mage during their lifetime. She was an ageing woman though, and frail, and as a result there were concerns that a new grand mage would soon need to be chosen from the five high mages that were currently within the tower.

Lorias had only spoken briefly with Galen, shortly after his unexpected arrival within the tower, and although she was welcoming and fascinated by the introduction from Alacatus, she remained tight-lipped about the tower's war preparations, which were currently taking place.

The tower itself was vast, almost inconceivably so. Galen had only explored a small area of the interior and there were areas of the tower that seemed to transform depending on the day of the week. He wondered if this was due to an enchantment or other mysterious effect but the puzzle remained unsolved.

On Galen's first day in the tower, he had been introduced to a number of other mages from a wide range of disciplines, and was amazed at the magical abilities that these incredible individuals possessed.

He had spent his first few days familiarising himself with the tower, its occupants and the bizarre new way of life that he now found himself experiencing. Galen had his own quarters, which were bland but spacious, and he felt at home in them, while his meals were mostly provided in one of the tower's community halls.

The meals themselves were well prepared by members of the mages guild and mostly made of vegetables and fruit that was grown and magically enhanced within one of the tower's botanical halls.

However Galen's favourite place, the one that really made him fall in love with life in the tower, was the great archive.

This enormous and awe-inspiring archive held an almost inconceivably large and incredibly captivating horde of tomes about magic and the arcane as well as books from various authors from the old world.

For Galen, it was beyond his wildest dreams and he had spent the rest of his time here, sometimes into the early hours delving deep into the depth of knowledge available to him.

In addition to the myriad of scrolls, tomes and tablets that adorned the shelves of the archive there were also artefacts from a wide selection of magical fields. Artefacts that held the power to influence the world around them and were simply priceless.

The archive was a deep and engrossing place, with darkened corners full of secrets beyond reckoning and it would take a lifetime to accurately take stock of them.

Galen sat in the quiet library section of the archive along with other members of the tower. His old ragged clothes had been replaced with one of the stunning white and gold robes providing Galen great comfort for the first time since the fall of Firexia.

He was deep in thought, pouring through a large black tome; Terrors beyond enchantments by Magi Vellis Briartongue, when there was a flash and a portal opened up nearby. Galen looked up from the book. He had become accustomed to these portals during his time in the tower, so was unsurprised to see that a moment later Plagar stepped out from the portal and gestured towards Galen to follow him.

"Come Galen, we must begin with your spellcasting lessons," he said.

Galen glanced back at the book one last time, took his staff from where it rested against the desk and followed Plagar through the portal.

A moment later he found himself standing in a large circular room. At the edges of the room were a number of wooden chairs and above them a large dome covered the ceiling with large golden steel supports criss-crossing in a beautiful ornate pattern.

Plagar immediately strode to the middle of the room and turned to face Galen as he withdrew a simple looking wooden wand from his sleeve.

"In order for one to weave a spell, one must first draw the mana from their surroundings. This process we call channelling." Plagar instructed, "In order to channel, one must learn a technique of concentration that will take you time to learn, but once it is mastered you will be able to channel at great speed. It shall become like second nature to you."

Galen watched as Plagar stepped forward and pointed at the blue gem atop the Staff of Vanis and it flickered slightly in response.

"The Staff of Vanis contains a powerful and unique gemstone believed to be from an ancient and long forgotten race known to us as the valian. It is the only known gemstone to still hold such a power, as the valian are all long forgotten." Plagar explained.

"At present the Armonis gem, as it is known, flickers randomly because you are channelling, even though you are unaware of it. This can be troublesome, and even in some cases, dangerous."

The last piece of information was somewhat alarming news to Galen. "Dangerous, how?"

"As an example," Plagar began, "The reason Alacatus was able to pull you into his mind was because you had inadvertently channelled when you were close enough to the void portal. The importance of today's lesson is to instruct you so that you only channel when and where you choose, in order to stop any accidental spellcasting."

Galen nodded and Plagar continued his instruction. "I want you to close your eyes."

Galen followed Plagar's direction.

"Focus your mind," Plagar continued, "I want you to picture the room around you." Galen could hear Plagar slowly stroll around him. "Picture my location, visualise everything you have seen."

Galen took a deep breath and did his best to imagine the training room, while picturing Plagar, who he assumed was a few metres behind him and to the right. To start with he didn't feel anything in particular, nothing that was out of the ordinary, however after a few moments of silence it was as if the room itself appeared before him.

"Good, you are connecting with the gemstone and it is allowing you to connect to the weave of mana energy that surrounds us," Plagar said, Galen could see Plagar now as he walked slowly across the room before him, it was like everything in the room, including Plagar himself, was made of light. Plagar particularly shone.

"Now. I want you to imagine everything around you is a well, which you can draw upon for your own purposes. I will give you a moment to do this, when you are ready you must draw mana into you from the room. This is channelling."

Galen did as instructed, and as his concentration continued he became aware of a world of energy that surrounded him, almost feeling its presence here within the training room. It was an incredible feeling, almost akin to an awakening of sorts, like a third eye had opened within his mind.

He decided that now was the moment and he willed the surrounding mana to him. It was slow at first, a trickle of magical energy entering his body. The feeling was like a warming touch upon his skin, welcome, but somehow unnerving at the same time. As his will continued, the flow grew ever stronger, until finally the mana was strong and he felt the staff resonate with the increased surge of power.

"Now, open your eyes," Plagar instructed and Galen did so. As the room came into focus Galen found Plagar standing before him, a big smile on his face as he gestured towards the staff. Galen followed his gaze and was amazed to see that the Armonis gem not just glowed but was shining a brilliant blue light around the room.

"Impressive indeed!" Plagar stated, "You have just produced your first spell, a basic but effective light spell."

Galen was still amazed, the feeling of drawing the mana was invigorating and exciting.

Plagar had an idea and strode across the room, collected a wooden chair and placed it in front of Galen. "You can release the mana in a number of ways - wait for it to fade over time or infuse it into a spell. The most simple of these would be a mana blast. I want you to point the staff at the chair and imagine the mana leaping from the Armonis gem and into the chair."

Galen nodded. He lowered the staff and willed the mana to leave the gem. There was an almighty crack and a blinding blue light filled the room for a split second, while trails of blue mana span and deflected across the room and around the walls, but the chair remained intact.

Plagar gave a gentle chuckle. "Ah yes, maybe you require further practice on that spell."

Galen smiled and lowered the staff, the gem was now dark and silent. "I apologise Plagar, I must have made a mistake!" He said, but Plagar assured him that all was fine.
"It is a learning process, my friend. You have progressed well with the channelling thus far." Plagar placed a reassuring hand on Galen's shoulder. "See, you are a mage after all."

Galen smiled and thanked his friend for his guidance.

Plagar and Galen spent much of the rest of that day on the process of channelling, along with the beginnings of teachings of other simple spells.

For Galen, once again, he was amazed and humbled by his current circumstances, but remained aware that the dangers of the world still awaited them outside of the tower's immense walls.

Out there somewhere, an army of dragons were systematically hunting the Allied Realms across the known world with one objective in mind. To utterly eradicate them, and at some stage, perhaps in the near future, Galen and the other mages of the tower would have to play their part in the war. Perhaps laying down his own life in the process.

It was a humbling thought, but one that brought further clarity. Galen would learn everything that he possibly could to give himself and those he would be protecting with his new knowledge the very best chance of survival that he could. He vowed to himself in that moment that with the many tomes and the fountain of knowledge available within that great library, that not a single stone would remain unturned.

If Galen were to ever face the dragons, they would know true fear once and for all.

The banquet

City of Hylia - 763 years ago

Talon Bloodborne entered Hylia Castle's great banquet hall to a round of applause from the gathered guests, and then took his position alongside his fellow dragonriders who stood shoulder to shoulder at one side of the hall.

Before them, laid out in a splendid display were rows of long dining tables full of well-presented foods from around the realms. The air was rife with pipe smoke and the smell of cooked meats and spices from around the kingdoms and the wine flowed freely.

A large number of high-ranking officials were already taking their seats at the tables amongst a throng of activity as servants moved swiftly to and from the kitchens, bringing out even more food for the feast and preparing drinks for the honoured guests.

However, the bloodborne's presence here was merely for show. To display to the various members of the realms that their kingdoms were in good hands, and of course to provide the grand master warlock Karl-Asvarian with increased support as the Bri-Tisa warlocks continued their dragon development.

Talon surveyed the room before him as the guests tucked into their meals and the servants attended to their every need. The guests gossiped amongst themselves as they did so and Talon couldn't help but feel uneasy within the environment.

The noise was intense, and Talon's senses felt overwhelmed. He wasn't the only bloodborne feeling this way - he could sense the wish to leave from his fellows but they had no choice but to grin and bear the display until they were instructed to leave.

At various times, one of the guests would approach and examine the bloodborne as if they were an ornament or a display within a museum, discussing their armour and musing at how tall the dragonriders were before losing interest and moving on.

Asvarian, meanwhile, was seated on the head table just a few places away from Queen Catherine herself, and was deep in conversation with a portly looking lord beside him who was dressed from head to toe in bright red clothing, lined with a golden trim.

Talon's eyes flashed to the rear of the room where the Queensguard dragon kin stood, their flaming eyes staring blankly back at him. They had been protecting the Queen for more than a year now and already proven their worth by thwarting an assassination attempt just a few weeks before the banquet.

The chatter came to an immediate stop as Queen Catherine stood to address the room.

"My esteemed guests, lords and ladies. As you may well be aware, in the last week reports have come from our front lines on Ruyan's Ridge. The Northern Guardsmen of the Flame, the Western Sun Magi and the 126th Legionnaires Battalion, in close association with Dragon Watch, Elder Voldestus, Surexx, Lord Graxilius and Princess Hazi. The shadeling invaders have been utterly defeated!" Queen Catherine declared to a resounding applause, cheers and celebration amongst the gathered guests.

The Queen let the cheers continue and smiled broadly while the pride was clear on Asvarian's face.

"The shadeling general, known as Vorv M'ladarr fell in battle, and as a result the remaining creatures are in tatters and the Allied Realms are safe from invasion once again!" Queen Catherine concluded, to more cheers.

"Know this! The Allied Realms will never again bow down to fear. We will never again feel the loss of a pillaged village, or be forced to watch as our families are tortured before us. Never again!" Glasses of wine were thrown in the air as the guests' cheers filled the banquet hall.

"Never again!" Came the response from the crowd and fists were drummed on the tables.

The Queen sat back down and the night's celebrations began in earnest, the musicians played and the guests continued in high spirits. As they did so, the bloodborne were ushered silently from the room one by one and out into an open courtyard surrounded by plants and trees under the light of a full moon.

One of the Bri-Tisa warlocks stood waiting for the bloodborne and as they entered the courtyard he told them, "you shall await Grand Master Asvarian here. When he is finished with the celebrations, he will address you directly."

The warlock moved back towards the courtyard entrance but remained watchful.

Talon relaxed a little but the entire event had been perplexing and a learning experience for him, the noise of the feast emanating throughout the castle grounds and out into the cool night sky.

He had never witnessed so many people together in this fashion. It was unsettling and something about it placed him on edge. He decided to stroll through the courtyard for a bit to clear his head and take in the beauty of this place while he could.

The bloodborne spent a large percentage of their lives in and around the grounds of the Spire of the Wyvern or in the dragonhold itself. The Spire did not offer carefully designed courtyards full of floral masterpieces or fountains with finely sculpted statues launching water into the air as if by magic.

What the Spire did offer its inhabitants was death, hardship and the constant smell of sulphur. It was a stark contrast to life here.

As Talon marvelled at the plants, of which there appeared to be thousands of various varieties on show, he was aware that a servant girl was watching him intently from nearby. Perhaps waiting to see if she could be of service.

"They are beautiful." Talon said, his voice deep and masterful but dimmed by the helm that he had sworn to never remove in front of others.

The servant seemed startled that a member of the bloodborne had spoken to her and didn't know how to respond.

Talon glanced up "The flowers I mean. They are beautiful. I have never seen them before."
The servant was surprised. "Never?" she asked. Something about the tone of her voice caused a reaction within Talon that he had not felt before, her voice was so soft and sweet, it was like it embraced him.

He shrugged it off and nodded. "Where I am from, we do not have such things."
The serving girl looked saddened to hear of this, she plucked a delicate purple flower and held it out to Talon. "Here, you can take it with you. It's called a Lilly of Luck, perhaps it will grant you a twist in your destiny."
Once again Talon was taken aback. "Bloodborne are forbidden to take gifts," he said, stepping towards the servant and gently pushing her hand back to her.
"The bloodborne are revered heroes," the girl responded with a smile, "surely they can do as they please," but Talon merely shook his head.
"I am afraid all is not as it would appear," he replied.

Meanwhile, within the great banquet hall, Grand Master Karl-Asvarian had been working his way between brief but meaningful meetings amongst the various leaders of the Allied Realms.

"Grand Master Asvarian, it is an honour to finally meet the great mind responsible for saving so many innocent lives," Asvarian turned towards the voice of Prince Karlak of Rinshire, a young and enthusiastic royal member of a vast land to the south, close to the southern marshlands, and rich in farming trade.

"Prince Karlak, thank you for your kind words. May I be of service to you, young prince?" Asvarian asked, bowing his head ever so slightly.

The Prince had clearly drunk a great deal of wine throughout the evening and he took another large gulp from his goblet before responding. "I have a need for dragon aid, some worrisome farmers outside my holdings are refusing to pay taxes owed for many weeks. I could use a dragon to go.. ruffle some feathers!"

Asvarian watched Karlak silently as he chuckled to himself and took another swig from his glass. "We don't do errands, young Prince. The dragons are not mercenaries for hire."

But Karlak simply stepped closer to Asvarian and leaned towards him to whisper in his ear. "I have reliable information that you may soon be considered for a chair on the council."

Asvarian nodded in affirmation before Karlak continued, "It is not going to go your way. The mages of the Tower of Light remain the thorn in your side," he took another swig before gesturing for a servant to refill his glass, of which he almost immediately spilt down his front as he took a careless gulp of the red liquid.

"I have the means to change that vote on your behalf," Karlak concluded and stepped back, looking pleased with himself.

Asvarian detested this kind of politics, but his desire to take a chair at the grand council was strong. "How many feathers do you need ruffling?" he asked and Karlak bellowed a laugh that turned some nearby heads.

"Let's just say I don't need the taxes," he said with raised eyebrows and a petulant grin.

Asvarian thought for a second. "Consider it done."

Karlak smiled but then he said, "Oh one last thing. The bloodborne you send simply must attend a celebration banquet once the job is done. It will not do to have such an esteemed warrior visit my estate and not have them meet my mother."

Asvarian nodded but then he asked, "I thought your mother passed away some time ago?"

Karlak simply laughed, "oh gods man, I can only wish!" With that the Prince strode off to mingle with the other guests.

Back in the courtyard, Talon's brief conversation with the servant girl was suddenly interrupted.

"Bloodborne!" A commanding yell echoed across the courtyard.
"I must go," Talon said and he turned to leave but the servant grasped his hand as he did so.
"My name is Choi, it was nice to meet you," she said. Talon nodded and then left the servant to return to the meeting area where the other bloodborne had already gathered.

Grand Master Asvarian strolled into the courtyard and addressed them.

"We have achieved a great and monumental victory for the Allied Realms, but there is still work that needs to be done. Mount your dragons at once and return to the dragonhold."

The bloodborne bowed and marched from the courtyard towards a large open space before the grand castle. It was here that many important royal events and announcements had been made for hundreds of years, but today, it was full of dragons of varying breeds, from Imperial Whites, their ice cold aura freezing the very ground below their feet; Blaze Tails, whose vicious nature made them unpredictable in battle and Deathclaws, whose poison was capable of bringing down the largest of prey.

Then there were the mighty elder dragons: Voldestus, Surexx, Lord Graxilius and Princess Hazi.

As Talon moved towards Surexx, Relaya moved to walk alongside him, playfully nudging him with her elbow as she did so.

"We shouldn't be talking with the servants," she stated.
"She seemed..nice." Talon replied calmly and Relaya laughed in response.

"If I see her with you again I may need to slit her throat," she said and she moved off towards Voldestus, who towered above his fellows, leaving Talon standing in bewilderment.
"I jest, of course!" Relaya called back as she mounted her dragon.

Relaya had been tethered to Voldestus just a week after Talon was tethered to Surexx and had told Talon that Voldestus was a difficult dragon to keep under her control, but she had handled the tether perfectly well ever since.

Talon wasn't sure if she was joking about slitting Choi's throat. It was hard to tell beneath the armour, but as he mounted Surexx, he noticed a small purple flower tucked into his armour. He smiled and climbed Surexx, who had lowered his head for his rider.

"How was your evening?" Surexx asked and Talon laughed.
"It was tiresome, but I did meet a new friend." Talon replied as Surexx leapt to the air and they flew away from Hylia Castle.

As they passed over the courtyard, Talon glanced down to see if he could spot Choi, but the courtyard was now packed with guests as the banquet continued and Talon sighed to himself.

Perhaps, one day they would meet again.

Eve of the eye

Fort Valian - present day

Arwin strode along what was now known as Market Street, proudly holding Joselle's hand as they browsed the makeshift stalls with a variety of items on offer, most of which were either found within the ruins of the city or critter meats of questionable origin.

The population of Fort Valian didn't have a currency to trade. What little gold was left from the old world had been hoarded by the dragons. Most trade was agreed over an exchange of items or services, but Market Street was a chance to gather and embrace some of the old ways, and as such it was a treasured part of life within the underground city.

Joselle and Arwin had spent increasing amounts of time together as the days had passed, mostly wandering the streets or finding some quiet space away from Heg and Barn or Joselle's father.

She was a good companion, light hearted and full of knowledge about the old world that she loved to share with anyone who would listen. Arwin looked at her now and felt blessed. She was slightly shorter than he was and close in age, though neither of them were able to recount their exact years, and she had the most beautiful bright green eyes that captivated Arwin every time he peered into them.

She smiled back at him with warmth that lit up her pale face and there was something about the way her long dark hair hung around her neckline that made Arwin's heart flutter.

The young man was the last of his family line and lost in a world of terror but here amongst the people of Fort Valian, he had found a home to be proud of.

However, Arwin had spent many nights haunted by the ghost-like vision and strange dreams that felt as though they echoed throughout the following day, and he had twice seen the female valian's image standing within the darkness, silently watching him.

Waiting.

The visions seemed to be gaining potency and just the night before, Arwin was almost sure he could have held a conversation with the apparition, but he had found that he was too afraid to speak.

Heg and Barn had been very supportive in trying to figure out a reason for the visits, and Heg had even asked some of the clerics within the city for advice, which resulted in a small party of them searching throughout the lower halls for any sign of undead activity.

The clerics were blessed with a powerful gift, which gave them the ability to detect spiritual anomalies and harboured additional magical spells that could clear away a spectral presence if one was indeed detected. As such they had proved extremely useful to Fort Valian as General Dervish cleared more living space for its citizens from the revealed areas of the city.

Despite the cleric's best efforts, however, they had not detected anything unusual from Arwin's experiences, nor any spectral activity around Arwin himself, and so the mystery had continued.

The sleepless nights were starting to take their toll on the young man and he became somewhat distant on occasion. Arwin would often find himself staring into an empty street or walking down an alleyway unexpectedly only to snap back to reality and retrace his steps. It was unnerving and was causing a lot of concern from those close to him.

Joselle squeezed Arwin's hand. "Are you still with me?"
Arwin nodded and smiled. "I'm just tired, we spent the whole day building storage for the lower quarter, but at least it's completed now."

"How about we head back? I need to get on with my lessons anyway," Joselle suggested and the pair made their way back up through Market Street and out towards a long side street.

Arwin's breath caught in his chest as the sight before him transformed before his very eyes. Instead of the aged, cracked stone street that was there just a moment ago, he found a brightly lit city street with plantlife dangling down from overhanging balconies and the rough stone was replaced with polished floors and walls, some of which had beautiful artwork painted across their surface in vibrant colours.

There were people everywhere, all valian, including children who played happily with one another, dancing and chasing through the street and around the legs of their parents.
Joselle was nowhere to be seen, and Arwin found himself reaching out for her but finding nothing but air.

He looked back down the street behind him to find more of the same incredibly refreshing surroundings and he could hear a strange chorus of voices echoing from the streets beyond, though he was unable to ascertain the language that they spoke.

"Help me Arwin!" It was the voice of the spectre once again. Arwin spun on the spot to find her standing at the end of the street, her ghostly form fading in and out of view.

Arwin couldn't pull his eyes away from the vision before him. She eventually turned, and walked out of sight, disappearing down an alleyway to her right.

Arwin followed, not really by choice but more an automatic reaction, as if he was being driven by an exterior force. His feet moving of their own accord as he tracked the apparition.

He reached the end of the side alley just in time for the ghostly form to lead him deeper into the lower part of the city, a section that had only recently been unblocked by the workers. As he followed the ghost from turning to turning, the surroundings grew darker and eventually returned to their real state, no longer brightly lit and covered with beautiful fauna but instead damaged, broken and long forgotten.

Arwin didn't really notice, he just wanted to follow the valian spirit further into the depths. However, It was becoming harder for him to keep up with the ghostly form as it led him through collapsed sections of the city and he often found himself climbing or ducking beneath rubble as he moved even deeper, still unable to release himself from the need to relentlessly follow.

Eventually Arwin was moving through pure darkness, fear overwhelming him. His attempts to stop moving were met with an almost painful jolt as the ghost led him on with an eerie glow. She appeared to simply pass through any obstacle and Arwin, through no will of his own, climbed, crawled and squirmed his way through the dark as if he had been down this route a hundred times before.

"Stop.." He tried to speak but was unable to get the words out of his mouth and he resigned himself to silently following the ghost's lead. "Do not fear, I need your help," the ghost whispered in his head and the hairs on his arms stood on end. It was hard not to feel fearful as he slowly but deliberately made his way ever deeper into the darkening tunnels ahead.

Meanwhile back in the city above, Joselle rushed through the streets as fast as she could towards Heg and Barn's camp. Luckily she found them and as she approached they looked up, immediately concerned by her appearance.

"What's happening?" Barn asked, a worried look etched across his face. Joselle was breathing heavily, clearly distraught. "It's Arwin! He's under some kind of spell!"
Heg immediately retrieved her metal hammer from beside the fire and passed Barn his bow. "Show us!"

Joselle, Heg and Barn hurried through the streets out to the edge of the city as quickly as they could, until they came to a boarded tunnel where a sign lay on the ground. "DANGER!" It read. The tunnel entrance was half collapsed, and only darkness welcomed them beyond the exposed archway. A section of the boarding was broken away, leaving a gap large enough for even Barn to pass through.

"Shittin' bricks, he's gone down there?!" Heg exclaimed with horror, Joselle nodded, she was clearly exhausted.
"I..tried..to..stop..him," she managed between breaths, Barn placed a large hand on her shoulder reassuringly.
"We'll get him back safe" he said and pushed himself through into the tunnels while Heg retrieved an unlit torch from her pack and lit it with a spark of flint.
"Go get help. Do not follow us. You hear?" She instructed and Joselle nodded before Heg too disappeared into the tunnel.

Deep within the darkness, Arwin moved on until he eventually stepped out of the confines of the tunnel into a large open space that disappeared into the distance before him. The ghost had vanished and he found himself able to control his movement once again. Relieved, he glanced around trying desperately to get some kind of a clue as to where he was.

Arwin held his hand up in front of his face but could barely see it, so he decided to kneel on the floor and slowly make his way forward while reaching out for anything that might feel like solid stone. It felt like an age as he moved barely a few feet, his heart still pounding in his chest and his mind reeling from the realisation that he might be lost down here with whatever lurked in the darkness.

Eventually a familiar voice echoed through the corridor behind him and Arwin nearly cried with joy. It was Barn!
"Arwin!" He called.
"I'm here!" Arwin responded, his voice was raspy and his throat dry.
"Heg! This way!" He heard Barn call out, followed by Heg's excited voice in response.

Arwin sat patiently on the cold stone floor as slowly but surely the light of a distant torch flickered its way through the tunnels and the voices and

footsteps grew louder and louder. Eventually Barn scrambled over a fallen beam and pushed his way to kneel beside Arwin.
"You OK?" He panted.
Arwin nodded meekly as Heg joined Barn shortly afterward. As he looked up at them he noted their confused expressions.
"Arwin. Your eyes, they're glowing!" Heg exclaimed.
"What?" Arwin replied in shock.
"Your eyes. They're.. glowing," Barn explained in astonishment.

Arwin's eyes were letting off a dim but clearly visible purple light and his irises were no longer blue, as they once were, but were now purple too.

The three friends took a moment to catch their breath. Heg and Barn couldn't help but keep looking at Arwin with clearly confused expressions. Eventually, Heg raised her torch in an attempt to bring light to their surroundings. They found themselves in what was once a wide corridor with what appeared to be several small rooms on either side and a stone desk of some description was nearby but it was empty and covered in dust and grime.

There was a very present smell here, perhaps a mixture of urine and faeces from whatever animals lived down here in the darkness.

Arwin pulled himself to his feet. He was unstable, but otherwise OK. Slowly and cautiously, Arwin, Heg and Barn made their way along the wide corridor and past the darkened rooms on either side.
"Did that spirit bring you here?" Heg asked quietly. Arwin nodded, his purple eyes still glowing and Heg gulped.
"Wait!" Arwin said suddenly, and he pulled Barn back towards him with his elbow. "There's something in that corner."

Heg stepped forward and raised her torch. To the group's utter horror, a large rat-like creature leapt from the shadows, nearly knocking Heg off her feet. It spun around and ran at them again but this time jumped forward in an attempt to strike at Heg, however, Barn swiftly grappled with the large creature.

"Hit it Heg!" He shouted as Barn and the creature slammed into the wall of the corridor with a thud that echoed throughout the forgotten ruins. Arwin released the short sword from his back and plunged it into the side of the creature. It squealed in pain as Heg clubbed it repeatedly over the head.

There was a sickening crunch and the creature went still before Barn slammed it into the floor in frustration.
"What in the light's name?!" He shouted.
Heg stepped forward and gave the creature one last kick. "Deni-rat. Used to get 'em a lot back home. Poisonous as well, did it bite ya?"
"Nah. It wanted to though, reckon there's more of 'em?" Barn replied.
Heg shrugged. "No idea, but we should get out of 'ere."

But Arwin shook his head and pointed ahead where a dim blue light leaked around a corner at the end of the hallway. "There's something ahead."
"I don't wanna find out what it is," said Heg but Arwin ignored her and started to cautiously make his way down the corridor. "It's her. I can feel it."
"Great." Heg huffed.

Heg and Barn exchanged nervous glances and Barn loaded an arrow into his bow as they followed the young man further down the corridor towards the blue light. Arwin carefully edged around the corner, slowly revealing the source of the glow. Ahead, at the end of this section of corridor, was a large doorway with a badly rotted solid oak door hanging off of its hinges. The glow was emanating from within the room beyond and Arwin was now aware of a low hum.

Just in front of the door lay a small pile of bones and cloth, perhaps once a valian. Barn stepped over the bones and checked the door would move, which it fortunately did, so he slowly opened it with a creak and rested it against the wall.

The room was now open and Arwin stepped forward again, his sword raised in front of him.

"We don't have much light left in this torch," Heg whispered and sure enough the torch in her hand was getting lower by the minute.

As they stepped into the room, the source of the glow became clear. Before them, suspended some six feet in the air, was what appeared to be an intact valian surrounded by a blue field of mana that hummed as the valian rotated in a kind of suspended animation.

Arwin looked closer and saw that the valian within the field was the very one that he had been seeing in his dreams and visions, and the one who led him into this very place.

Barn watched Arwin carefully. "That's her, isn't it?" He asked and Arwin nodded, his eyes transfixed.
Heg circled the suspended valian, her eyes wide with wonder. "Incredible."
"She can't be alive in there?" Barn said, a kind of half-question, half-statement.
"She asked me to help her." Arwin stated as he stepped closer to the Valian.
"Careful kid, you don't know what'll happen if you touch the.." Barn stopped mid sentence.

Arwin inexplicably reached out and placed his hand directly into the magical field. Barn tried to reach Arwin in time to stop him, but to his surprise, Arwin was unharmed. He simply reached into the magical field, cradled the valian in his arms and stepped back calmly as both Heg and Barn watched open mouthed.

"Are you mad?" Heg mumbled in frustration at the young man's reckless behaviour, but Arwin's purple eyes were burning brighter than ever and his expression was blank. Heg and Barn watched as Arwin lay the valian gently on the floor and placed his hand on her head.

She was frail, her skin almost pure white with some kind of light scaling across the surface and she was dressed in grey robes. Her eyes were closed and her breathing shallow, but she was alive.

She was small, perhaps no more than four feet tall and had an almost bat-like face, with tiny eyes, a small, flat nose and large ears that folded back behind her head. Her hair was grey and short and her arms were extremely thin but long, with lengthy fingers at the end that seemed to have more joins than a human's or elf's might.

After a few minutes of complete silence, the valian's tiny eyes flickered open to reveal pure black orbs that struggled to focus, and at the same time Arwin removed his hand and seemed to be able to control his movements once again. She began to speak, her voice weak and fluctuating and in an alien tongue but a clear voice in the common tongue also echoed in Arwin, Heg and Barn's minds. "You saved me, I am forever grateful."

"She's in my head." Barn complained as he tapped on his skull while Heg nodded in agreement.
Arwin shook his head, "I.. I don't understand. I was unable to control my own actions, what did you do to me?"
The valian female reached out weakly to touch Arwin's face. "My apologies, I felt I had no choice and my powers were waning, we had no time."
Arwin grimaced, his head was pounding. "Who are you?"
"My name is Arlestra, eve of the eye and light of Narfanu. I am the one who must see, for the others can no longer see." the Valian replied.

Arwin's heart was still pounding. He wasn't sure if he should drop the valian to the floor and draw his sword or remain by her side.

Arwin's confusion was evident. "How long have you been here? Where are we?"
"I have been here since Narfanu fell. Since it was attacked," Arlestra replied.

Arwin glanced up at the others before returning his concentration to Arlestra. "Narfanu? You mean Fort Valian?"
"You know it as Fort Valian? To my people it was Narfanu, the Holy City," Arlestra confirmed.

Barn stepped forward and knelt beside Arwin and Arlestra. "You said the city was attacked. Was this before the earthquake?"

Arlestra shook her head and explained that there had been no earthquake, but instead that the city had been attacked. Much of the population had perished in the attack but she believed some had also managed to escape through the tunnels deep below the ravine.

"Who attacked you?" Barn asked cautiously.
Arlestra sat up a little. "A powerful spell caster by the name of Karl-Asvarian came to Narfanu many years ago, and deceived our king. He gave this man the gift of Armonis."
"Armonis?" Arwin asked.
"Our magic works differently to many others. Armonis is mostly a creation magic, though still incredibly powerful if used in other ways. Our ancestors were forced to travel across planal existence and in doing so, their own inert magical powers began to fade. In their desperation they imbued their powers into the very earth itself, creating Armonis gems."
Arlestra reached into her robes and pulled out a small trinket. Within it was a tiny blue stone that emanated a faint light.
"Each valian who showed the gift would be destined to carry Armonis with them, the original magical power of our people, imbued within the gems so that it may continue to live in this new world." Arlestra concluded.
Arwin nodded his understanding. "I see, and this man, this Asvarian? He took the Armonis and attacked the city?"
"He was a man of immense power even before he took up the Armonis gift, but he aided the city and our king in many matters and gained much favour. However, after some time had passed and he had won our trust, Asvarian began to delve into our libraries and he spent many years learning, looking for something. I do not know what it was that he sought," Arlestra replied before continuing.
"The people grew suspicious as Asvarian came and went, and eventually the king confronted him and demanded he explain his actions, but Asvarian struck him down without remorse and then attacked Narfanu itself. The Armonis's powers of creation were twisted into destruction, and Asvarian became even more deadly. Our spell weavers were unable to stop him, not even standing together as one."

Heg frowned. She had heard the name Asvarian before but couldn't quite place where or in what context. "Where do you fit into this? How did you end up here?" She asked.

Arlestra thought for a moment before she responded. "I escaped the attack but myself and a few others were trapped here when the corridor collapsed. The one I was with, his bones lay outside this room."

She pointed to the bones just outside of the door and continued. "He placed me into stasis, poured his Armonis into a field that would hold me until help arrived. He had no idea it would be this long. He was skilled in his art. Even now, years after his death, it held me within."

Arwin sighed and relayed to Arlestra how sorry he was about the loss of her people and of the city, but then a thought occurred to him.
"Why me? Why did you bring me here?" He asked.
Arlestra gazed deep into Arwin's now purple eyes for a moment as if she was deep in thought.
"You are imbued with Armonis," she said at last.

Arwin, Heg and Barn were clearly confused.

"You sayin' Arwin has the Armonis stuff inside him? Like that gem?" Heg asked, her surprise at this news was evident for all to see.
Arlestra however just shrugged. "I do not have this knowledge, I am sorry. All I know is I sensed your presence and was able to guide you to me."

Arwin sat back, he was feeling a mixture of confusion and shock. He had so many questions that needed to be answered but Arlestra was weakened by the stasis and needed to rest. Perhaps with time she would be able to help him piece together the puzzle.

As voices and torches echoed through the corridors behind them, Arwin knew that General Dervish would have many of his own questions. He hoped that he would give Arlestra the time she needed to rest following what must have been an incredible ordeal.

She would be as confused as he and would likely find the sight of her once resplendent city now in ruins a tough pill to swallow as she became accustomed to all the changes that had taken place here since she was gone.

The exile's return

Thalindor - present day

Drakarim, Nia and Giggles stopped at the edge of the next rise. To their left, a small path led back up into Mount Voltaris, or at least a lower section of it, snaking its way into the mountain's treacherous eastern pass where many adventurers, human and elf alike, had vanished without trace.

The last few days had remained quiet, with no further sign of the orc raiders, but the companions had remained alert for the duration of their journey. The fresh morning breeze blew across Nia's face as she gazed down into the thick mass of trees and shrubbery that lay ahead. She was apprehensive about what was to come, but she knew that she must confront whatever waited for them at Thalindor and garner the aid of the Ancients.

She looked back at Giggles and found herself smiling once again. This little girl had overcome so much and yet she was still so brave. She had become a huge part of Nia's life now and as a result Nia felt once again that she had a purpose. Perhaps, with the help of those elves in Thalindor, she might be able to secure a better future for Giggles or even a permanent home.

Drakarim's large head appeared over Nia's shoulder, "She'll be fine. I give you my word," he said reassuringly.
Nia nodded and sighed, "If I don't return in a few hours you must take her and flee this place, for it would mean that I have failed and they will be coming for you."

She turned and made her way towards the dense foliage ahead, where Drakarim lost sight of her. He turned and curled up next to Giggles who almost immediately cuddled into his long tail.

"Nia won't be long," he whispered and they lay in silence, listening to the Nedai trees creak as they swayed with the wind and the birds as they continued to sing their song. Drakarim breathed in the fresh glade air and bathed in the comfort of these new surroundings..

Meanwhile, Nia weaved her way through the dense foliage until eventually she stepped into a small clearing where the trees formed a kind of natural domed roof across a small, carefully laid stone circle, which was covered in dappled light, leaking its way through the trees where it created warmth upon the ground.

Several sconces stood around the circle. They were unlit when Nia arrived here but as she approached the circle they flickered to life of their own accord. She positioned herself in the centre of the circle and placed both hands out to her sides with her palms facing upwards.

A long moment passed.

The sconces flared and then several elven guardsmen stepped through the other side of the clearing and surrounded Nia. The leader, an older elf male with long pure white hair pulled back in a ponytail and a stern looking face gave Nia a cold smile and addressed her.

"Well well, Nialandra Kalin'tor, it is a surprise to see you here," he said with a smirk and Nia smiled politely in response. The elf continued, "Especially as you are banished. Very brave indeed."

Nia knew the leader of these guards as Araneth Blackthorn. His family were well placed within elven nobility and he was a stickler for the rules. This was the last person that she wanted to greet her here, but Nia was not ready to walk away without a fight - too much was at stake.

"Then you would know that I wouldn't come here without good reason, Araneth. I come with a dire warning for Thalindor, I am no threat. But you already know that, don't you?" Nia responded pointedly.
Araneth stepped forward from the other guards and lowered his voice.
"You are no longer a member of the council little girl, so run off and enjoy your time with your beloved dragons and human filth."

Nia didn't move an inch, instead she glared into Araneth's green eyes with determination. The two elves shared a long history but very different views. Both of them had once sat on the Thalindor council but an incident resulted in Nia's permanent banishment and Araneth's relegation to guardsman.

"The information I have is for the council's ears only," Nia said, she reached into her belt pack and pulled out a small silver coloured coin and held it up for all in the clearing to see.

"I hereby claim the status of Elunara, you shall let me pass," she said loudly. On seeing the coin Araneth's eyes widened and the guards immediately relaxed.
"How did you.." Araneth started but Nia side-stepped him and strolled past the guards.

Beyond the clearing and down a long winding path, there was a giant archway made of twisted wooden vines that twinkled with light. As Nia passed under this, the rest of Thalindor revealed its breathtaking beauty, fading into existence before her piece by piece, house by house and street by street.

It was as if the trees themselves had grown high above providing complete cover from the sky while wonderful lights trickled through the greenery to illuminate the city below, which was in turn nestled across the landscape as naturally as foliage growing upon a hillside.

The smells of the city struck Nia almost immediately and brought back many treasured memories. Herbs lined many of the streets, hung upon the outside of the elven homes and along the pathways a myriad of colourful flowers blessed their edges providing a beautiful and stunning visage as they ran into the distance, weaving between the houses and shops.

A mixture of small, elegant looking structures made from smoothly crafted wood and polished stone made up the largest portion of the city's outer area. At its centre was a large spiralling tower that weaved its way up into a circular elevated platform, with beautiful carved wood supports that overlooked Thalindor's streets.

The scene nearly brought Nia to tears. She loved this city and its people with all her heart and she missed it dearly.

She wasn't born here, but had travelled far from the Eastern Isles many years ago on her mother's orders. The orders that eventually got her banished from Thalindor. It was a banishment that Nia was determined to overturn, so that she could send a message to her people in the east that this was a safe place for all elves to live and prosper.

Nia slowly made her way through the streets, closely followed by Araneth and his guards. They made no attempt to block her, but they were watchful in case there was any need for intervention. Nia could almost hear Araneth seething at the sight of the coin of Elunara but he had no choice but to respect its status and allow her passage.

The climb to gain an audience with the Ancients was long and arduous. In other areas of Thalindor there were lifts and even some short distance portals for quick travel, but the climb to the Ancients had always been a symbolic one, for to finally gain an audience with the great ones you must first present your determination.

As Nia continued on the path upwards, her thoughts returned to her mother, whom she had not seen nor heard from for many years. Her mother's determination to bring about a greater change to the world had influenced Nia greatly But her mother's views were not shared by all the elves in Thalindor and although her mother was named Queen of the Eastern Isles, her influence here was limited, especially following the purge.

But Nia had to put these faults aside and focus on the task at hand, to bring about awareness of the greater threat but also the possibilities of a stronger future. A future standing side by side with dragon kind.

Up ahead the pathway ended, through another smaller, but equally stunning archway and through this sat the High Council, alongside them the three great Ancients of the Thalindor elves.

Those who were present watched Nia closely as she approached and made her way to the centre of the large circular platform.

"Nialandra Kalin'tor, your return is a surprise. Would you care to enlighten us?" A tall, elegant elven female with long blonde hair and striking blue eyes stood and addressed the gathering. This was Princess Seraphina Darkthorn, Araneth's older sister and ruler of the Thalindor elves.

"Indeed, I claim the right of Elunara, I seek counsel," Nia wasted no time, she raised the silver coin for all to see. The response was one of surprise from the council members but one of the Ancients stepped forward and rested on a finely crafted walking stick. Her aged, friendly face was a warm welcome to Nia and she was close to tears at the sight of her old friend and ally.

"Elunara, I return to you your coin," Nia said, she knelt and lowered her head while holding the coin out towards the elderly elf, who approached and retrieved the coin from Nia's outstretched hand.

Nia stood once again and to her surprise, Elunara hugged her and looked her up and down.

Elunara was still beautiful in her advanced years and was perhaps the most respected of the three Ancients, all of whom were alive before the time of the dragons. Elunara wore a long dark green gown and her pure white eyes, although unnerving to some, were the most friendly eyes that Nia had ever seen.

"I accept my coin and your return, Nialandra Kalin'tor. You may address the council," Elunara said as she stepped back to give Nia some space. "I am afraid that I will bring a mixture of good news, and also a dire warning," Nia said.

She glanced at Araneth before continuing, "Orcs are gathering in the Great Glade, raiding local settlements and expanding in number by the day. I have never before witnessed an army of this size."

All eyes were on Nia as she continued her report. "My party disturbed such a group just a day's travel from here. They appear to have magic users amongst their number."
"Impossible," Princess Seraphina began. "The glade does not allow creatures like orcs to walk its hallowed ground."

There were nods of agreement around the platform, but Nia was insistent on being heard.

"They are using some kind of charm," she said as she pulled the charm that she had recovered and handed it to Elunara. "With this, they are able to walk freely. It appears to have been carved by elf hands."

This caused quite the stir amongst both council and Ancients alike. Elunara examined the charm closely in silence as discussion broke out between the members present.

"What would the orcs want here? Salvation perhaps from the dragons?" One of the council members suggested.
"This is extremely concerning," Princess Seraphina said. "No matter how we proceed, we must ensure that our borders are not breached."

The council members murmured between themselves before Seraphina addressed Nia once again. "You mentioned a party that you travelled with. Where are they now?"
"I felt it prudent to not lead them directly to the portal entrance and they remain outside until my return." Nia stated as Elunara watched her closely.

Meanwhile, the remaining two Ancients watched intently. Nia did not have the close companionship with them that she had with Elunara and she was cautious of their influence over proceedings here.

One of them stepped forward. He too had an ornate walking stick. This was Oranlire of Oakland, a very powerful sorcerer from what was once known as Direfolk Moor. In the past, he had been instrumental in Nia's removal from the council but did not wish for her to be banished.

He was an elderly man but he oozed power and would be a fearful combatant in any battle.

"This party that you speak of. One of them is a dragon, is it not?" he said curtly. Nia's breath caught in her throat.
"What?!" Araneth yelled in horror and he stepped towards Nia threateningly as Seraphina gasped.
"You brought a dragon to our very doorstep!" She yelled, and her voice echoed around the platform.

Another council member that Nia did not recognise joined in, yelling for the guards to act and the platform became a noise-fueled mess as Nia desperately tried to calm the elves around her.

"Silence!" Elunara yelled suddenly. Her surprisingly powerful voice overcame everyone on the platform and the noise subsided. "Let Nialandra speak!"

Nia could sense the anger at her from the others. She needed to explain herself fast, so she started at the beginning with the night in the village and the experience with the human child who so desperately needed help.

She relayed to them how close Drakarim had come to death and how, following his battle with the dragons, she and the child had tracked him back to the cave, where he lay severely wounded and at times near to death.

The council listened as Nia described her numerous visits to the dragon, and also of his battle against the orcs as he tried to defend Thalindor and ensure it was not discovered.

She also told them about Giggles, her acceptance of Drakarim and his utmost desire to do all that he could to help bring balance back to the world.

Finally, she told them of Drakarim's belief that there were other dragons out there of likemind, those that would wish to aid in the removal of King Voldestus and return peace to the world once again.

There was a prolonged silence as she finished.

Seraphina spoke first. "Do you still believe, as you did all those years ago, that Empress Meduz-Larr and her husband are friendly to the Allied Realms?"
Nia locked eyes with Seraphina and nodded. "I do."
Araneth scoffed loudly in response and said, "Utter madness!"
"I do not recall you being a member of the council," Oranlire snapped sternly and Araneth bowed his head in shame.

The third Ancient stepped forward now. Another male, slightly younger than the others with a heavily deformed face that he received during a battle against an elder dragon named Princess Dajax during the purge.

It was a battle that the elf won.

Alaric Stormblade was an incredible combatant with skills that were legendary amongst the elves. He had been an important leader amongst his people long before he gained the status of Ancient.

"The dragon who has travelled with you. What does it require from Thalindor?" He asked, his voice barely a rasp.
"Answers to his past," Nia replied. "He has visions that he is unable to understand and does not recall his name." Nia reached into her backpack and pulled out a shattered piece of Drakarim's scale. She stepped forward and handed it to Elunara.
"I had hoped that perhaps you would sense something from this, Elunara." Nia said.

Elunara held the scale in both hands and closed her eyes. She began to glow ever so slightly as she fused mana and scale alike and delved into her senses to ascertain more about Drakarim and his past.

The silence was palpable. Nia looked between the other elves present, then to Araneth who simply returned her gaze with a cold expression. Nia was deeply concerned at what may be the outcome of this meeting, but she tried to remain hopeful.

Several long moments passed until suddenly, Elunara's pure white eyes opened in utter surprise, her mouth hanging open and she glanced around the members present.

"It.. cannot be?" She said, her gaze settled upon Nia. "Nialandra, you have found him!"

Broken chains

Spire of the Wyvern - 759 years ago

Voldestus had grown weary of late. The poor treatment that his brood mates had suffered at the hands of their warlock creators was weighing heavily upon his mind. The warlocks were constantly driven towards improving the dragons, and ensuring that they always had more to throw into battle should any fall.

The dragons were not impervious, and certainly not the lesser breeds, some of which would vanish regularly and the elders were sure that they had been lost to one dark experiment or another.

Despite constant victories on the battlefield, the destruction of the shadeling general and the dragons obeying every whim of their masters, each and every night the experimentation, the torture and the suffering continued without pause.

The Bri-Tisa warlocks would stop at nothing to improve their creations.

In the past week, at least six dragons had been condemned to the pit - a giant hole that ran deep into the earth, where failed experiments were resigned until they died of starvation in the darkness below.

In addition, after each battle the dragons were chained in the dragonhold and enchanted so that they were unable to summon their flame.

The warlocks were evil manipulators of the arcane; their magic was dark and twisted and as a result, the dragons that they created were a chaotic mixture of breeds, depending on the process used to create them.

The oldest and most powerful of the dragons were branded elders and their abilities would dwarf the smaller dragons in many ways. Their leadership was a valued element of controlling the brood.

The eleven elder dragons, each with their own unique powers and abilities were an incredible asset to the warlocks but also a huge concern, as their loyalty and controllability varied and these highly intelligent beasts would, if given the opportunity, turn against the warlocks.

Queen Catherine and the high council were unaware of the dragons' abuse and the experimentation the warlocks had used on so many small and helpless children to create the bloodborne. Asvarian had concealed his actions well, and the council members whose task it was to report back to the high council were well paid for their silence.

Asvarian was power hungry and ignorant of the dangers that he toyed with, perhaps overrating his own ability to keep his creations under control, especially as the elder dragons grew in power and influence, far beyond his original intention.

The most dangerous of the elders was Voldestus.

Voldestus had become a powerful leader. He was an immense beast, perhaps twice the size of most of his elder brothers and sisters and five times larger than the other dragons. He was also the only golden dragon amongst the brood and thus he had gained a great deal of influence.

However, the great dragon had, as a result of his abuse at the hands of the warlocks, garnered a genuine and great hatred for all the peoples of the Allied Realms, openly stating this fury to the other dragons increasingly over time.

His views had, on occasion, caused confrontations with the fire dragon Surexx, who was known for his love of the Allied Realms, but the one thing the two dragons agreed on was their wish to break free from the warlocks' grip.

Each night over the past few months, Voldestus had grown more vocal, at first between the elder dragons with whispers and mentions of revenge running late into the night. However, over time, Voldestus grew in his boldness, until eventually his patience had been pushed to its peak and Grand Master Asvarian personally visited the dragonhold, with a view to publicly punish Voldestus in front of the other elder dragons.

As the sun dipped down behind the Spire of the Wyvern and a light rain blew lazily across the surrounding marshes, the grand master came to stand before the gathered dragons.

Voldestus glared at Asvarian, his large, black eyes emanating his fury as Asvarian demanded his obedience. The old warlock oozed power; the fear that the dragons felt when he was present was very real, for many of them had at some stage suffered the tyrant's abuse.

"You will obey!" Asvarian shouted as he thrust his twisted wooden staff into the ground, and immense pain immediately erupted within Voldestus' chest.

The golden dragon roared in agony. With his free hand, Asvarian pulled an ornate wand that many of the dragons had seen before from his cloak. The wand had a golden shaft carved into the shape of a dragon that twisted its way around the wand and its tip was imbued with a small purple gem that glimmered in the dimming light.

Asvarian thrust the wand towards Voldestus whilst chanting a dark curse, his voice echoing across the courtyard. Purple light spewed forth into the elder dragon and Asvarian slowly and systematically began to rip several scales from Voldestus' side causing the Dragon to screech in agony. The other dragons watched helplessly, pulling at the enchanted chains that held them to the ground, but it was futile.

Surexx tried with all of his might to break free of the chains that bound him to the earth, but the magical constraints on him were also too strong. He roared loudly, but Asvarian ignored him and continued regardless, and this time he gripped the ornate wand with both hands and chanted as he did so until Voldestus writhed in pain, desperately trying to pull himself free of the offensive magic.

Asvarian seemed to be enjoying dishing out the punishment to his prize dragon and strolled forward confidently until he was able to reach out and touch Voldestus.

"For too long have you nurtured your ideals of freedom." he said as a jolt of mana shot from his wand straight into the open wound that he had created moments before. "You are mine. I created you. I command you!"

Voldestus tried again to free himself, but Asvarian drove another painful spell through him with a simple gesture of the wand.

"Hear me!" Asvarian shouted at the surrounding dragons. "The punishment for any of you, should you dare to question me, is DEATH!"

"You will NEVER have freedom!" He shouted directly at Voldestus, his face was alight with fury and hatred.

As Voldestus' punishment continued to be dealt unto him, several of the other warlocks had moved from the edge of the scene and were individually punishing other dragons who dared to struggle against their chains or raise their voices in protest.

Surexx glanced across the dragonhold and found himself locked in a gaze with an elder with whom he shared many views. The crystalline dragon known as Meduz-Larr shared the desperation that he felt. She was much smaller than the other elder but she too struggled against her chains and called out for the punishment to stop before she looked deep into Surexx's eyes.

To Surexx's amazement, Meduz-Larr's voice entered his mind as if she were standing right in front of him.

"I can loosen your chains," she said and Surexx's golden eyes widened in surprise. She could communicate through his mind?!

A moment later though she too was in pain as a warlock began to chant and cast his own curses into her, but Meduz-Larr managed to glance at

Surexx one last time and in that moment her eyes ignited briefly with a powerful blue light.

He looked down and examined the chains around his body, each of which was magically secured to the earth but Surexx sensed that something had changed and he tugged at his bindings as hard as he could.

Two warlocks noticed his intention and Surexx found himself screaming in agony as the warlocks approached and pummelled him with their offensive magic. He could hear other dragons roaring in anger as the onslaught continued, but Voldestus was still suffering more than his brothers and sisters and was now surrounded by currents of mana that whipped and stabbed his body as they moved.

The pain that Surexx was under was excruciating, and it felt like it would never end, but then, just as suddenly as it started, it stopped, and Surexx opened his eyes to see a humanoid figure pushing the warlocks back, a flaming curved blade in each hand.

It was Talon!

"Now!" Meduz-Larr's voice commanded in his head and he pulled with all of his might, his muscles bulging as he roared in anger.

Just as he felt that he couldn't break the chains there was a sudden and incredible crack and huge chunks of steel shattered across the dragonhold.

Almost as soon as the chains split, Surexx could feel his inner fire return and his entire body re-ignited with an intense flame.

Without hesitation he took a deep breath in. With all of his might and every ounce of strength he had, he blasted out the most destructive and furious jet of flame he had ever produced, directly at Asvarian, who vanished within the blinding torrent of fire that ran all the way to the base of the Spire of the Wyvern.

Surexx wasted no time. He took several steps forward, glanced down at Talon who was still deep in combat against two warlocks and took the chains that held Voldestus in one huge flaming claw, ripping them from the ground and setting Voldestus free at last.

There was an almighty ear splitting roar of anger and Voldestus slowly pulled himself up to his full height, dwarfing the surrounding dragons. The powerful beast spread his wings as wide as he could and the air around him heated as he drew on his inner fire. The dragonhold shook and one by one, the warlocks became aware of the dire situation they now found themselves in.

At that moment, a flaming figure leapt from the ground and flew upwards into the air as it rained down magical attacks onto Voldestus.

Asvarian!

The warlock was not so easily defeated and he soared around the Spire and fired a piercing jet of magical fury that pierced straight through Voldestus' wing, but the dragon took to the sky with an almighty beating of his wings and returned fire with a golden jet of flame and a furious roar.

Surexx moved as swiftly as he could from dragon to dragon, freeing them as more warlocks and some bloodborne emerged from the tower to join the battle raging outside. He took a moment to check back on Talon and noted that he was now moving through the battlefield engaging each and every warlock or guard that he could.

The skies above were now full of red clouds as dragon fire burst forth in all directions, some of which struck the Spire of the Wyvern, sending huge chunks of debris flying across the dragonhold and crushing any who stood below.

Surexx searched the skies for any sign of Asvarian or Voldestus. There were golden streaks of light illuminating the red clouds of smoke and Asvarian's purple lightning returning fire but no sign of either of the combatants.

As Surexx moved through the battlefield, searching for dragons that he could help, he noted that some who had been set free had immediately abandoned the area, perhaps grasping their freedom while they could, in fear that it may soon be taken back from them, if Asvarian defeated Voldestus.

Many of the elder dragons remained in the fight though and one or two had taken to the skies in an attempt to aid Voldestus. To Surexx's right, a pure white dragon named Firax fought alongside the ice twins Frostfang and Shatterclaw who had already frozen many of the warlocks, bloodborne and tower guards where they stood.

Surexx felt a sudden pain in his side and spun to find three guards, one of which had thrown his spear into the dragon's leg. Surexx unleashed a torrent of flame that incinerated all three guards until there was nothing left but black ash, and ripped the spear free before spitting it onto the floor in disgust.

The battle raged on for what seemed an eternity, but as the warlocks slowly succumbed to the immense power of the dragon horde and their guards fell, it became obvious that the dragons would emerge victorious.

Surexx located Talon and they approached one another as roars of victory emanated from all around.

"You are free now, my eternal friend," Talon said and to Surexx's surprise he removed his helm to reveal a handsome but scarred young man, with blazing purple eyes and a shaved head. It was the first time that he had seen his friend without his armour.

A second later there was an almighty crash of thunder from above and Voldestus burst through the clouds to land upon the battlefield. The ground shook with the immense impact and Voldestus looked exhausted and in a great deal of pain.

The dragons gathered around Voldestus, whose hide was seared with burns, blood and ash, and their mouths fell open as they realised that he was holding Asvarian's limp and unresponsive body.

"This is the day!" Voldestus bellowed to his brothers and sisters, "that dragon kind claims our freedom from our oppressors!"

The gathered dragons roared and blasted flame into the air in triumph.

Voldestus raised the body of Asvarian into the air and as he did so the ornate wand slipped from his robe and clattered to the muddy ground.

"We do not take flight when YOU command us! We do not burn those YOU choose to burn," He circled around, showing the body to all of the dragons before continuing, "Our inner fire is OURS to command and OURS alone!"

With that he spun and launched the lifeless body into the Spire of the Wyvern, following it with an incredible jet of golden flame that he held in place for what seemed an eternity.

Eventually the tower itself began to crumble and an entire side of it disappeared into a cloud of dust. Then, with an almighty roar, all the dragons joined in, throwing all their fury at the once proud Spire of the Wyvern and sending its debris flying in every direction. The ground shook and the air burned as the Spire slowly disappeared into a pile of molten rock.

There were cheers as Voldestus turned and approached Surexx, who stood with Talon.

"You have done well, my brother. You have set us free." Voldestus then glanced down at Talon, "Now I must set you free."

Voldestus reached forward and before Surexx could react, he crushed Talon under his enormous claws and Surexx staggered backwards in total shock.

"No," he stammered. "NO!"

Surexx felt the tether he had with Talon snap as the bloodborne's life ended and he grimaced with agony and glared at Voldestus. His flaming body flared brightly as the rage fueled his inner fire to burn even brighter.

Voldestus grinned. "Dragons rule this world now! We will feast upon the bones of these pitiful creatures that once commanded us until NONE are left standing!"

Surexx couldn't breathe. He murdered Talon?

"Kill them all, feast on their children, burn their world, I want to see NOTHING but ash!" Voldestus commanded and many of the dragons cheered, although some, including Firax and Meduz-Larr remained silent as they feared what would come next.

Sure enough, Surexx roared, his whole body flared in a fiery display and he drew everything he could from his inner flame, opening his mouth wide he unleashed a blinding spear of powerful fire directly into Voldestus chest, catching him off guard and driving him backwards as he dug his claws into the earth. He churned up the ground around him as he struggled against the blast and tried to regain his footing.

The dragons around them began to battle against one another as allegiances were formed and broken. Dragons of all sizes ripped into one another with claws and teeth, or flame and ice.

Surexx pushed forwards with his unrelenting attack on Voldestus, who was unable to break out of the fire, which was slowly breaching his outer armour. Surexx's fury was on display for all to witness, the incredible fire dragon, whose entire body flashed now with so much fire and anger that a huge area around him was also burning brightly.

Voldestus pushed back though, his immense bulk finally gripping the earth and he managed to return Surexx's flames with his own fire and the two elder dragons became locked in a powerful battle of wills.

However, as dragons raged around them, the supporters of Voldestus had gained the upper hand, thanks to their overwhelming numbers. Unknown to Surexx, Frostfang and Shatterclaw had flanked him, and they unleashed a devastating vortex of ice shards straight into his back.

Surexx soon disappeared amongst a mass of ice and steam as his body's flames extinguished, but the twins didn't stop, casting all of their might into Surexx to ensure he was defeated once and for all.

Voldestus strode to their side as the ice rage continued. He took a deep breath and then released a huge golden fireball that exploded when it hit the ice. The entire battlefield felt the impact as shards of ice and dirt flew in all directions.

Frostfang and Shatterclaw shielded themselves with their wings as ice rained down, thudding into the earth around the dragonhold.

Then there was nothing but silence.

Slowly, as the mist cleared and Voldestus emerged once again, the dragons searched the scene for Surexx's body only to find a huge crater, covered in ice and smoke but no sign of him.

Voldestus slumped, he was exhausted. His underbelly was completely black and his blood was splattered over his golden frame as well as across the grass itself. The battle had taken its toll and he would need to rest.

Meanwhile, unseen at the edge of the battlefield, Meduz-Larr skulked away and her eyes dimmed as she released the mana from her body.

As dense smoke drifted across the battlefield and Voldestus's supporters sought out and put to death any who dared to stand against them, a new age dawned upon the world of Nefi. An age of terror and destruction like no other.

An age of fire and ash.

A fire burns

Outskirts of Thalindor - present day

Drakarim watched as the large group of elves, including Nia, Elunara, Araneth and a number of guards approached from Thalindor.

Drakarim carefully placed Giggles, who was still fast asleep, against the trunk of a nearby tree and moved as silently as he could towards the newcomers.

Nia smiled and nodded as she approached. "It is OK, they mean you no harm."

Nia proceeded to introduce the elves to Drakarim, some of whom were openly nervous in front of the mighty crimson dragon and he in turn introduced himself.
Elunara, meanwhile, was in awe of the sight before her. "You are wondrous!" she exclaimed as she took a step forward.
"Don't give him a big head Elunara," Nia smiled and Drakarim huffed, sending a small amount of smoke drifting from his nostrils.

As Elunara examined the dragon, she recalled the months before the great purge, when the shadeling army had been vanquished and news arrived back from the eastern heralds.

"There were songs sung of dragons who breathed lightning and lit up the skies as they defeated their enemies, tales of Moonwing, a ghostly dragon who passed through enemy lines and vanquished a feared ogre Groxgigar in one devastating slash of her claws."

Elunara looked at the little girl huddled by the trunk of the tree, smiled gently, and continued.

"There are many epic and intriguing stories of the elder dragons, who were rumoured to tower above even the largest giant and engulf entire armies in their fury."

Elunara turned and placed her hand gently on Drakarim's claw. "However, the most enthralling of the tales I heard were of a wondrous dragon, whose entire body would become flame as they soared across the skies."

"This Dragon and its bloodborne rider were heroes amongst the people, visiting town after town along the most affected areas where they would help to rebuild and show the people that there was nothing to fear."

She looked up into Drakarim's huge golden eyes as he watched her.

"This dragon gained its title simply through the good deeds it bestowed upon the people. His name was Surexx the Kind. His heart was pure and his love for those around him was clear for all to witness."

She closed her eyes but continued to speak. "When the purge began, this mighty dragon, so it is rumoured, stood his ground against the tyrant king Voldestus, perhaps with help from others. However, sadly, he fell in battle alongside his bloodborne and Voldestus emerged the victor."

There was silence now, as Elunara chanted in elvish quietly and a light breeze whipped through the surrounding woodland. The great Nedai trees creaked and rustled their leaves overhead and the birds sang their song as daylight twinkled through the dense forest ceiling.

Nia could feel the hair on the back of her neck tingle - so much hung on the next words that Elunara spoke. She trusted her old friend and mentor. Their history was a deep and important piece of Nia's upbringing and she knew if anyone could gain the answers that Drakarim sought, it would be her.

Meanwhile, Elunara delved deeper into Drakarim's mind and he too closed his eyes and embraced the silence while focusing on the elven incantation that the Ancient whispered.

As Elunara drifted deeper into the void, she felt Drakarim's emotions touch her own, his breath became her breath, his heart became her heart.

The mists settled and Drakarim awoke with a start. He lay on his side, slumped against rocks and shallow grass. He took a breath of clean, fresh mountain air and groaned as his body ached from head to tail.

The world around him swam in and out of focus, but he could feel the coolness of the damp grass against his brittle and damaged hide. He blinked, but didn't wake up, instead slumping back down in a heap as he drifted into his regenerative state.

The mists swirled once more and Elunara floated through reality, her head now pounding with pain as she became Drakarim once more.

He walked slowly, dragging each heavy leg, and he was unable to raise his tail from the ground no matter how hard he might try. His wounds were not healing as they should, his body was rejecting it somehow and he felt guilt, betrayal and fear all at once.

He stopped to lick the water from a cool mountain stream and caught his reflection glancing back at him. He was bare, his crimson scales no longer burning with dragon fire, and he felt so much smaller, no, he was so much smaller than he remembered.

The water was soothing, he lay his head in it and let it wash over his horns. How he got to this place, he didn't know, nor could he recall who he was or where he came from.

It didn't matter, it was too much. He took another few steps and lay down beside the stream, listening to the water as he did so. Yes, sleep was needed, and he fell into a deep slumber.

He awoke some time later. Something was licking his face and he opened his eyes to find the most wonderful creature standing before him. It was much like him, only more vibrant in colour and much smaller, with a kind and innocent face.

He blinked and arose. The mountains around him were shrouded in a light mist as the sun cast its wonderful warmth across the land.

Drakarim looked around, there were more of those beautiful creatures, like miniature versions of himself, all in lovely bright, vibrant colours and full of the presence of mana.

They were tiny compared to Drakarim, but they made him feel safe. Like he was at home.

The mists swirled once more and Elunara travelled across time before she was Drakarim once again and he was stronger now, but his mind was still lost and confused. He felt he needed to learn more about his past, to re-discover and re-learn what he had forgotten.

It was time for Drakarim to leave the smaller creatures behind, he felt sorrow and loss, but love and thanks. He wished to see them again one day.

Perhaps.

His journey was long but he was able to fly again, and he took to the skies and felt the wind rushing against his face. He felt pleasure, and wanted more of this feeling.

As he flew above the earth, he could see small beings travelling across a mountainous path, a dangerous route for ones so small and fragile, and he circled above them, curiosity filling his mind.

Something larger, dark and evil, followed the small beings around the mountain path. Drakarim felt alarmed - he sensed the danger and noticed that the small beings were fleeing their pursuers.

He flew lower and then circled once again to investigate further. The pursuers wore armour and carried large weapons. They were inquisitors. A breed of dragon. He remembered now - these were hunters.

He watched as the pursuers grew closer, feeling urgency within and his inner fire began to burn once again.

He swooped low, between the fleeing prey and the hunters, and landed on the edge of the mountain path, his claws gripping deep into the rocks.

"Move! This is our hunt!" One of the inquisitors demanded as they came to stand before Drakarim.
"Hunt your prey elsewhere. These beings are under my protection," Drakarim responded.
"Protection?" The inquisitor scoffed with a growl. He did not hesitate any further, the conversation was over and he launched his sharpened spear at Drakarim, who batted it away like it was nothing before unleashing his fury at the aggressors.

Elunara recoiled at the sight of blood, the feel of ripping another creature apart tore away at her very soul. However, she also felt a sense of accomplishment as the last inquisitor fell down dead.

Drakarim took to the skies once again as the mists encircled him.

Time and time again, over many years and many months, Drakarim sought to regain what he had lost. He leapt into battles, took many wounds and defeated many of his enemies as he roamed the lands over countless miles.

As Elunara drifted from one space to the next, she felt closer to Drakarim. She became all the more aware of the dragon's innermost drive, his compassion and his longing to make the wrongs right once again.

Finally, she watched as he saved a small child from a burning village. She felt his heartache at losing the mother and experienced his anger and pain as he battled against the other dragons who attempted to bring him down on that day.

Drakarim barely survived that encounter. Yet all he could think about was the child. He blamed himself for not doing more and he cursed the dragons who burnt the settlement to the ground.

Elunara had seen enough.

She released her hand and stopped chanting. She slowly drifted back through the mists, their colours changing from crimson to a deep green until she was once again standing before the other elves.

She looked up at the dragon who opened his eyes and looked back, wonder and appreciation etched across his face.

"I.." Drakarim stammered.

Elunara patted his claw and smiled the most brilliant of smiles. "You, my wonderful and kind friend, are the great elder dragon, Surexx the Kind."

The gathered elves gasped loudly and Nia fell to her knees, tears streaming down her face.

Drakarim stood in shock. He had travelled those memories along with Elunara, experienced those feelings, and seen the wonderful mountain that he now missed so much, as more memories flooded back to him like a torrent.

These were his memories, this was his story.

He recalled the fateful night when Voldestus began his rule and they had battled one another. But how had he survived under the twins' ice blast? And how did he arrive on that mountain top, with the small creatures who had nurtured him back to health?

Perhaps it was Meduz-Larr. She had shown that she had learned to weave mana much as the magi had. Perhaps she had used that ability in those moments and removed Drakarim from harm.

He still had so many questions, but now he had some answers. The pieces of his puzzle were finally coming together.

He looked over at Nia, who was still in tears as she gazed back in awe. The other elves who had been hostile and guarded towards Drakarim were now simply staring at him in bewilderment.

Finally, Drakarim felt a small hand on his leg and he looked down to see Giggles, who had awoken and wanted to know what was happening, and he smiled.

Perhaps now, with the answers that he had and the support of the elves, he could locate more of his brothers and sisters who also sought peace. Perhaps Firax survived that night, or the Seer, or any of the others who might help stand against Voldestus.

It was a possibility that could not be ignored, but where could they start?

"Surexx, we must inform the council of our findings. Please understand that it might be best if you wait for us here so as to not cause panic within Thalindor," Elunara said.

Aranath nodded politely to Drakarim and he led the guards back into the trees, closely followed by Nia who waved at Giggles as she left.

Drakarim looked down caringly at the little girl. "Hello sleepy one," he said but Giggles looked confused.
"Why did they call you Surexx?" She asked, "Your name is Drakarim."
"Yes it is. I no longer wish to be called Surexx." he answered and then, a moment later, "You spoke!"

Drakarim was amazed, the little girl beside him laughed and then said, "Oh, yes I did!"

Together the giant crimson dragon and the small human orphan laughed and chuckled and chatted as they caught up on lost time.

Drakarim felt more free than ever before.

The survivor

Fort Valian - present day

Since the discovery of Arlestra, a valian survivor found deep within the vast underground city of Fort Valian, the city itself had become a hive of activity.

Arlestra's wealth of knowledge about the ancient city was paramount to the excavations and she had provided detailed maps to aid the work that would help Fort Valian grow and thrive once more.

As her magical strength slowly returned, she was also able to help reconstruct some of the more complicated structures including the old city hall and entrance to the scholars' quarter, where the great library once stood.

Alestra had grown close to Arwin's partner, Joselle, and they spent hours talking about the old city while Joselle had learnt much about the valian themselves, their deep and vibrant history and the fascinating powers that they could wield.

However, General Dervish had kept strict surveillance over the valian, and she was banned from leaving the city, but this didn't bother her too much as the people of Fort Valian accepted her aid and many were fascinated to meet her.

Arwin's eyes had never lost their purple glow which started the night that he discovered Arlestra., It was unnerving for both him and the others around him. At first, he felt Joselle pull away on a few occasions but eventually she grew accustomed to his new look and accepted the changes.

Arwin had spoken in depth to Arlestra about the imbuement that she mentioned when they had first met. She wanted to learn more about what caused the change in his eyes and also discover more about the changes that they may have to deal with in the future.

Arlestra thought it possible that the Armonis had lain dormant until Arwin arrived in Fort Valian, and as he spent more time within the fallen city, his connection to Arlestra became stronger until his imbuement became obvious for all to see.

This only added to the unease Arwin felt and his nights were full of restless sleep as he struggled to become accustomed to the news that he was someone imbued with an ancient and unpredictable magic.

He had relayed his concerns many times to both Heg and Barn but both had been fully supportive and had proven themselves once again as great friends.

"Arwin!" Heg called as she strolled swiftly towards him, "I've been looking everywhere for you."

Arwin was sitting at the edge of the outer ravine path, which wound its way down into a vast cave system that sat beneath the city.

He looked up as Heg approached, "Sorry Heg, what's up?"
"You have got to come and see this! Quick!" Heg said as she gestured for him to follow.
Arwin tossed one last stone down the ravine and pulled himself to his feet. "What's going on?"
"Come on, you'll love this!" Heg said excitedly, eager for Arwin to follow.
As they strolled up the pathway towards Fort Valian, Heg placed a hand on Arwins arm supportively, "you ok kid?"

Arwin nodded but didn't feel much like talking right now. Apart from feeling exhausted, he really didn't know what to say. Instead, they just walked in silence and Heg hummed an old dwarven tune to keep them company.

They moved through the hustle of the town, passing the market square where a new blacksmith's had been constructed and the sound of hammer on steel rang out across the city. There was a great deal of excitement and chatter as Arwin and Heg pushed their way through a throng of people until they passed down into the scholar's quarter.

As they arrived, large chunks of marble and stone passed them by in mid-air, surrounded by a familiar magical aura. Then Arlestra appeared up ahead, her long, slender arms outstretched before her as she guided the stones away.

Beyond her, surrounded by a small crowd was a large archway that extended from the floor through to the cave ceiling above, and through it was the most incredible sight that Arwin had ever seen.

The great archive had finally been revealed. Lines and lines of books, tomes, ancient slabs, artefacts, artworks and more filled the space that ran deep into the rock face and was well lit by a combination of bright blue enchanted orbs that seemed to hang effortlessly in the air.

Above them, there were huge slabs of marble that spun quickly as if they had a mind of their own, resulting in a constant cool breeze throughout the great library.

Arwin's mouth hung open in amazement at the site that stood before him and Heg grinned openly. "Told ya!"
Just then Joselle came running excitedly to hug Arwin, "Isn't it marvellous?!" she said.
"I can't believe it," Arwin stammered. "Did Arlestra do all of this?"
Joselle shook her head. "No, the library was almost intact, though it had some damage deeper inside. It has its own Armonis that was dormant until Arlestra activated it again," Joselle said, she grabbed Arwin's hand and pulled him into the archive, where she began to excitedly point out the incredible things she had found.

Joselle explained that the valian's library was not just about dusty old books and ancient knowledge, but was also a primary museum of artefacts, a storage of records and that it held an almost religious significance to the valian that used to live here.

It was the heart of the ancient city, and it was beating once again.

Arwin walked through the rows of books, letting his fingers drift across the various items that had sat undiscovered for almost eight hundred years. It was an overwhelming feeling of discovery and it almost felt like he had a connection with this place that he was unable to put into words.

As he glanced around, he noted several people thanking Arlestra as she gazed at the library once again. She looked deeply emotional and also incredibly moved as she smiled towards Arwin.

Her voice entered his mind, "We can find so many answers here!"

Arwin nodded and smiled, deciding that he would spend the rest of his day here, not to read the books as they were all written in a language that he couldn't understand, but he was intrigued by the incredible collection of artefacts, some in glass cases and others strewn about the floor without a home.

It wasn't long before General Dervish had instructed his militia to lock down the great archive until they could be sure that the items that lay there were not dangerous, and the disgruntled crowd was ushered away.

Arwin, however, was allowed to remain, along with Joselle and a number of others who had been instructed to catalogue as many artefacts as they could.

Amongst the items found were an enchanted pair of gloves that created their own light, a small metal orb that seemed to allow the user to see through some surfaces and a musical instrument that played its own beautiful tunes.

However, the most incredible discovery was in a chamber off to the side of the main library, through a thick metal door that took some effort to open, thanks to heavily rusted hinges.

Around the outer edge of the chamber, each on their own pedestal, were five equally spaced individual metal frames of varying designs that resembled the frames of floor to ceiling mirrors.

Each frame had a small Armonis stone set within the top and before each of them was a different word, etched into the floor itself.

Upon investigating, Arlestra had informed the team that these words related to old locations in the world, but they were in an ancient valian dialect that was difficult to understand. The Armonis embedded in each of the frames was non-responsive leaving the chamber one large, un-answered puzzle.

Arlestra had reasoned that perhaps these were transportation portals, not unlike the ones used deeper within the city, but she had never seen nor heard of this chamber before, so she and Joselle had decided to look through the records for an explanation about their purpose.

As the others moved off to search for more information, Arwin followed the steps up to the nearest frame and examined the intricate metalwork up close. The base of the frame had been crafted to resemble rocks, and as the frame progressed upwards, the rocks became a hundred spears and swords, intertwining until they arched over the top of the frame and encapsulated the Armonis gem at the top of the arch.

It was a wonderful item to look at and more impressive than many of the architectural wonders he had witnessed around Fort Valian.

As Arwin was about to turn away from the frame, he noticed a tiny animal figure etched onto the rocky base, he knelt down and gently ran his finger over the surface. The animal was a small lizard-like creature, and as Arwin examined further, he noticed more of them, dotted about the rocks in various poses.

"Draklings, the original form of what you now know as dragons," Arlestra's voice entered Arwin's mind and he turned as she stepped into the room. "How they once were, innocent and one with the world around them."

Arwin was puzzled, "Dragons were different during the time of the valian?" He asked.

Arlestra nodded. "Something happened that transformed those peaceful creatures into something monstrous. The dragons your people know today are very different from the ones my people knew of eight hundred years ago."

Her mood seemed to dip and she stared silently at the red frame before them. Arwin suddenly realised just how difficult this must be for Arlestra, rebuilding a city she once knew as vibrant and full of life.

Valian life. Now just ghosts amongst the ruins.

"I've never had a chance to say how sorry I am about your people. I hope that the wizard that attacked the city and killed so many met a fitting end after the battle." He said. Arlestra was grateful for the support. "My people are gone now. Most perished in the attack or were buried in the rubble, but I can only hope that some escaped and perhaps made a new home elsewhere." She said hopefully.
Arwin nodded, "I'm sure they did, and one day I'll help you find them."
"Arwin, Heg is looking for you," Joselle announced from the doorway.

Arwin got to his feet and passed Joselle, giving her a quick kiss as he did so.

Heg was pacing up and down outside, a worried look etched across her face. "It's Barn, his unit hasn't come back from the ravine!"
Arwin was confused. "They went into the ravine?! Why?"
"No time, I'll explain on the way. Grab Arlestra, I think we'll need her!" Heg replied and Arwin immediately ran off to gather Arlestra and any other scouts he could find before meeting Heg at the top of the ravine path.

Thanks to Arwin's quick thinking, they had managed to gather a rescue party of five, several of whom were seasoned trackers who had been into the ravine before. They were all dwarves, part of a caravan of travellers who arrived at Fort Valian more than twenty years ago.

As they moved swiftly down the ravine path, Arwin caught up to Heg, who he had never seen move so fast.

"Heg, what was Barn doing down there?" Arwin asked.
Heg pulled Arwin down to her level and whispered, "Routine patrol. Barn don't usually go and the dwarves do it all, but Barn reckons this lot were up ta somethin' so he went along."
Arwin thought for a second. "You mean I just asked more dwarves to join us and they might be trouble?"

Heg just nodded and made the face she made when things weren't going well. It was a face Arwin had witnessed too often.

"You think they found something down there?" He asked.

Heg nodded again and explained that Barn should have been back hours ago but hadn't returned.

"Did Dervish authorise this?" Arwin asked.
"Not exactly," Heg replied. "He knew of the problem but didn't want anyone else risking their lives down here. We've lost people in the past."
"Great," Arwin sighed as the party followed the narrow pathway that led them into the depths of the ravine, occasionally stopping to light the numerous sconces that were fitted into the rock face for additional light.

Eventually they reached a point where the path dipped into a large cavern that vanished into the darkness ahead. Water droplets could be heard in the distance but other than that, it was silent.

Arlestra stepped forward and raised her hands into the air. She chanted for a few seconds and then several spheres of light left her frail body and hovered out across the cave. They weren't bright enough to light the ceiling of the cave, but it was enough to provide guidance throughout.

"There's a small entrance to the next cave over there somewhere. That's where they would have gone" Heg whispered as she pointed westwards. Arlestra guided her spheres across the path and sure enough in the distance, Arwin could see a smaller cave entrance.

Was that the flicker of a light that he saw beyond the entrance?

As the party moved carefully across the cave, several of the dwarves began to moan about the task that they now faced and Arwin did his best to listen.

"Fwayn knew about the dangers, they weren't deep enough to.."
"Shut ya mouth Koll, we have work to do."

Heg stepped in front of them and turned angrily.

"What in the five hells are you talkin' about?" She demanded and Kol, the oldest of the five dwarves looked sheepish.
"Wait, please tell me ya didn't start mining down 'ere?" Heg asked.

"It were only a small dig, we ain't hurtin' nobody n there was already a mine so we just kinda carried on." Kol replied but Heg grabbed him by the scruff of his neck and pulled him close.
"Dervish ordered you idiots that no dwarf was to mine down 'ere, it ain't worth the risk!" she said angrily, but still kept her voice to a whisper as best she could.

One of the other dwarves stepped towards Heg and Arwin reached for his sword instinctively but the dwarf raised his hands apologetically. This one was called Harnis, a rough looking middle-aged dwarf with an even rougher sounding voice. His beard was a tangle of brown and grey and Arwin was sure there was some food lodged in there somewhere.

"We just wanted to 'elp, its wot we do, Heg. We found gemstones!" Harnis said.
"What in the name of the old gods would we need with gemstones?!" Heg asked but Harnis just shrugged.
"Ok, we said sorry," Koll shrugged and Heg pulled him closer.

"If you got my mate killed, I'll toss ya off the ravine," she growled before releasing him with a shove.
"Do you think they disturbed somethin' down 'ere?" She addressed Arlestra who nodded.
"It is possible, there are many other creatures in the deeper tunnels," he replied.

The party crept towards the entrance ahead, where a small torch light flickered. There was another sconce here on the wall which had already been lit and the cave itself had a number of valian-made items around, including rusted tools and containers. The cave was nothing more than a rather slim mine shaft that seemed to split into two paths up ahead.

"Is that a.." Koll said, Arlestra nodded, her dark sight was better than the rest of the party.
"A corpse, another dwarf, he has an arrow in his back," she said.
"It's Fwayne," Koll whispered. He pulled a small pickaxe from his side harness, while other members of the party readied weapons for whatever lay ahead in the darkness.

Arlestra released the light spheres from her control, lowering the light and increasing the chance of the party moving un-noticed.

Arwin struggled to see now and made sure he stuck close to the others as they moved forward, but as they passed the dwarf corpse, it became clear that one of the paths ahead was well lit the deeper that it went.

As they crept on, they found more signs that there had been a skirmish, and there were a number of bodies, some were clearly residents of Fort Valian but others were fairly small creatures, with long snouts and fur-covered bodies.

"Cave gnolls," Heg whispered. Arwin noticed she was growing more anxious and seemed to be closely scrutinising each body that they passed. He placed a hand on her arm and told Heg that he was sure Barn was OK.

The cave widened out just a few steps further down the shaft into what appeared to be a work area, complete with a table and more tools. A gruff voice echoed from ahead.

"Where from?!" It growled menacingly in a strange accent that Arwin was unable to place.
"I've seen puppies that are more menacing than you," Barn's voice replied weakly. Heg went to run forward but Arwin pulled her back and placed a finger to his lips.

He crept past Heg and then crawled to the back of a large rock to get a better view on the dangers that lay ahead. Once in position, he peered cautiously around the rock, counting the enemies as he did so, then he turned back to Heg and held four fingers up.

Arlestra's voice echoed into everyone's mind, "I can blind them with a spell, beware though, there may be more gnolls ahead."

Arwin nodded and readied his sword, while the dwarves did the same. They would have to strike fast.

Arlestra flicked a hand forward and suddenly the corridor was full of light. Arwin spun around the rock and leapt forward at the nearest gnoll, managing to plunge his sword deep into the creature's side and bringing it down immediately.

As he looked for his next target, Heg swung her hammer at the cave gnoll that had been interrogating Barn, who appeared seriously wounded, his tunic covered in blood. The gnoll took a hit but stepped backwards and attempted to swing at Heg with its stone axe but, still startled from Arlestra's blinding spell, it hit nothing but air.

There was a roar accompanied with more angry shouts from further down the mine shaft, as other gnolls became alerted to the skirmish. Meanwhile one of the dwarves fell to the ground with a large wound to his head, but Koll stepped forward and finished his assailant with a clean swing of his pickaxe.

Arlestra quickly threw another blinding spell down the corridor to slow the gnolls reinforcements from arriving, and launched a number of crates, rocks and other items down the corridor with her impressive powers.

"Heg! You came!" Barn smiled, his face was covered in dried blood and he held his hand tightly to his side.
"You're an idiot!" She shouted as she swung again at the gnoll but he managed to block the strike with his axe.
"Listen! There's a whole army down 'ere, fuckin' hundreds of em!" Barn struggled to shout as the sounds of combat filled the mine.

Another gnoll fell to a crunching strike from one of the dwarves, but as he celebrated the kill, an arrow implanted itself in the back of his skull and his eyes rolled up in his head before he slumped to the ground.

Harnis roared with anger, ran forward to the gnoll nearest him and grabbed it before smashing its head into the rocks at least four times, sending blood splatter everywhere.

Arwin meanwhile had moved up. As he passed Heg, he spun and decapitated the gnoll that she had engaged before readying himself for the reinforcements that were coming from the mine, narrowly avoiding an enemy arrow as he did so.

Heg was impressed - she had never seen Arwin fight before and this was quite something to behold, but the gnolls outnumbered the party and it was time to leave. She helped Barn to his feet and together they struggled back towards the entrance as Arlestra threw another blinding spell.

Several arrows hissed through the air and ricocheted off the mine's rocky walls as the party made their way back up the tunnel, but new voices and a scurry of feet up ahead told them that the small cave entrance through which the party had entered the mine was now blocked.

"The other tunnel.." Barn struggled to talk and he looked weak. Arlestra moved closer to Heg and Barn and placed her hands on his wounds and started chanting. A second later her hand was aglow with magical energy.
"This will help, but it is only brief," she said.

Heg and Arwin led the party back down to where the tunnels split in two. The gnolls were close now and a war trumpet sounded from further down the mine. Together they struggled into the darkness of the unlit tunnel, stumbling over various items and rocks as they did so.

"There's no way out and we can't fight in the dark!" Arwin warned.

Arlestra spun towards the approaching gnolls and whipped her hands across the air. Blue spirals twisted and coiled from the ground, spinning their way around the top of the mine shaft where support beams began to shudder and contort.

"Brace yourselves!" Her voice echoed in the minds of the party members as the entire mine entrance collapsed in a torrent of rock, wood and soil.

Seconds later, the party was standing before nothing but rock. Arlestra created her spheres once again but she was close to exhaustion now and the remaining dwarves lit torches as the dust settled.

Arwin placed his hand on Arlestra's shoulder "It's OK. She nodded, releasing the spheres and slumped to her knees.

Heg thought quickly. If the gnolls found a way round the blockage, they would be on the party in no time.

"We have to keep moving," she said. There was a collective sigh but everyone knew the situation could change in a heartbeat and together they began to make their way down the tunnel.

Behind them, beyond the fallen passageway, the cave gnolls were scrambling to break through, but they were also aware of the shadows that they themselves had been fleeing before they arrived here.

For if those creatures were to discover them once again, it would be a bloody and terrible battle.

Unity

The Tower of Light - present day

Plagar watched intently as Galen proceeded to channel mana from the surrounding environment before sending a shower of ice and cold water across the room at a makeshift target against the far wall.

"Good," he said, "that spell is known as a frost vortex."
Galen nodded and smiled. "A weak one."
"It's actually an advanced spell, so you should be proud of yourself," Plagar said sternly and Galen grinned.

Plagar was just as cold and to the point as he ever had been and lessons with him were short compared to the other mages that Galen had learnt from over the last few months. However, his talent was clear and his instruction solid, which worked well for Galen and he responded to Plagar's tuition positively.

Between his lessons, Galen had also explored outside the Tower of Light with a number of other mages. The cold, snow covered wastelands surrounding the tower were treacherous at best, with deep snow storms occurring often even during the warmest months of the year. There were some terrifying beasts that wandered the wastes and it was a strict rule that excursions were to be conducted in groups of no less than five mages to ensure their safety.

Though Galen had never witnessed such a beast, Ice Giants were rumoured to roam openly which was actually something of a comfort to Galen, for he knew well that the giants and dragons had a long history and Voldestus was not keen on starting any wars against giant kind, at least not while he still had the Allied Realms biting at his ankles.

Galen's exploration of the tower had taken him to many extraordinary rooms, and each discovery was just as incredible as the last, but there were still questions that plagued his mind constantly.

The Tower of Light, for example, had stood for many years, evading the eyes of dragons and providing those within, a safe and secure environment, though the number of non-magical inhabitants was lower than Galen had expected. This led him to understand that the Tower of Light was not reaching out for survivors, nor was it offering solace to anyone other than their own.

It was an unnerving thought and something that did bother the old scholar a great deal, for he had witnessed first hand the suffering that many were enduring out in the harsh reality of the world, and they could have had solace here within the Tower of Light.

"Walk with me." Plagar said as their lesson came to an end. Galen did as instructed and the two men exited the practice chamber and made their way outside.
"You are, of course, aware that there are five schools of arcana." Plagar said as they walked into a long corridor lined by marble statues depicting a number of historic magi who had once learnt their arts right here within the tower.

Plagar continued, "the staff that you carry does not follow any of these schools, which is why it is unique. You see, a magi will follow one or maybe two schools, they would be unable to wield anything more than this."

Plagar extended his hand, palm up and created a small flame that flickered as they proceeded on their way. "For example I specialise in the school of the flame, but I can also extend my skills into the school of wind, and as a result I am unable to push my abilities any further than this, it is a natural barrier that is arcana's way of ensuring there are no masters of all."

Galen nodded, "I understand, so why is this staff so different?"

"Ah!" Plagar exclaimed. "The gem imbued within your staff is not of this world, thus it does not follow the same rules. Instead, what it appears to do is simply draw mana from the weave and allow you to create using that mana. I am unsure as to the limits of this ability but it is this that Master Polus Vindwaar utilised for such powerful healing spells during his lifetime."

"Fascinating," Galen said as he took this new information on board, "and if I were to lose the staff or it would be destroyed?"
"Then I believe you would be unable to manage a single spell, but I would not advise on testing this theory, for it may hamper the connection you now have with the gem within your staff."

Galen understood. He had grown attached to the staff, certainly more so since he had dwelled within the Tower of Light and learnt to use its powers. He couldn't put his finger on it, but he did now feel a certain connection with the magical item.

As the two mages continued their conversation both were seemingly unaware that the walls around them were changing, slowly and subtly. Slabs were shifting silently, phasing between one another. Behind them where there was once a straight corridor lit by many magically infused torches, there was now a junction draped in shadow.

It was Plagar that noticed the changes first. He paused in his tracks and the conversation stopped abruptly.

Galen noted the look upon Plagar's face as it changed into one of confusion "That's peculiar," Plagar said quietly.
"What's happening?" Galen asked, but he already knew the answer.

For before them, rather than the usual corridor that they had walked many times over, was a large metal doorway, inscribed with an array of arcanum symbols that neither Plagar nor Galen were able to decipher. The door was open just a touch and a circular room sat beyond.

It was as if they had been transported unknowingly to a completely different area of the tower, and both mages were bemused at what lay before them. Galen and Plagar slowly and cautiously edged forwards, Galen feeling the panic growing within his chest as they drew closer to the room, which appeared to be well lit from within.

"Caution is advised." Plagar whispered, Galen noted that he had his hands up, mana already drawn to them in case it was needed. He closed his eyes and tried to focus, but he found it difficult to draw the necessary mana while his mind was racing. Eventually he found his calm and the gem atop the staff lit up brightly.

As they drew closer, the interior came into view. Five pedestals were equally spaced around the room, upon which were five very different looking mirror frames that stood around the height of a small doorway.

Galen walked cautiously inside, followed by Plagar, and they noted that each mirror frame had a gem embedded within the top, a blue gem. The magical aura within the room matched that of Galen's staff and he immediately felt a connection with it.

"The gems." Galen pointed, and Plagar seemed to notice as well.

Galen's curiosity got the better of him and he ascended the steps to the middle mirror frame, which was made of a pure black metal with no shine to the surface whatsoever.

The frame was carefully crafted into a beautifully detailed twist of vines, complete with sharp thorns, that arose all the way to the gem sitting within the centre of the arch above the frame. Galen was about to reach out to touch the frame when suddenly the gems in both his staff and the frame itself began to glow brightly.

Before Galen could react the centre of the frame sprung to life with a crack and he stepped back in shock as it revealed a dark energy, pulsating and reverberating across the open surface.

Galen stood in silence as he took this new revelation in. Slowly, Plagar ascended the steps and he looked astonished at the sight before them.

"This appears to be a portal of some description," Plagar pondered.

The surface that had appeared across the mirror frame shimmered in and out of focus. As it did so, Galen could just make out small details amidst the dark images - perhaps he was looking into a room that was mostly devoid of light?

He channelled some energy and created a light source atop his staff, but despite lighting the very room in which they now stood, it did nothing to the space beyond the portal.

Galen stepped back from the portal and retrieved his small notepad from his robes, proceeded to tear a blank page from within and after screwing it up into a tight ball he threw it at the portal.

However, as the parchment collided with the black surface of the portal there was a loud crack, a spark and the parchment deflected across the room engulfed in flame.

"I guess we won't be touching that," Galen mused with a smile but Plagar was not impressed. Galen stepped back down to the centre of the room, and, as he did so, the portal closed with a loud *CRACK* and the gem dimmed once again.

Plagar, who still stood beside the portal turned to regard Galen, utterly gobsmacked and Galen leant on his staff with both hands as he considered their findings.

"It would appear you are the one that is activating the portal. Perhaps even your presence was what allowed us to discover this chamber in the first place. Leave your staff there and approach it again." Plagar instructed.

Galen complied, leaning the staff against the outside wall of the room, and then stepped before the black portal gateway once again. This time, however, it did not activate.

This confirmed it. Galen's staff, the Staff of Vanis, had a direct link to the portals within this chamber. Galen thought back to his time with Alacatus, and recalled his words: "The stone brought you to me."

Perhaps then, Galen was sure that the staff had brought him to this chamber to show him something. Perhaps there was a link here to Alacatus, or there was more to learn from the other portals.

Plagar, meanwhile, looked at the portals individually: a frame of red metal, one of green wood, the black metal frame where he currently stood, the next was polished silver and finally one of rough stone. Surely they couldn't be, but it matched perfectly.

"The Pillars of Twilight! Of course!" He exclaimed in excitement. "Each of these portals represents one of the arcane towers. The Tower of Light has a direct link to all the other arcane towers! Absolutely incredible!"

Could these portals be passable somehow? Plagar summoned his will and reached out with his mind but something powerful was blocking him from his search. Perhaps an enchantment of some description had disabled the full use of the portals.
"It appears someone does not want us to pass through these portals." he said as he opened his eyes.

Galen nodded, retrieving the staff, and made the decision to try each portal, one at a time, starting with the left side of the chamber.

He glanced at Plagar for reassurance, who nodded in encouragement.

Galen made his way up the steps until he stood before the first frame. This one was painted in a dark red paint that had faded away over the years. Galen brushed away the dust layered over its surface until he could see many small draklings atop a rocky framework that blended into twisting swords across the archway.

Seconds later, once again the gem atop the frame began to glow brightly and with a crack, the portal re-activated.

This time Galen was able to view a circular room, not unlike the one in which he was standing right now, but it was empty, and although late afternoon light was pouring in through the open door, the room appeared to be dark and in a state of ruin.

A single skeleton lay slumped against the far wall, covered in dust and grime. A journal lay open just a few feet away, its pages worn away by the passing of time.

Plagar stepped forwards. "The Red Moon, situated in the Western Wastelands. Once held by the Flamewalkers of 'Inith."

Galen felt he already knew the answer to this test, however, he once again screwed up a page from his notes and threw it at the portal where it ignited and flew across the room.

Galen made a few notes and tucked the pad back into the pocket of his robes. He then made his way to the next portal, which was made of a slightly different material to the last two, a type of green wood, tough and smooth to the touch, that he was not familiar with. The frame was slightly thicker than the others and the artwork depicted healthy looking trees surrounded by many woodland animals. As this frame extended upwards, it was as if the tree canopy itself made the arch and the Armonis stone at its centre was nestled deep within the leaves.

Galen ran his hand gently across the dusty surface as the portal cracked into life.

A wonderful scene of vibrant greens and brilliant bright sunshine was a welcome sight for Galen's tired eyes. He stepped back to admire the impressive view extending before him. It was a dense forest canopy, where light streamed through the thick coverage and dappled the area, but it seemed as though perhaps the frame at the other end of this portal link had fallen over and was now facing upwards.

Plagar strolled slowly across the room to the portal and pondered for a moment.

"The Tower of the Vine, its location remains a mystery. Could the tower be no more than a ruin now?" He questioned.

Galen once again tossed a small piece of paper at the portal and as before it deflected away with a crack. Each time he made his notes, keeping a detailed record of what he was experiencing here, and he moved along to the next portal, but as he passed the black framed portal at the centre of the five he asked Plagar which of the arcane towers this could have been connected to.

"The Spire of the Wyvern," Plagar sighed, "where dragons were created, and it is said our nightmares began. This tower was rumoured to be destroyed on the same night that the dragons turned against their masters."

Galen made some notes and then ascended the steps to the next of the frames, which was a smooth, polished metal and angular in its design. He stretched out a hand and brushed it across the surface of this frame, but this time neither his staff nor the gem embedded within the archway reacted to his presence.

"Curious." he mused, and glanced at Plagar. "Which of the towers is this?"
"I would imagine the Silver Moon Spire. It stood over the Ardune Sea and commanded the waves and the creatures within to heed," Plagar answered.

Galen stepped back and made some notes specifically about the possibility of a damaged portal. Then he moved across to the final one. This was stone like in its design, huge rocky pathways extended around the base and merged with what appeared to be a city, built into the rocks themselves.

"This one would be the Bastion of Shade, a mystery to me where this would be located," Plagar said.

Galen nodded and placed his hand on the surface and a moment later the portal jumped to life. Again, there was a room beyond the portal of a similar size and shape as the very one in which Galen now stood. It was well lit, with some kind of sconce upon the wall emitting a blue light into the room.

This time, however, Galen was amazed to note that he could see movement just beyond the doorway to the room at the other end of this portal link. He glanced back to Plagar, who also looked surprised.

The two mages stood in utter silence for several minutes, unsure how to react in case the movements created at the other end of the portal link were that of hostile creatures. At one moment Plagar felt they needed to shut the link off but curiosity spurred him on.

They listened intently, and it was only now that Galen realised there were no sounds coming through from the other side of the portal link. In fact, he hadn't heard anything from any of the others, not even the trees and bird song from the forest portal.

"Hello!" He said loudly, but if there was someone beyond the door it seemed as though they were unable to hear him.

Plagar came to stand alongside Galen as he paced to and fro, deep in thought.

As he walked past the open portal he suddenly noticed a figure standing within the doorway of the room at the other end of the portal link, making him jump somewhat.

"Galen!" Plagar exclaimed as he too noticed the figure.

A young woman, perhaps of teenage years with shoulder length black hair, stood, clearly shocked with what she was witnessing. It was Joselle. Standing within the chamber at Fort Valian, her heart beating fast and eyes wide with surprise. She appeared to be trying to speak and Galen also attempted to make conversation, but she was unable to hear him.

As she stepped forward into the room a sudden realisation hit Galen and he held his hand out before him as a signal to stop. As Joselle paused, he scribbled in his notes as clearly as he could and then turned the pad around to show Joselle his message.

DO NOT TOUCH PORTAL, DANGER

Joselle read the note and nodded her understanding back to Galen. He then scribbled another note and showed this next.

MY NAME IS GALEN DINN

Joselle smiled, then she held a finger up and left the room for a moment before returning with some parchment and a quill. She placed an ink pot on the floor before her and dipped the quill before scribbling on a portion of the parchment.

My name is Joselle. Where are you?

Galen smiled, this was a wondrous moment indeed. He scribbled his reply excitedly and displayed it for Joselle to read.

TOWER OF LIGHT

Joselle's eyes widened and she wrote a reply.

Fort Valian

The valian name immediately piqued Galen's curiosity further, but communication was proving slow between himself and Joselle.

Plagar stepped towards Galen and placed a hand on his arm, "Caution, we do not know this person and we cannot be compromised."
"I understand." Galen replied.

Hours passed by and Joselle and Galen continued to write long into the night, as Plagar reported their findings back to the grand mage. Galen and Joselle were each keen to learn from the other, each equally excited and enthralled to be using such a powerful magical device to converse.

Perhaps, together, they could find a way to allow passage between the portals, bringing the two immense Pillars of Twilight together once again.

A perilous journey

The Great Glade - present day

Drakarim, Giggles and Nia had spent the last few nights nestled within the safety of Thalindor.

Since the Ancients had discovered that Drakarim was once the great Surexx, a dragon who had saved thousands of lives through his own risk and pushed back the deadly shadeling horde so many years ago, his treatment here had immediately improved.

Drakarim and his travel companions were now well fed and free to explore the elven city as they saw fit, though wherever they travelled there seemed to be quite the crowd gathered to welcome them. However, for Drakarim, each day spent within Thalindor was another day wasted, when he could be out there trying to gather support from his fellows, for without other dragons alongside him, it would be impossible to defeat Voldestus no matter how pure his intentions.

Nia had spent the earlier part of the day liaising with Elunara, who had agreed that for Drakarim to have any chance of raising a force against Voldestus, he would need to travel swiftly and remain undetected for as long as was possible.

Elunara shared a vast history with Nia and her affection for the young soulwalker was certainly strong. At first she had tried her best to talk Nia into staying at Thalindor with Giggles, however Nia was stern in her response. Drakarim needed aid, and she was the perfect person to provide it.

Besides, as she explained to Elunara, Drakarim had become a friend and she would not let the dragon down in his hour of need.

Something was troubling the Ancient. After some time together, Nia decided to push for an answer as to what it might be.

"The charms you discovered upon the orclanders," Elunara replied. The extended name for the orcs was a historical difference and many of the Ancients referred to them this way. "The charms were indeed elven craftsmanship. This is most vexing."
"Do you believe we have a traitor? Perhaps a f'airen out for revenge against us?" Nia asked, but Elunara shook her head.
"I am unsure, the connection was cloudy when I held the charm. It could be that the orclanders discovered these charms somewhere within the glade," she answered as she turned to Nia. "I advise caution until we ascertain more information."

Elunara did have one last piece of advice to bestow upon the younger elf.

"When Drakarim finds his allies, you will be in great danger. A battle between dragons is no place for any of our kind. Please, Nialandra, promise me on the light of the leaf that you will return immediately."

Nia understood, and she nodded before hugging her mentor one last time before returning to Drakarim and Giggles, who awaited her on the walkways below.

As Nia approached the dragon, Drakarim huffed loudly.

"Why do we linger?" He asked, as Nia led them across a huge bridge between two ancient Nadai trees that towered above them.
"I need some equipment. I have a friend here who should be able to help," she replied.

Drakarim looked out across Thalindor as they neared the far end of the bridge. It was the most impressive place he had ever visited and as his memories from his past life returned to him, he had a sudden realisation that he had visited other elven settlements over the years. Those settlements must now be long gone but they too were places of beauty.

As his thoughts wandered, he found himself recalling his good friend Talon, who he had been tethered to more than seven hundred years ago, and Talon's fate beneath Voldestus' claws on that fateful night when the dragons rose up against the warlocks.

Thinking about that moment now all these years later was hard for Drakarim. His damaged mind had never really mourned the loss of Talon, nor that of his dragon relatives who had fought and died that day.

It was memories of Talon's death that drove Drakarim to recall Grand Master Karl-Asvarian, and even now, many years after the destruction of the Bri' Tisa, the hatred within the dragon still ran strong. His death was both a blessing and a curse, and Drakarim couldn't help but blame himself for what followed his own actions that day, for without his attack against Asvarian, he would have continued to punish Voldestus and perhaps even eventually murdered him.

How could he have seen that his brood brother would move on to be so destructive. To murder so many innocents?

He replayed the moment of Asvarian's death over and over, watching as the old warlock's limp body was displayed to the other dragons for all to see, re-living the sounds of the dragon horde cheering and celebrating as one on the birth of their freedom.

Drakarim stopped abruptly and Nia turned "Are you ok?" she asked.

Drakarim had recalled one specific moment, when a wand slipped from Asvarian's robes and fell to the ground, unnoticed by the other dragons.

"Asvarian had two magical weapons. A staff and a wand." Drakarim said.

Nia listened as Drakarim described the staff, a twisted quarterstaff of dark wood which the grand warlock often used for most of his spell casting.

However, in addition to the staff, Asvarian had an ornate wand adorned with a purple gem that glowed ominously when he weaved its magic.

This wand was the one he switched to when he used his dark magic to pull the very scales from Voldestus's body, a feat that was seemingly impossible by any other means.

Drakarim had witnessed Voldestus in battle many times. His greatest victories were against two powerful opponents, the giant Ol Grimm, whose stone-like body was unable to break through Voldestus's armoured hide and Queen X'in, a demon from the hellspawn whose claws split two Thunderhide Dragons but barely scratched Voldestus.

This wand and the secret powers it held within could be the key to destroying the great golden dragon.

As Drakarim finished his description, Nia was already on the move again. "Where did you last see this wand?"
"On the day that Asvarian fell, so too did this wand. There was much chaos that day, and heavy rains. Perhaps it remained where it fell," Drakarim replied. "If it did, I would sense it no matter how deep it may be buried."

Nia quickened her pace, seemingly frustrated with their ponderously slow progress and suddenly infused with a new drive. This weapon could be the very key that they needed. No matter how unlikely it may be that they re-discover this wand, they had to try.

"Wait for me here, I'll be back," and before Drakarim could respond, Nia had vanished ahead, leaving him standing at the edge of the bridge with Giggles.

Drakarim looked down at the child and noted that she was placing various leaves between his claws.

"Pretty." he boomed and Giggles laughed cheekily.

Nia made her way along a winding lane that led towards her old friend's workshop. She hadn't seen Tobbin for many years, but the cantankerous old gnome would be a pleasant sight nonetheless.

As she approached the hut, which was nestled within the very bark of a Nadai tree, a familiar high pitched voice broke the silence.

"If yer come fur me donation I already told ya other guy I ain't a believa!" Nia smiled to herself and she replied, "typical gnome! No manners and no gold!"

There was a clunk and a grouchy yelp as Tobbin dropped something. A moment later, the cloth curtain at the front of the hut flung open and a middle aged, chubby, grey skinned gnome with one half-gnawed ear and dressed in a leather apron and blacksmith's clothing stepped out to greet Nia.

"Nah, me shits be givin', it fuckin' is ya!" the gnome yelled and he bounced towards Nia and threw his long arms around her.
"Hey Tobbin, you ok?" Nia asked and Tobbin stood back, gobsmacked and with a tear or two running down his face.

Gnomes were an interesting creature, and many of them chose to live in solitude away from others, but Tobbin had made his home within Thalindor a long time ago as he fled the wrath of the dragons. He was a skilled craftsman, capable of creating and blessing a range of magical tools and weapons and had been honoured to find a permanent place within the safety of the city.

"Course' I'm crappin ok! Bloody toes Nia! I thought yer banished like?" Tobbin said grinning, he ushered her inside the hut as they continued.
"I'm not banished anymore Tobbin, I'm here with a dragon named Drakarim. We.."
"Dragon! Ye crappin pissin' in me supper?? Nah!" Tobbin sputtered. It was incredibly hard sometimes to fathom what the gnome was saying but Nia did her best to keep up and pretty much caught the gist of it, even through Tobbin's colourful language.

"I need your help, Tobbin, we don't have much time I'm afraid," Nia explained, "Do you have any of your enchanted arrows?"
Tobbin looked pleased with the request and nodded enthusiastically.
"Course' I do!"

He turned immediately and pulled a number of quivers from the back of his workshop. "Crappin good ones," he said as he handed over some impressive looking arrows.

Nia recognised some of them straight away, amongst the selection were arrows that would shatter on impact and ensnare her target in thick vines. She selected a number of these and placed them to the side before examining a few that she didn't recognise.

Tobbin pointed to the shaft which Nia noted was vibrating ever so slightly. "Aimy arrow!" He exclaimed proudly.

Nia nodded and placed a few of these arrows to the side, together with some that Tobbin described as "flashy" and another he dubbed "boomin."

"Crappin good," Tobbin grinned enthusiastically.

Nia thanked her old friend, but before she could leave, he instructed her to wait and then rummaged through the back of his workshop excitedly. Eventually he came back with a long leather bound bow case and placed it on his workbench in front of Nia.

"Open go un," he said and Nia did as instructed. Her mouth opened in awe as the bow within was revealed.

Inside the case was a beautifully crafted green and gold long bow. The finery in its design was exquisite and Nia could sense a magical aura about the weapon from the moment she lay eyes upon it.

"It's incredible," Nia said, she was in awe.
Tobbin pushed the bow towards Nia. "Made it fur ya long time ago. Take it will ya."

Nia felt a tear come to her eye. She and Tobbin had once travelled together on many adventures and they had experienced heavy loss together as well.

"Are you sure Tobbin? I have nothing to give." Nia asked, but Tobbin insisted and he seemed more than pleased when Nia took up the bow and placed it over her shoulder.

"Where ya headin?" Tobbin asked his old friend.
"Spire of the Wyvern, or whatever is left of it," Nia replied and she handed Tobbin her old bow which had travelled with the elf for many a year. The old friends embraced one another, and Nia pulled back the curtain and stepped out into the streets of Thalindor.

As she headed back towards Drakarim she glanced back one last time at the small workshop and Tobbin who stood waving her away. She hoped in her heart that she would see her friend once again, but found solace in the knowledge that he was safe here within Thalindor.

As Nia turned the corner, she chuckled at the sight of Drakarim, who was lying down while Giggles sat atop his head. She had been pulling leaves from the tree above her and was placing them on the dragon's head.

"I needed a hat," Drakarim mumbled and Nia burst out laughing.

As Giggles climbed down, Drakarim sat up and the leaves fell from his head in a flutter.

"She won't be safe with us." he said, looking at the small child who would be in grave danger if she stayed with them on this journey.
Giggles immediately ran to Nia and clung to her legs tightly, "No!" She screamed.
Nia met Drakarim's gaze directly. "I promised her, Drakarim. I promised I would never leave her again."

Drakarim watched the two thoughtfully for a moment. They were his family now, his brood mates. He would never be the same again if he lost either Nia or Giggles, but Nia was right. This little girl had nobody else to turn to, and to push her away now when Nia and Drakarim may not return for many months or even years was not the right thing to do.

The three companions made their way out through the gates of Thalindor and looked back as the city faded from view once again and the power of the etherveil re-activated to conceal its location.

Drakarim, Nia and Giggles travelled for a number of hours to ensure that they were well clear of the borders of Thalindor before they attempted to hasten their travel.

"It is time," Drakarim said.

Nia nodded. "Just so we are clear, if we encounter any dragons, our first priority is to escape, OK?"

Drakarim sighed and nodded solemnly, then he lowered his great head to the ground and said "Climb on."

A few moments later the three companions burst through the canopy of trees that towered over the Great Glade and with a mighty beat of his great crimson wings, Drakarim took the companions to the skies.

They knew not what would face them, and re-visiting the dragonhold after all these years would be a harrowing experience for the elder dragon, but if that wand still lay where it fell more than seven hundred years ago, it could hold the power that the world needed to wrest the tyrannical rule from Voldestus and finally deliver an everlasting peace.

A darkness approaches

Tearstoke Mine - present day

The sounds of pursuit grew louder by the minute as the cave gnolls gained ground on their prey.

Arwin, Heg, Barn Arlestra and the dwarves were running out of options fast. With each new passageway came more confusion and it was hard to judge if they were getting any closer to Fort Valian, with the gnolls in relentless pursuit.

"Even if we get back to the city, we put everyone there in danger!" Arwin managed through exhausted breath but Heg shook her head.
"They are too close to the city as it is, they will find it. We need to warn them," she replied.

The current shaft ran down into a wider mining area with multiple tracks running in various directions and an assortment of mine carts, tools and other equipment discarded throughout. Some were of valian origin, but there were signs of a dwarven workforce amongst the equipment that may have dated back to before the construction of the city above.

"I thought dwarves had a nose for this kinda thing," Barn muttered as he gripped his wounded chest.
"Shut ya face, we dunno this mine!" The dwarf named Harnis grunted.

Arlestra had been periodically healing Barn's wounds as the group travelled, with short rest breaks in between, but he would still need further aid once the group reached Fort Valian.

The other dwarf named Kol pointed up ahead, there was what appeared to be a steep rise which vanished into a large open tunnel. "That's a breachin' line, it'll run up to the next stagin' area."

"It's our best bet, let's go!" Heg ordered and she helped Barn back to his feet before moving forwards into the darkness.

The party moved on, mostly in silence, struggling as best as they could, given the uphill climb they now found themselves faced with. As they passed a rusty cart, Arwin had an idea.

Without a word, he pulled at the brake lever on the side of the cart with everything he had. It was rusted tight but after a few attempts the lever released and the cart began rolling. Arwin helped it along with a swift push and it gathered momentum into the darkness below with a clatter and a loud bang. The aim was to hopefully misdirect their pursuers when they heard the noise of the cart crashing somewhere below.

"Here!" Kol said excitedly as he led them into the large tunnel and along the tracks.

It was difficult to see exactly where they were heading, especially for Arwin and Barn who couldn't see as clearly in the dark as Arlestra and the dwarves could, but they still made progress. The large tunnel ran in a smooth, continuous slope and as they moved along it the sounds of pursuit slowly died away. It felt as though they were in the clear, and just then Heg seemed to spot something.

Sure enough, as the party gathered around Heg it became clear what she had discovered. A thick, sturdy looking ladder headed up into a moonlit exit twenty or so metres above. Heg instructed Kol and Arwin to move first, with Barn, Arlestra and then Harnis and Heg last.

Slowly but surely, the party made their way upwards. Barn found the task especially hard and as he gripped the ladder he moaned in agony, but grimaced and carried on. The group proceeded to climb in silence as they ascended from the darkness of the mine, until eventually, they reached the surface.

The cool night air was a welcome feeling as Arwin pulled himself from the ladder and staggered to a heap where he tried to catch his breath, taking in the surroundings as he did so. This entrance was part of what must have been a mining camp many moons ago, but it had long been destroyed by weather and the rot of time. They were not far from Fort Valian, and in fact this entrance lay a fair distance down the ravine itself. Luckily enough they were on the right side of the ravine so they could make it back to the city within half a day's travel.

"I recommend we keep moving." Arwin suggested and Kol grunted angrily but Heg shook him.
"We have to warn Dervish! Remember?!" She growled, clearly still angry about the danger that the dwarves had unleashed from the depths.

As the party gathered their energy for one last push, Arlestra laid her hands once more on Barn's wounds and chanted until her hands glowed. Barn placed one of his large hands on Arlestra's and thanked her sincerely.

"Don't get soppy ya old fart," Heg said and Barn chuckled at his friend.

The journey back was uneventful, with several stops to gather their bearings. As the sun came up over the ravine, Fort Valian's walls became clearer amongst the shadows. It was a welcome sight indeed.

"Dervish is gonna be pissed." Heg mumbled and Arwin nodded wearily.

By the time the party had reached the main square, they were utterly exhausted. Heg had moved immediately to find a cleric, who had assured her that Barn would recover from his wounds. Meanwhile it seemed it had fallen to Arwin to inform Dervish of the gnoll presence just below the city.

Dervish was, as expected, furious at the realisation that the dwarves had taken to mining the tunnels below but his main focus was on protecting Fort Valian and preparing its populace for the possibility of an attack in the coming days or weeks.

"You need to head to the library. Joselle has made an exciting discovery, and you need to inform me of any changes." Dervish instructed and Arwin left immediately.

As Arwin and Arlestra made their way towards the library, the atmosphere within the city was already very different. Word was spreading of the approaching gnolls and of the deaths of the dwarves.

Arwin found Joselle sitting inside the room with the five portal frames, but he noted that there were guards posted both on the outside of the room and also within. As he entered, the sight that welcomed him stopped him in his tracks, Arlestra not far behind.

Joselle sat cross legged, surrounded by scraps of parchment in front of the white stone portal, which was currently active. A very similar chamber to the one in which they now stood was on display within the white frame, shimmering in and out of focus.

Arwin was utterly shocked when he noticed an old man dressed in a clean white and gold mage robe, sitting on a chair on the other side of the portal window. When the old man noticed Arwin and Arlestra enter the room, he stood immediately, smiled and bowed. He looked aghast as he set his eyes upon the valian.

Joselle turned around with a huge grin on her face.

"Where have you been?!" She asked excitedly, but Arwin ignored the question and moved to stand directly in front of the active portal. Unbeknownst to him, his eyes were glowing brightly with purple light, but all he wanted to know was who the old man was beyond the portal.
"Can.. can he hear us?" He asked. As Arwin spoke, the old man on the other side of the portal suddenly looked both shocked, and excited.
"I can hear you!" He exclaimed at once and Joselle stood up suddenly.
"We can hear you too!" She said excitedly, "Galen, we can hear each other!"
Arwin looked at Joselle. "You know his name?"
"Joselle and I have been writing to one another." Galen said and he held up his notes.
"Who are you? *Where* are you?" Arwin asked and Galen laughed.

"So many questions, I have them too. You must be Arwin?" He said and Arwin nodded in response. "I've heard a lot about you. Your eyes are quite striking I must confess."

Galen looked past Arwin to Arlestra and his eyes widened. "Oh my, you must be the valian I have heard so much about, it is an honour to meet you."
Arlestra's voice echoed through the minds of those present. "I am Arlestra, Eve of the Eye, it is a pleasure to meet you."

Galen was once again in awe at the method of communication and he scrawled some notes quickly, while Arwin turned to one of the guards at the rear of the room and instructed her to inform General Dervish of the change in circumstances. She left immediately to locate him.

"Let me bring you up to speed young Arwin. I am within the Tower of Light, and I am in possession of a powerful staff we call the staff of Vanis. There are many magi here, who are training day and night in order to prepare for what they believe will be a war against the dragon horde," Galen explained.
"The item you call the Staff of Vanis is a valian construct. It is an Armonis gemstone and would have once belonged to a valian," Arlestra stated as she gazed upon the staff in Galen's hands.
Galen admired the staff. "Fascinating," he said, as General Dervish entered the chamber and moved to stand alongside Joselle and Arwin.
"Galen Dinn, can you hear my voice?" He asked and Galen responded with a nod and welcoming smile.
"Excellent, we are still unsure exactly how this is working but it is imperative that I speak to the grand mage. We may not have much time."

Galen nodded and glanced back at Plagar who stood at the back of the room. "I will be a moment," Plagar said, he moved his hand through the air, creating a portal of his own and then stepped inside, vanishing from the room in an instant.
General Dervish looked impressed, "I haven't seen that magic in a long time."
"You say you need urgent aid," Galen said. "Can you tell us more?"

"Yes, the city is in great peril. A day ago we discovered a large cave gnoll settlement just below us. They are aware of our presence and will likely raid us, and we lack the defences to hold off a force of this size," Dervish replied.

"Grave indeed." Galen said. I'm sure the Tower of Light can assist, but I must inform you, Fort Valian is no city, General. It is in fact one of the six Towers of Twilight. Arcane and powerful constructions that hold immense importance." Galen informed those present before explaining that Fort Valian was in fact an inverted tower which ran down into the earth itself.

"Of course!" Joselle exclaimed suddenly, "that makes so much sense!"

"Fascinating as this is, we have a gnoll army on our doorstep and unless we move fast, this place will be overrun," Dervish explained and Galen looked troubled.

"We are unable to pass through the portal General, please watch." Galen screwed up a page of his notes and threw it at the portal, to his surprise it passed right through and hit Arwin in the stomach.

"Oh, that's new!" Galen exclaimed.

Joselle moved towards the portal and Galen held his hand up to stop her. The parchment may have passed through the portal without issue but Galen was unsure if a human could do so.

"Let me, young lady, I'm just an old man," he took a breath and reached tentatively towards the portal.

As his hand made contact with the surface it rippled and shimmered and within a second his hand pierced through the light within Fort Valian. He immediately retracted it and checked himself for wounds.

"OK, that seems to work. Though it does feel somewhat unsettling, I do have to say," he reported with some relief.

Something seemed to be troubling Arlestra and Joselle moved to her side.

"Are you OK?" she asked.

"You were unable to communicate with Galen until we entered the room. I believe that it is our link to the Armonis that is allowing us to speak with Galen and perhaps move through the portal."
"Ok and this is bad?" Joselle asked, somewhat confused.
"If, for example, Galen were to step through to our side of the portal would this then sever the link to the Tower of Light? And vice versa, if myself and Arwin were to pass to the other side - would that sever the link to Fort Valian?"

The concern was now certainly shared between Joselle and Arlestra. This would be something that they would have to remain aware of moving forward. They could not allow for either party to become stranded at either end of the link.

There was a flash of light behind Galen and Plagar appeared alongside a number of other excited looking magi. The grand mage, Lorias Kwin had also joined them.

She stepped forward and addressed those present, "General Dervish?" Lorias asked as she approached.
"I'm Dervish," the general answered.
"You have an urgent situation I hear. Cave gnolls?" Lorias asked.
"Yes," Dervish replied, "a large number of them approach the city, and we do not have the defences to repel an attack like this, so we urgently need aid."

The response was not as Dervish had hoped, Plagar and Lorias exchanged concerned looks and spoke quietly amongst themselves before Lorias addressed Dervish once more.

"I am afraid that we cannot risk sending mages to aid you in this battle, General." Lorias said, Dervish looked taken aback but tried to remain calm, perhaps there was room for negotiation.
"May I ask why?" He said.
"If a single survivor of the attack were to inform Voldestus of our existence, it would endanger the entire world and bury any chance that we have of surprising the dragon king."

Dervish sighed and nodded. He understood the value of surprise that the mages needed, but Fort Valian would fall without their expertise and many innocents would die. His only task was to protect his people.

"I do understand, but we are in desperate need here. There are hundreds of men, women and children that will surely die in this attack," Dervish pleaded.
"May I?" Galen addressed Lorias and she watched him expectantly.
"We have space here, we could evacuate Fort Valian to the tower and then sever the connection," Galen's suggestion was solid and it gave hope to Dervish and the others. Even Plagar seemed to approve.

Lorias was still hesitant, but she too understood the gravity of the situation and could not bring herself to leave the residents of Fort Valian in need.

"Very well. Begin the preparations to evacuate Fort Valian."

The golden dragon

Shadekull Plains - present day

More than seven hundred years ago, the dragons of dragonhold broke their chains and wrought a terrible vengeance on their creators, scorching the world with dragon fire, tooth and claw, until nothing remained but ash and ruin.

The dragons crowned a new king, the great golden dragon Voldestus, whose fury would see them become the new ruling power of the known world. His eye was always watchful, his inner fire always burning and his rule was never in question.

However, Voldestus had struggled. He was unable to gain favour with one specific group of dragons, who resided in the far eastern lands and controlled the city of Jumunpek, where his sister ruled along with her husband, surrounded by powerful dragons who would die to protect their empress and emperor.

Voldestus, though, was wise as well as powerful, and he forged an alliance with those in the east, so that dragons would rule without question, and their might and powerful will would be respected by all races of the world. So, by exchange of talon, the alliance was forged. The dragons to the east would have the freedom they so desired, with just one rule that they must abide by.

To eradicate the Allied Realms wherever they may be found.

For Voldestus saw the smaller races as nothing more than a vermin that needed to be stamped into oblivion. It was only with their utter destruction that his people could really be free.

With this agreement in place, Voldestus could watch over his lands safe in the knowledge that none such as the Bri-Tisa warlocks of old could ever again exist on this mortal plain.

However, as the years passed by and the Allied Realms were wrenched from wherever they attempted to find refuge, they still continued to snap at the dragon's heels, and the elves specifically seemed resilient and able to evade harm better than expected.

Time drained the king's patience, and Voldestus grew increasingly frustrated. His hunting parties would often return empty handed or worse, not at all. For the elves could still be formidable when the need arose, despite the destruction of their fabled Loreweaver's Hearthstone around three hundred years ago.

The hearthstone held the essence of a powerful and ancient tree and through its continued use, they were capable of commanding nature itself to hamper the dragons' expansion, but even without this powerful relic, somehow the elves remained a threat.

The dragon king's spies had informed him of an elven city buried somewhere within a forest of immense size known as the Great Glade, and several of Voldestus's most trusted generals had strong opinions about burning through the entire glade to erase the vermin that hid there.

Voldestus, however, was aware of the dangers of such an act, preferring to keep his forces away from the Great Glade. Its natural defences were brutal and the elves that defended the glade were strongest within their own elemental space.

King Voldestus had other plans to push the elves from their precious glade, out into the open and it would be then that he would strike, severing the head of their revered Ancients and breaking their spirit before ending the elven race once and for all.

It had taken many years to bring his plan to fruition, but the time for change was nigh.

Voldestus arose from his slumber, opened his black eyes and looked out across the plains of Shadekull. It was a mostly barren and open land, with little to offer most species except the dragon horde.

For it was here that the Dragons had space to move, with easy access to surrounding lands and an open view for miles around, should a hostile army ever dare to approach.

Voldestus didn't have a throne, for he did not need one. Here, below the stars, his rule was absolute. His nest, made of plunder and the broken bones of his fallen enemies was all that he required.

He did not fly often, and when he did it was with purpose, for his injuries from the battles against Grandmaster Karl-Asvarian, and Surexx, were extensive and deep. Even with constant regeneration, he was unable to restore the scales that had been ripped from his body by Asvarian's dark magic all those years ago.

The thought of that night brought him to anger even now. To suffer at the hands of such a pitiful little being was not fitting for a creature as vast and majestic as he, and his brother's betrayal so soon after he had released Voldestus from his chains was such a moment that he would never forget nor forgive.

The ironforge dragonkin had constructed Voldestus a mighty breastplate made from black darian steel, the same material once worn by the bloodborne, and fused it to his body to conceal his wounds, and as much as the pain still ran deep, the breastplate served as a reminder to Voldestus to never trust even his closest allies.

In the distance, across the large expanse of the Shadekull, the dragons' roars could be heard as they moved around freely, nesting, hunting and feasting just as their ancestors did before them.

The skies were busy with activity here and silhouettes of dragons of varying shapes and sizes flying past were now a common sight.

Voldestus's attention was drawn to a large black orb that rested alongside him. The ancient device, created long ago by a necromancer who was foolish enough to stand against the dragons had proven itself useful for Voldestus attaining his vision, and as it burst into life with a hiss and a small flash of light, the king expected this news would give him a new direction.

The ghostly image of a mighty orc feral warlord floated ominously just above the orb which now vibrated. Its face and upper shoulders were covered in tribal tattoos, his face wore a variety of scars and it was adorned with an assortment of jewellery made from the bones of his fallen foes.

Grimwolf was the lord of the Fangs of Felondon; a large alliance of smaller orc tribes that had banded together when faced with two simple options.

Serve Voldestus or be destroyed.

Given the overwhelming support for survival, the orcs reluctantly put aside their ancestral differences and moved forward with the purpose of serving the dragon king until such a time as they would be strong enough to withstand his will and claim his head.

"Grimwolf, what do you have to report?" Voldestus asked.
"My liege, we have not yet located the elven stronghold but my spies assure me we are closer by the day." the orc reported. His mastery of the common tongue was surprisingly good, but Grimwolf was substantially more intelligent than many of the other warlords.
"I don't allow failure, Grimwolf. Our agreement was, you drive the elves from the glade and we burn them. If you fail, I will not hesitate to order my forces to feed on orc corpses as opposed to elven ones," Voldestus replied pointedly.

Grimwolf didn't seem phased by the threat and instead continued. "We both know you can't start another war, don't bark your empty threats. I will deliver you news, that is all."

Voldestus scoffed and almost laughed at Grimwolf's brazen response. "Go on, enlighten me orc."

"One of my scouting parties was attacked by a great dragon. Just one survivor made it back to camp to report the incident," Grimwolf said.

Voldestus, now intrigued, sat up a little more. "My dragons would not attack you unless I gave the order, do you have a description?"

"I am no expert, but it was crimson in colour and it devastated the unit as they searched the glade for the elven stronghold." Grimwolf answered.

"Impossible. The Great Glade would not allow the dragon there." Voldestus retorted. "There are no elder dragons left alive that match your description. Are you certain of this scout's report?"

Grimwolf nodded. "As certain as I can be," he watched Voldestus closely, trying to read his response.

Voldestus recalled that there had been multiple attacks against his kin over a long period of time, indeed perpetrated by a mysterious crimson-coloured dragon. Each time it attacked, it killed his forces and then vanished afterwards without trace.

"Some months ago, I arranged a trap for this dragon. My soldiers finally defeated it and we assumed it was dead." he said. "Perhaps not."

"Double your efforts. Next time this conversation will be very different." Before Grimwolf could respond, Voldestus had already cut the connection and with a flick of his claw he rolled the black sphere away from him.

He sat thoughtfully for a moment. Dragons were present in the Great Glade and somehow welcomed by it. Meduzz-Lar had promised that she would send her forces to scout for the elves, but perhaps they attacked the orcs instead. Could this have been a plot by his sister?

Meduzz-Lar knows full well that the orc clans are serving dragon interests. Perhaps she needs some reminding of where her loyalties lay.

He stood and blasted out a jet of golden fire into the sky. Moments later, a small grey dragon landed before him. It bowed silently, placing its head on the floor. It was a tiny creature, almost appearing to be a child, and it shook with fear as it knelt before the king.

"Find the one who walks minds, Romal Kaan. Inform her that she is to accompany me to Jarmunpek," Voldestus instructed.

The grey dragon stepped back, head bowed low, then turned and leapt to the skies.

Romal Kaan was not an elder dragon, but had a curious ability to detect the thoughts of other dragons that she conversed with. She had proven useful to Voldestus on many occasions when he had cause to doubt a dragon's loyalty, and she would prove useful once again.

If the empress and emperor were plotting against the horde, their armies would be a difficult foe to overcome. Perhaps, with some careful planning, Voldestus could cut off the head of the snake in one single stroke and bring the dragons to the east under his rule once and for all, cementing the expansion of the horde past the eastern kingdom out towards the unknown seas.

Voldestus was not keen on making this journey, but if he must confront his sister, he would rather it were a surprise that would be hard for her to evade. One thing was sure as day turns to night, if Meduzz was plotting against Voldestus, she would die an agonising death, but not before she revealed the location of the elven stronghold if she knew it.

He scooped up a large dead wildebeest from before him and consumed it in one loud snap. As blood dripped from his enormous fangs, he eagerly awaited Romal Kaan's arrival.

A dark past

Black Marshes - present day

Drakarim, Nia and Giggles had spotted many distant dragons during their journey to the Black Marshes, which were home to the now ruined Spire of the Wyvern, but thanks to some quick thinking and Nia's careful guidance the travellers had managed to avoid any entanglements.

Drakarim thought that there would be more activity the closer that they got to the tower, but Nia had been assured by the best elven scouts that many dragons avoided the old site of the dragonhold, perhaps fearful of the area.

They were approaching the tower through the usual poor weather that was known in the region and a heavy fog lay over the landscape while rain pelted the marshes below. Visibility may have been poor, but Drakarim's keen dragon sight aided him as he circled the site of the dragonhold from above.

The remains at the site were mostly buried now, the years that had passed since the purge had seen the remaining pens, cages, chains and array of equipment, either rot away or disappear beneath layers of mud thrown up by the weather system.

The Spire of the Wyvern sat to the side of the dragonhold, its pathways no longer visible and much of the rubble that fell during the battle all those years ago had fallen around the perimeter, this too was now covered in mud, moss and natural plantlife.

But despite the heavy damage, there were portions of the tower that appeared to be accessible, at least from this vantage point.

"It looks safe enough to land," Nia said.

"Very well," Drakarim replied, and he began a cautious descent, opening his senses to their surroundings as much as was possible, for if they were attacked, Giggles would be especially vulnerable.

Nia hugged the small child close and whispered instructions in her ear should she get into trouble. Giggles nodded, her nerves clearly on edge as Drakarim finally touched down beside a broken cage that rattled in the wind's embrace.

Drakarim's heart sank and it suddenly hit him just how much he hated this place. Despised it with all of his being, and yet it was here that he spent his valuable time with Talon and his dragon brothers and sisters. He tried to shake it off, aware that time was short and he looked at Nia, who was already dismounted and searching the area.

"Can you remember much of this place?" she asked.
"Yes," Drakarim replied. "The ruin that you stand next to was my pen, where I would be chained to the ground until they needed me."
"They locked you up?" Nia asked.
"And worse."
Nia looked back at Drakarim with a respectful nod. "Not anymore my friend, you are free now."

She moved off and disappeared into what remained of the doorway to the pen as Drakarim continued to get his bearings. Although there were no signs of warlock, guard or bloodborne corpses here, there were a few dragon bones half concealed in the surrounding mud. It would appear as though the battle continued long after Drakarim was transported from his frozen tomb to Mount Voltarf by Meduz-Larr's magical abilities.

Nia appeared once more. "Do you recall where this Asvarian fell?"
Drakarim strode towards the Spire of the Wyvern and stopped when he felt he was around the area that Voldestus once held Asvarian's corpse aloft for the dragons to see.

Then, he opened his mind. If the wand was still nearby, he would be able to sense its presence even if it was buried deep below the surface. Slowly but surely, Drakarim's mind cleared and he reached out around him, digging with his senses as he did so. The sounds of the battle echoed around him as the ghosts of a time long forgotten danced by. He could hardly hear Nia's voice as he delved deeper, but still nothing revealed itself to him.

"You are free now, my eternal friend," Talon's voice echoed through the darkness as the rains fell and Drakarim looked up, alert now, his eyes fixed on the tower's remains.
"Are you OK?" Nia asked, watching him intently. Drakarim didn't answer. Instead, he slowly walked by, his senses stretched in every direction, but it wasn't the area around the dragonhold that was drawing him near, but the darkened remains of the Spire of the Wyvern.

Twisted lumps of black rubble lay strewn across the area, half buried in the muddy earth and moss of the marshlands. Small wildlife scattered from Drakarim's path as he approached, inching ever closer to the tower itself, which still stood some one hundred metres up, leaning ominously as the foundations slowly eroded away.

"Drak?" Nia said from behind him. He didn't turn but he did answer.
"There are still magical essences at work here," he said slowly as he sniffed the air cautiously, "almost dragon-like, but I am unsure."
"I'll scout, stay here." Nia said and she moved ahead of Drakarim, slipping her new bow from her back and notching an arrow. She moved with the skill and dexterity of an expert hunter as she proceeded in near silence, leaping up onto the rubble in order to get a better view of what lay beyond.

Nia could see well into the open remains of the tower now, its enormous expanse lain out before her. This was the old grand entrance area. The large wooden doors that once stood proudly astride the arched entrance were long gone, perhaps simply rotted away from years of rain and exposure to the elements, but the metal hinges remained, clinging onto the building like a fearful child to a protective parent.

The chequered floor tiles were still here, though many were cracked or simply buried beneath the muddy land and the plantlife had burst through from beneath to climb and encase the stone statues that once dominated the hall.

The statues that once stood here depicted Asvarian, and a typical warlock in various imposing stances. They were carved at the time to infuse a sense of fear to those that visited the tower and there were rumours that Asvarian sought to imbue the statues with the same animation spell as that which enchanted the mighty statues of Feraxia, though he had never managed to master the advanced spells required for such a feat.

Nia approached with the utmost caution. Apart from anything else that they might meet here, she was unsure whether there were traps, perhaps set by Voldestus's minions before they left this place to rot away. Forgotten, and abandoned, as it deserved to be.

Water dripped down noisily from overhead as the rains found their way down every nook and cranny in the fallen stonework and gathered into large muddy puddles that dominated the way ahead. Nia's keen elven senses were delivering a slew of information. There was something here that was not sitting well with her at all. A cold, unsettling feeling that drifted from the rotten corridors up ahead. Perhaps this was what Drakarim had warned her about.

This place was cursed. She was sure of it.

As she moved past the interior hallway, she found herself in sufficient cover. The floor above had managed to withstand the destruction to a degree, and aside from a number of holes where sections of the ceiling had collapsed, there was sufficient structure in here to make out specific rooms, but the entire floor was overgrown with long marshweed. The buzz of insects was almost as strong as the smell of the stagnant waters that lapped around Nia's boots as she progressed deeper.

But how far should she investigate? Surely the wand that Drakarim spoke of was no longer here, or if it was, it simply rotted away with everything else and they would need to source an alternative tool to bring about Voldestus' destruction.

However, Nia continued to move deeper into the old ruin, her bow primed for a quick shot should she need it.

Meanwhile outside, Drakarim kept close to Giggles, his anxiety rising the longer that the companions lingered in this foreboding place. Drakarim didn't think that it could get any worse here than it once was, but it seems he was to be proven wrong, for this was utterly dire and Giggles' nervous face said everything that Drakarim needed to know.

They needed to leave, and soon. Perhaps coming here was a mistake. Where was Nia?

As the minutes passed, Drakarim found himself glancing around nervously at each and every sound around them. Just as the feeling of imminent dread hit its peak, there was movement from the ruins and Drakarim felt relieved that Nia was returning at last from the hellish place.

However his relief was cut short when the archway entrance burst outwards in a shower of rock and lumps of mud, forcing Drakarim to swiftly arch his body around Giggles to protect her as several slabs slammed into his side. He just managed to peer back as a large black and brown mass launched itself from within the ruins and landed with a thump, sending water spurting across the dragonhold.

The harrowing sight that stood before Drakarim would give even the hardiest mountain giant nightmares. Perhaps once it was a dragon, but now, as the twisted arcane energies had seeped from within the Spire of the Wyvern across the landscape, they had infused into the rotting corpse and animated it with an unearthly and hellish curse.

Half of the dragon's mid-section was simply rotted away, and what remained was a gaping hole, dripping with rain water over the remaining hide and revealing bone and innards within. The dragon's face was a mixture of ripped flesh and protruding skull, emanating an unsatiated hunger for death.

It wasted no time in lumbering towards Drakarim with an ear splitting, hellish scream that felt like it burnt into the very soul.

Drakarim swiftly lifted Giggles to his back and she climbed aboard, screaming as she spotted the awful undead dragon approaching at speed and he spun around, smashing his tail into the creature's face as he did so before attempting to get some distance.

He would struggle to engage this beast in a full-on battle with the child on his back and would have no choice but to flee. All he could think about was Nia, but she was nowhere to be seen. He had no option, and leapt for the air as a half rotten claw cleaved at him, just behind Drakarim, barely missing its mark.

Drakarim managed to release a blast of fire at the undead dragon, but it just shrugged it off and leapt into the air, spreading its wings in an attempt to pursue Drakarim, seemingly forgetting that the only wing it had left was nothing but bone causing it to come crashing back into the ground where it rolled and slammed into the side of one of the remaining cages in the dragonhold.

Drakarim, now airbourne and feeling secure, hovered in place and unleashed a burning blast that he hoped would have more effect on the zombified dragon below, but once again it shrugged it off as rotten hide burnt away from the bone underneath.

"Where is Nia?!" Giggles screamed, but Drakarim had no time to answer. At that very moment a small figure launched itself from the ruins, leaping nimbly off of a large piece of rubble and released a glowing red arrow towards the undead Dragon. It was Nia!

The arrow sliced through the air with an effective hiss and on making contact with the undead dragon's skull, exploded in a forceful blast of energy that sent the undead beast flying to one side, kicking up mud and debris as it did so.

Drakarim hovered in place as Nia launched herself onto his back and they gave themselves some distance. Below, the smoke cleared and the undead dragon appeared once more, this time half its skull was smashed and its jaw hung loose below.

To Drakarim and Nia's shock, the dragon called out to them as they ascended. "She calls you to her!" it hissed menacingly.

Drakarim's eyes widened but he wasted no more time, beating his wings, as they rose upwards into the air, out into the safety of the sky.

"What in the name of the leaf was that?!" Nia exclaimed, looking over her shoulder nervously.
"It appeared to be a fallen dragon, risen again from the dead," Drakarim replied.
"Well it's behind us now, let's agree never to revisit that place again, OK?"
"Yes." Drakarim agreed.

The mystery of Rinshire

Klascombe - 763 years ago

Surexx landed in the middle of a dusty field, just outside Klascombe village, a small farming community which was located on the outskirts of Prince Karlak's holdings.

A few days prior, Talon Bloodborne had been summoned by the warlock high commissioner and handed a missive giving instruction to visit the area. According to the report supplied, the village had been overcome by bandits and they were to be eradicated by any means necessary, returning control back to Prince Karlak.

The instructions were very clear. Do not deviate, purge the area and attend to Prince Karlak before return. However, the high commissioner had not realised just how different Talon was to his fellow bloodborne. He was constantly intuitive and overtly aware of the impact of his actions. These traits would see the young bloodborne to tales of glory over his time serving the Bri-Tisa.

Today was such a day.

Talon, saddled atop Surexx, eyed the scene carefully as he considered his options. However, almost immediately after they landed, a mob of angry villagers appeared, armed with whatever they could find, children included.

The area was a dusty shadow of its former self and Talon recalled just how lush the farmlands usually were around Klascombe and the extended Rinshire region. However, as he looked to the distant fields and surrounding hills, it was a very different story.

He slid from Surexx's saddle and stepped towards the villagers, who had been standing with outstretched pitchforks since they had arrived.

"We don't want ya here, piss off bloodborne!" One of the older villagers yelled and several of them spat towards Talon in disgust. He held his hands up apologetically.

"I don't understand, we are not here to harm you," he said, attempting to quell the anger.

"Then get back on ya pissin' dragon and fly away!" A woman shouted from the back of the crowd. This was followed with shouts of "Why are you here then?" and "Down with the queen!"

Talon remained calm, his hands held up before him, palms outstretched. "Please, I had been informed there were bandits in the area," he said.

"Bandits?! Ha! That's what they call us now is it?!" Another villager shouted and the crowd's hostility continued.

Talon removed his twin blades from his back and placed them on the ground before him, then he took a few steps back with his hands raised once again. He turned to Surexx, who nodded his understanding immediately. The dragon's flames reduced in furiosity until they were barely visible and he lowered his head to signal that he meant no harm.

Upon seeing these actions, one of the villagers who stood at the front of the crowd slowly lowered his pitchfork and signalled to the others to do the same. Some obliged while others huffed and remained defensive.

"I am serious. I mean you no harm, and you have nothing to fear. I just need to know what's happening here and if I can help you, I will," Talon assured them.

The man stepped forward. He had grey hair and a messy grey beard and his clothes were typical of a farmer or worker. What struck Talon though, was just how thin and malnourished everyone appeared to be. These lands were supposed to be some of the most prosperous farming areas within the Allied Realms.

"Why is the land so dry? Where are your crops?" Talon asked. The man's face said it all, desperation and concern were written across his brow.

"It's something that *he* is doing to us, the animals are dying, crops ain't growing. We have nothing left," the farmer said.

Talon took a moment to glance between the members of the crowd that had gathered, everyone had that same look. "You live here? In the village?" He asked.
The farmer nodded, "Course we do, been here all our lives."
"Who is *he?*" Talon asked.
"That fucking prince!" One of the villagers shouted from the crowd and there were jeers of agreement.
"Karlak? He is responsible for the drought?" Talon asked and once again the villagers nodded.
"Gotta be. Other villages are empty, nobody there. You see his castle and grounds, it's expanding. He's building something," the head of the village said.
"He's the devil!" someone shouted and to Talon's surprise, there was agreement amongst the villagers.

Talon thought for a moment and then said, "If I send Surexx here to fetch food for you all, would you allow me to investigate the village and crops?"
The villagers seemed to agree, so Talon signalled to Surexx who leapt to the air in order to hunt and Talon was welcomed into the village proper.

Talon was shocked to witness the state of the village, buildings in serious need of repair, dead cattle and poverty like he had never seen. The villagers were in dire need of help, and they certainly weren't bandits as he had been informed.

There were children here, some were dying. It was clear to see and heartbreaking to comprehend.

As the villagers showed him slowly through the town, Talon witnessed further evidence of foul play. The well that had been providing the village with fresh water for hundreds of years was inexplicably drawing rancid water, full of disease and clearly a danger to drink.

They moved on, and Talon was accompanied to the fields. Once resplendent with yields of corn and grapes, now simply dust and decay. The man who walked with him was known as Theobald, and as he showed more to Talon, he seemed grateful that someone outside of the village had taken an interest.

"Nothing grows, even with rains," Theobald said. As they stood before the empty field, the sound of Surexx's return filled the area. He landed just outside the village carrying several dead deer.

As Talon and Theobald approached, Surexx had cooked the meat with his dragon fire and villagers rushed to take their fill, grateful for the help the dragon and bloodborne had provided.

"You are very kind, Bloodborne," Theobald said as he retrieved some meat for himself.
"You may call me Talon, Theobald." Talon turned towards Surexx and mounted the dragon with a nimble jump.
"Stay within the village. We will bring more aid but we must visit the Prince first." Talon instructed and he and Surexx flew away from the village in the direction of Rinshire Keep.

As Surexx and Talon glided across the landscape, their shadow drifting across dried field after dried field, Talon decided to ask Surexx for advice.

Surexx thought for a moment and then responded. "I am sensing a dark essence from the area of the keep. The villagers may be correct that the Prince is responsible for the region's woes. I advise caution."

Talon knew all too well how poorly it would be taken that a dragon and bloodborne might confront a member of royalty and ignore their orders. However as they approached Rinshire Keep, which stood atop a clifftop, overlooking the fields below, it felt very much to Talon as if confrontation would be inevitable.

The keep had clearly expanded recently. A large wooden defensive barrier was currently the outskirts of the structure, but within was a hive of activity. It appeared that large extensions were being constructed from the base of the main tower and a strange dark mist surrounded the area, while the tower itself was supported with construction platforms, and men and women were busy building.

It was almost as if the keep was being prepared for defensive measures. Perhaps the prince felt the hostility of those villagers who occupied the area.

"Land in the courtyard, Surexx. Let's make an imposing entrance," Talon suggested and Surexx was keen to please.

Those people within the keeps walls, both guards and workers alike, scrambled for cover as Surexx touched down in front of the main tower, his flames flaring around him as he did so.

As they came to a stop, Surexx let out an almighty roar, causing Talon to smile. "Bit much," he said calmly.

Surexx stood for a moment, glaring at the men and women in the courtyard, but there was a real mixture here. Some appeared to be mere guards, dressed in the prince's family crest, each of them uneasy at the arrival of Surexx and Talon, while some were workers who appeared more like slaves than hired help, and finally, scattered amongst them were what could be more accurately described as mercenaries, dressed in an odd black leather garb and carrying almost foreign-looking weapons.

One thing was sure though, and that was that nobody seemed pleased to see Talon and Surexx.

Eventually, one of the guards did approach, albeit very slowly and cautiously.

"Can we help you?" He stammered awkwardly.

Talon decided to stay where he was, leaning forward to address the guard, but before he could speak the doors to the main tower flung open and Prince Karlak emerged from within with a flourish of his arms. He was dressed from head to toe in expensive red and blue clothing and a long billowing cape.

He stopped though, just within the doorway and exclaimed loudly, "Ah! You've arrived! Finally! Come, come bloodborne, we have a banquet laid out!"

With that, he turned, and vanished back within the tower. Talon was uncomfortable with the invitation, but he dismounted and whispered "Stay alert."

Surexx did just that, extending his dragon senses around him, analysing the dark essence that wisped around the base of the tower as he did so.

Talon followed Prince Karlak into the tower. Inside, it seemed dark and dreary, with very little in the way of light and more of the mercenary-like soldiers were posted within. There were several doors that lined the internal corridor, but most of these were closed.

The sergeant at arms stepped towards Talon. He was a stern looking man of middling years with a nasty scar that ran from his left cheek down his neck and vanished behind his tabard. He was a tall man but looked tiny when standing against the enhanced height of a bloodborne, Talon was around two feet taller and broad shouldered.

"It is tradition here to hand over your weapons when in the presence of the prince," the man said, as he held his hands out expectantly.
"It's a bloodborne tradition to never hand over your weapons," Talon responded and walked straight past the sergeant without another word.

Prince Karlak noticed the exchange but didn't appear flustered as he led Talon into a large drawing room where the walls were covered with paintings, animal trophies and some weapons that Talon guessed were either gifts or family heirlooms. Once again, he noted no windows in this room. Perhaps there used to be, but the lower portion of the wall was now wooden panelling that ran the length of the room.

In the centre of the room there were two large armchairs facing each other, alongside a large fireplace providing the main source of light for the room. The prince sat down in one armchair and with a flourish, he signalled for Talon to sit opposite him.

It was only once Talon was sitting down that he noticed a young woman with long dark hair and pale skin, standing in the very corner of the room, partly concealed in shadow. He made a point of looking directly at her but she neither responded nor moved from her position.

"Please, young bloodborne, drink with me." Prince Karlak said and a servant appeared at his side with two large glasses of red wine. Karlak took one and sipped it immediately, as Talon took the second from the servant and immediately placed it on a small ornate wooden table next to him.

The prince laughed. "Ah yes! Of course, you are not allowed to remove your helm! Ridiculous rule." Before continuing, "the bandits are eradicated I presume?"
"There are no bandits." Talon replied.

Prince Karlak's face changed, a look of confusion briefly appearing before it returned to one of jovial indifference. "I beg your pardon? Those bandits have been murdering these poor farmers for weeks, spreading nothing but chaos and despair. Perhaps they deceived you."

"No, there was no deception, just villagers struggling to survive in this blight," Talon said. "What happened to the farmland?"
"Bandits! If you had followed your orders, they would have been purged and those poor villagers could start to rebuild," Prince Karlak replied, his voice taking a darker tone. Talon noted his eyes also seemed darker than before somehow.

The prince stood up suddenly and swigged the last of his glass. "It is a shame you didn't follow your orders. It does complicate things somewhat, but hey ho," he said.

Talon detected the changes around him and he went to leap from the chair but found he was unable to move his arms or legs. The woman, who had been standing in the corner of the room, moved forward, but instead of walking, she slid in complete silence, and as the light of the fireplace drifted across her Talon was mortified to witness her expressionless face, bereft of a mouth, and her eyes completely black. Her arms ended with long, boney fingers and sharpened claws.

Talon was now in a state of near panic, still unable to remove himself from the chair. It was only when he managed to glance down that he realised with horror that it was the chair itself that held him in place, alive now and rippling with pulsating skin of the darkest reds.

"You must be wondering what is happening. I don't blame you," Prince Karlak continued. He picked up Talon's discarded wine and started to drink it himself.

"She really wants your blood, it's very simple. I'll explain as we take you to her. She doesn't like tardiness," the prince continued and he led the way out of the room. Talon felt the armchair moving and realised he was being carried along behind Karlak, while the woman in black followed in silence.

"Your blood is very special isn't it? Quite precious, some might say. Unique, certainly. Part of you is a dragon, a little secret that Asvarian likes to keep to himself and as she wishes to feed, you shall provide her with new powers. New abilities. She will be more beautiful than ever!"

Talon tried to think fast as they continued down a dark corridor. It seemed the further they went, the darker and more twisted the environment around them became, the beams of the corridor itself were writhing and shifting, creaking and pulsating.

"My dragon will destroy you," Talon said, trying to sound calm, but Karlak just laughed as he turned to look at Talon. His face had completely changed to one of rotten flesh, and his mouth was full of fangs.

"We will feast on the beast come nightfall." he growled, his laughter echoing around the corridor as darkness embraced them.

In the heat of the moment, Talon had forgotten his tether to Surexx. It was a power that he preferred not to use despite insistence from Vandire to do so.

He focused on Surexx, closing his eyes and pictured the dragon waiting patiently in the courtyard of Rinshire Keep. It was his last viable option before a certain death at the hands of these creatures.

The mystery of Rinshire part 2

Rinshire Keep - 763 years ago

Surexx's senses searched the nearby area but the mist that surrounded Rinshire Keep seemed to stop him locating Talon, increasing his anxiety.

He glanced around his surroundings and noted that several of the guards and mercenaries out here had taken up strategic positioning, their eyes alert and weapons ready. Surexx was almost certain this would become hostile any second and as the sun was slowly dipping down for the start of evening, he grew concerned about Talon.

Surexx stepped towards the keep and lowered his head to the ground, listening intently for any signs of a skirmish within the tower. The last thing he wanted to do was to create a situation if there wasn't one, regardless of the actions of the men outside, who looked more nervous now that the dragon was on the move.

It was as Surexx got closer to the tower that there was a sudden pain in the back of his skull and he lurched forward with no control over his body. He looked around, but the men and women in the courtyard remained in their positions, it wasn't an attack from any of them.

Again, the same pain, and his head lurched forwards several times. No matter what Surexx tried to do, he had no control over his actions at all. Again and again, it was as if someone was pulling him towards the tower.

It was then that he realised what was happening. *"Of course!"* He exclaimed to himself, it was Talon!

Surexx's eyes widened at the thought that Talon was trapped inside, and he knew that from the moment he acted, these well trained fighters outside would engage him. He assessed that they shouldn't be a threat to his thickened dragon hide, but there could be a surprise here that he was unaware of, so he did what dragons do best.

With one smooth motion, Surexx leapt from the courtyard directly towards the main tower, extending his claws before him, and within a second he landed on the edge of the tower, claws gripping deep into the stone work and rubble falling to the earth below, sending many of the guards scrambling for cover.

Surexx wasted no time, arrows and crossbow bolts rained down on him as he clung to the tower's edge. He drew on his inner fire, building up enough power for a lingering blast of flaming death, opened his giant maw wide and unleashed the attack on the guards and mercenaries below.

The entire courtyard swiftly became a burning pit of death. Flaming men and women ran helplessly and blindly around, only to slump onto the floor in a fiery heap seconds later, and anything made of wood was instantly burning brightly as the last of the day's light was replaced with that of the blazing courtyard.

Surexx drew back and slammed his claws into the side of the tower, ripping as large a hole into its side as he was able, sending more large chunks of debris flying in all directions. Once he was sure there was a large enough hole, he peered inside, but there was no sign of Talon.

Surexx realised that perhaps Talon was still on the large ground floor of the main keep and so he leapt back into the flaming courtyard and proceeded to the front doors.

Arrows still rained down from the remaining guards and mercenaries, but they bounced off the dragon's hide or were incinerated by the flames that surrounded him. However, as he approached the gate, he suddenly detected a dark presence around him and he stopped in his tracks. From within the flames, there were many dark figures, and they were approaching at speed.

Before Surexx could react, several of them leapt from the flames and clung directly to his side. He spun around immediately, and rolled across the floor in an attempt to crush them before managing to grip one between his giant claws.

The creature was one of the mercenaries from the courtyard earlier, but its true form had been revealed and it was very much like a dark-skinned devil, with pure black eyes and ferocious looking claws that Surex could feel ripping into him.

He immediately reacted, biting the creature in half and spitting the top half of its body at the victim's allies.

"Not good!" Surexx thought to himself as he threw the rest of the victim directly at another mercenary.

Meanwhile, deep within Rinshire Keep, Talon remained constrained to the pulsating red chair as he was carried into a large circular chamber made completely from stone, but with some kind of dark liquid running down the walls, across the floor and into a circular pit at the centre of the room.

Seconds later a large scream erupted from the pit and a number of long spider-like legs emerged, much like a spider rising from a plughole, until a horrific looking creature from the shadowed abyss finally stood before Talon and the others.

The creature's legs ended in a twisted mass of what appeared to be multiple human bodies, culminating in a half-naked female form with dark black skin and long arms covered in spikes.

The creature's face was a mass of teeth, no nose to speak of and two piercing white eyes that seemed much larger than they should be, while its head was bald and misshapen.

"Yes, my queen," Karlak said, responding to a voice that Talon couldn't hear, and he gestured to the chair that restrained Talon to move towards the hideous spider queen.

Talon continued to struggle, but he just was not strong enough to break free of the grip in which he found himself, and he reached out to Surexx again. One thing he had noticed was that there were noises now from the courtyard, so he was sure Surexx had engaged the enemy forces.

Sure enough, mere seconds later, a huge rumble shook the room and dust fell from the ceiling above.

The prince looked suddenly concerned, and it appeared the spider queen was speaking to him once again. In this moment, Talon sensed Surexx was close, perhaps directly above the room, and he used the opportunity and momentary distraction to pull on the tether once again.

There was another, louder crash and a chunk of the ceiling slammed down beside the spider queen. She screamed in anger, while Talon detected in that second that the grip on him had loosened, so he twisted his body with all of his might and found he was able to free one hand. Talon reached back and released one of his twin blades, ignited it and drove it backwards immediately.

Purple goo shot out from the side of the chair creature and it squealed in pain, releasing its grip on Talon as it did so. He took the opportunity, spun from the creature and sliced deep into its pulsating flesh again and again until it slumped to the ground from the flaming wounds inflicted upon it.

Talon reached back and unsheathed the second of his twin blades, ignited it and stood ready before the remaining three creatures: the prince, who looked in a shocked state, the spider queen, and the mouthless female.

"You made a mistake picking me as your victim," Talon said calmly. His imposing form, black plate armour, dragon helm and twin flaming blades would have been enough to cause concern to even the darkest of the world's creatures.

There was a moment of silence within the chamber as Talon stood ready to defend, and the creatures circled him.

The first to attack was the mouthless female. Her attempt was swift, she lunged forward with an arm that became impossibly long, almost like a finger spear, but Talon's reactions were honed to perfection and he dodged aside as another rumble shook the room, causing several of the torches to go out.

Talon danced through the shadows, his flaming twin blades hissing around in a deadly flurry of attacks, ripostes and blocks as both the mouthless female and Prince Karlak tried with all of their might to bring the bloodborne down while the spider queen seemed to bide her time, watching the combat closely with those large white eyes.

Several times during the fight, Talon attempted to get close enough to deliver a blow to the queen, but he was blocked by the others in one way or another. It was this response that gave the young bloodborne an idea.

First, he drove towards Prince Karlak who sneered and attempted to bite or claw Talon in response. Just as the flurry of blows built to a momentum, Talon spun away and threw one of his blades directly at the spider queen's head. It was not so much as an attempt to hit her but more to draw the mouthless female to try and defend her queen. She reached out and caught the blade mid-flight, but in doing so had overextended and opened herself to a strike.

Talon drove his remaining blade home, directly into the stomach of the mouthless female where it remained for a good second. It seemed the moment hung in the air, as the flames from Talon's blade lit up the mouthless female's face as life drained from within it.

As she fell, Talon retrieved his blade from her hand and stepped back to prepare his defence once more.

Prince Karlak looked furious, crouching down low, like a leopard about to strike. Long fingers, with deadly claws extended out in front of him ready to cleave into Talon's armour should he make the wrong move.

Talon's gaze passed from the prince to the spider queen, who had yet to make her move. Talon noticed that she was grinning at him like a maniac, making her mouth appear even larger than before.

The prince sensed that Talon was distracted and he launched with tremendous speed. Talon barely managed a block before Karlak was on top of him, clawing relentlessly at his armour, so much so that sparks went flying across the room from each impact. Karlak's speed was unbelievable.

Talon eventually shoved the prince back and then retreated swiftly, whilst bringing his twin blades up to defend. What he hadn't counted on was that this retreat had taken him within range of the queen and she screeched with joy as she spat out a stream of acidic breath which struck Talon in the side.

This wasn't all she did though. One of her spider legs slashed forward in an attack of its own piercing his armour and finding his flesh beneath. The pain was excruciating and Talon struggled to retreat once again whilst defending himself against the prince at the same time.

Just as all seemed lost, the ceiling behind the spider queen caved in and a giant flaming dragon head appeared through the resulting hole. It was almost humorous as Surexx scooped up the Queen and vanished once again from view.

"NO!" Karlak screamed and he turned and leapt from the room, through the hole in pursuit of Surexx and the spider queen.

Talon took a second to glance down at his side, where blood seeped through his armour, then gave chase. Leaping from the room and scrambling up fallen beams and rubble until he emerged in the night air.

The scene before him was one of utter carnage. Scorched bodies lay strewn across the courtyard amongst half-eaten demon spawn and piles of debris that Talon guessed once belonged to Rinshire Keep.

Down below, rolling around in a frantic battle, were Surexx and the spider queen, who looked worse off. Talon could have sworn the queen was missing a few legs now, but she was ripping at Surexx, stabbing forth with her legs and spitting her acidic breath. It appeared she was impervious to his flames and there was a slight shimmer in the air around her, perhaps a magical shield of some description.

As for Prince Karlak, he was nowhere to be seen. He had vanished into the darkness, but he had to be around close, so Talon ran swiftly across the rooftop until he reached a vantage point and he knelt down. If Karlak showed himself, he would be ready to strike.

Surexx's hide was becoming a smoking mass of bubbling acid as more of the spider queen's spit rained down across his back, and she scrambled around behind him, still clinging on but able to avoid his claws and teeth. It was a constant battle of wills as the two large creatures struggled for an advantage, the spider queen using her agility and Surexx his pure might.

However, the queen had taken some heavy wounds and eventually she slowed. Each time Surexx rolled across the courtyard, the weight of the dragon on top of her brought more harm. The spider queen tried one last time to bite into Surexx's neck, but he managed to twist and gripped one of her extended legs in his teeth, causing her to scream in agony.

Then, with one last turn, Surexx launched the spider queen across the courtyard slamming her into the side of the keep just below where Talon had knelt. As she scrambled to get up, Talon dropped from above, plunging his twin blades deep into her upper body and she stilled for a final time.

As Talon dropped to the ground beside the slain spider queen, there was a shout from across the courtyard and Prince Karlak appeared, sprinting towards Talon but his legs gave out and he slumped to the ground, and he struggled to pull himself across the dusty floor.

Talon and Surexx watched with curiosity as the prince writhed in pain, his face a contorted mixture of his devilish guise and the prince that the world once knew.

"She.. promised me power.. not.. this," Talon stepped closer and Karlak continued, his voice a raspy struggle as his life seemingly drained away. "There is darkness below.. all.. around us. She promised.. me."

With one last struggle for breath, Prince Karlak finally moulded back to his original form, the young prince who foolishly made a deal with the shadowed abyss. His eyes rolled up into his head, and his body went limp.

Talon stood, breathing heavily from the exertion of battle, before the fallen corpses around him and Surexx stepped to his side. He too was breathing heavily.

"Took your time," Talon panted and he glanced up at Surexx, who just stared at him for a moment with a blank expression across his face. "Better late than never," the dragon finally replied.

In the days following the skirmish at Rinshire Keep, the villagers reported life returning to the local area. On Queen Catherine's orders, a number of elven druids and spiritwalkers had been dispatched to the region to cleanse the area of the curse from the shadowed abyss. However, it was possible that there could be a larger and more significant threat growing in the abyss and this would need investigating, so the keep had been secured for this very purpose.

In the meantime, Surexx and Talon had once again made a name for themselves and tales of their brave assault on Prince Karlak's forces, together with their kind provision of food supplies spread from village to village, giving birth to the name Surexx the kind.

Talon reported his findings before both the queen and Grand Master Asvarian and there were serious concerns regarding the spider queen's interest in Talon's blood and the powers it would have granted her or her masters, had the ritual been completed.

Asvarian, as always, was several steps ahead. He understood the threat posed by the shadowed abyss; the reasons for its thirst for bloodborne blood and the additional powers that it would provide *her*.

His actions had angered a darker being than the spider queen. One who would not rest until she had what she desired.

What was once hers.

The siege of Fort Valian

Fort Valian - present day

The cave gnolls had approached much faster than expected. There was a veracity and an almost desperate element to the assault that took the Fort Valian defenders by surprise.

Within the portal room, a surge of refugees poured through the Tower of Light portal as quickly as they could possibly manage, with the women and children of the city passing first. Joselle had refused to leave with the initial group, preferring instead to help retrieve what valuable artefacts, food supplies and clothes she could, along with many others.

The panic had intensified as the surge of gnolls pushed up the ravine path, breaking the initial line of defenders and dispersing into the city itself, rampantly destroying anything that they could find and murdering without restraint. The gnolls were ferocious creatures and their numbers were immense, but there was something else driving them forward.

Arwin, Heg and Barn had joined the defenders in an attempt to buy those evacuating through the portal a little more time to get clear, while Arlestra had to remain within the portal room in order for it to stay open.

It was heartbreaking for Arlestra to hear her city once again come under assault. If it were to fall this time, it would surely be the last time she would see her home. She pushed these thoughts to one side and concentrated on saving the lives of the people around her.

Meanwhile, elsewhere within the city, Arwin's sword slashed through another of the gnolls, spurting blood and sinew across the stone floor of the main market before he moved forward to his next target. Heg was once again surprised by the young man's veracity in battle, and his fighting style was like one who had trained for many years under a swordmaster, rather than that of a desperate survivor.

Barn let loose an arrow that struck a brutish looking cave gnoll straight between the eyes as it clambered over a stone wall. For a second the gnoll seemed oblivious, continuing on its way until its brain shut down and the beast slumped forwards onto its dog like snout, but they just kept on coming and Barn was quickly running low on arrows.

"Fall back to quarter two! We've lost too many!" Heg barked out her orders and the defenders slowly backed away, shields raised to deflect gnoll arrows and spears.

"Any word from Dervish?!" Arwin said breathlessly as they backed down a narrow tunnel that would be the next bottleneck for the defenders to hold. Heg shook her head. Concerns were growing for the General and his unit who had tried to flank the attackers. Without a clear line of communication, it would be hard to judge when to call the full retreat and sever the portal link between Fort Valian and the Tower of Light.

Across the battlefield, down a maze of corridors now abandoned by those who called this place home, General Dervish and his men were deep in battle. Their attempts to flank the enemy had been met with furious resistance and the gnolls had inflicted heavy casualties on Dervish's men. It was looking more and more desperate as they themselves were now surrounded.

Dervish dropped a gnoll and managed to step back as another lunged forward in an attempt to impale him on a sharpened stone spear. He was running out of options fast, as he watched one of his close friends and lieutenants take a fatal wound, causing them to disappear into the throng of gnolls that were pushing forward.

"Fall back!" Dervish shouted. He would make his last stand in the old factory works. His defenders had prepared a few surprises that were initially intended to be used to thin out the enemy numbers when the attack came. Now it would be his tomb, but he could use the resulting explosion as a signal to the other defending units to call a full retreat.

The factory works were essentially a series of underground warehouses that once saw a great deal of activity, but had recently been used for additional camp space. Families had sheltered here and many of their items were still present, scattered across the area. A clear sign of the desperation of the evacuation.

The gnolls were relentless in their pursuit of Dervish's men. Good, honest fighting men and women were falling to the crazed beasts, their blood soaked fur and teeth adding to their bloodlust.

Dervish attempted to step aside as an arrow came towards him but he was too late. It embedded itself in his chest, forcing him to his knees for a moment as blood soaked his tunic. He used his long sword to push himself back on his feet and one of his fellow soldiers aided him to retreat.

The gnolls grinned with glee as they realised they had their enemy surrounded. Many of them circled the factory unit, clambering through the windows at the sides and rear and entering through several other doors at the far end of the structure.

But as they slowly closed in, becoming more and more confident about their victory, something was happening at their flank, deep within the ravine. A chorus of noise was growing louder and louder, echoing from the darkness below.

It was the sound of death.

Dervish became aware of the change as the gnolls' expressions switched from confidence to abject panic and the chatter between the beasts altered almost immediately. Howls of agony, terror and desperation echoed from their rear ranks. Seconds later, a mass of dark forms emerged from the ground, the air and across the walls of the city, eviscerating the gnolls, spewing forth their blood and guts across their fellows.

The noise was deafening. Whatever had emerged from the ravine let loose screams like they were from the five hells, ear splitting and terrifying.

The last remaining soldiers from Dervish's unit were asking each other what they were witnessing. Initially they were pleased to see the gnolls being attacked in such a fashion, believing that the shadows that were weaving their way towards them were the result of a friendly spellcaster.

But those that were cheering soon changed as the darkness ascended upon them.

"Ghasts!" a soldier yelled from across the unit floor, just moments before he was cut down with devastating efficiency.

Another soldier just a few feet from Dervish managed to time his attack perfectly and a ghast was destroyed, evaporating with a loud hiss, but then he fell to a gnoll who swung wildly at anything that moved around it.

Dervish watched in horror as both the gnolls and his own defenders began to flee in panic, and as the screams from both sides intensified, he fell to his knees, weakened from the fatal wound to his chest.

He didn't have much time.

Dervish crawled past the bodies of his soldiers to the contraption. This device once provided power to the city, but on advice from Arlestra, could be used as a weapon of sorts in one last stand. He wanted to give his unit more time to retreat, but unless Dervish acted now, both ghast and gnoll would move into the city centre where there were still civilians.

He took a deep breath, drew back his sword, before swinging it down with all of his might upon the device.

Arwin had heard the screams from the outskirts of the city. Something was going very wrong.

He exchanged looks with Heg and as they hurried to usher more civilians towards the portal room, there was an almighty explosion, its origin directly where Dervish and his forces had been battling against the gnolls. The city shook to its core and rubble fell from above.

"NO!" Heg exclaimed, and Barn had to pull her back towards the great library.
"Retreat! Retreat!" He shouted and the other defenders around them pulled back away from the confused gnolls, who were now glancing back to their flank, hearing the strangest of screams.

"Arwin! We are out of time! We have to close the portal!" Heg called amidst the panic.

Arwin disengaged and started to make his way back towards the great library where he hoped most of the civilians had made it through the portal link to the Tower of Light, cutting down any stray gnolls that got in his way.

As they reached the great library, it became clear that most of the civilians were out, with just a small number running for their lives towards the portal room, but the screams behind the retreating forces were growing louder and louder.

Arwin turned to witness the first ghost as it flew swiftly across the pathway, engaged with a gnoll who swung its axe but missed and paid for the error a split second later with its own life. Then the ghost hovered in place and turned to look at Arwin.

It was human in shape, but made of a ghostly black mass that shifted and phased in and out of view. If it had eyes or any facial features, they were not evident in its appearance. It seemed like an eternity passed as the ghost and Arwin stared at one another. He felt the hairs stand up on the back of his neck and a real feeling of fear came across him.

It was only when the ghost suddenly moved that Arwin snapped out of it. It flew towards him with terrifying speed, zig-zagging its way past Barn's arrows. There was no time to think. Instead Arwin readied himself in a defensive stance, lowered on his haunches, blade at the ready. His timing would have to be perfect.

Arwin swung and side stepped at the same time, a motion that allowed him to move his body away from harm but still slice cleanly through the ghast. There was a loud hissing sound and the ghostly form evaporated.

Arwin just had time to glance at Barn who was looking past him with wide eyes. "Run!" Barn yelled and without hesitation, the three companions and the other remaining defenders ran as fast as they could into the great library, but the ghasts were already on their backs, cutting down any who were unable to keep up.

They finally reached the portal room where Arlestra stood waiting, looking deeply concerned as Arwin and the others arrived. The last few defenders passed through the portal to the Tower of Light, until it was just Arlestra and Arwin who remained.

"Is everyone out?!" Arwin shouted and Arlestra nodded. Arwin pushed Arlestra through the portal as the first of the ghasts flew into the portal room with blinding speed and he barely managed to dispatch it before he himself stepped backwards through the portal, leaving Fort Valian for good.

There was a flash of light around Arwin as he passed through, his skin felt as though it was pulling itself apart, though he felt no pain. A second later he found himself stepping back into Barn, who still had his bow raised and aimed at the portal.

Arwin quickly glanced around him. Arlestra had arrived safely and Heg and Barn were here as well as a few of the tower mages, including Galen and Plagar.

All of them were watching the portal intently and Arwin followed their gaze.

The portal room at Fort Valian was now full of ghasts, one of which flew directly at the portal, exploding in a flash of light. The others just hovered in place, staring at the portal with their hollow faces.

"Shut it down," Plagar instructed and Galen closed the portal once again.

The room fell silent. The defenders were exhausted, breathing heavily from their efforts, and some were sobbing openly.

"Arwin." Arlestra's voice echoed into his mind and he turned to see her, tears running down her cheeks.

"It's Joselle. She didn't make it."

Unwanted guests

Jarmunpek - present day

Empress Meduz-Larr had ruled Jamunpek with Emperor Graxilius since the purge began seven hundred and sixty three years ago. On the fateful night when Voldestus broke his chains and led the attack upon the Bri-Tisa warlocks at the Spire of the Wyvern, it was Meduz-Larr who had freed Surexx from his bonds, using a power that only Meduz and Graxilius had been aware of.

That power, a method of mana weaving that had long been dormant amongst dragon kind would have been Meduz's death sentence if the warlocks had discovered it, but as the opportunity presented itself, the desperation to be free of the warlocks' captivity drove Meduz to use her new found powers to change the course of history forever.

However, it was mere moments after she had freed Surexx that Voldestus had revealed his true plans. That he wanted to utterly destroy the Allied Realms, including every innocent man, woman and child dwelling across the known world. Once again, she would be forced to use her powers to escape that dreaded battle, along with Graxilius and several other dragons who did not share Vodlestus's view of the new world order.

As the months passed and word spread among the dragons that Meduz and Graxilius had taken control of the Eastern Realms, their numbers there grew and they carved out a solid empire of their own, built on the foundations of a once barbaric land. One that the dragons residing there could be proud of, with established trade routes to many of the smaller dragon tribes now dotted across the world, and of course to Shadekull, where Voldestus ruled the majority of the dragons across the biggest area of land.

But Meduz and Graxilius harboured a secret, one that if Voldestus discovered, would mean that he would come for them with all of his fury, and rip away everything that they had built, before claiming their land as his own.

Meduz had always had a close affinity with the elves, and she had spent some time amongst their Ancients, garnering knowledge and forging a close bond with their people. She had no issue with humans, dwarves or any of the other Allied Realms and Graxilius shared these views.

And so they gave the Allied Realms safe harbour within the cavernous underground service tunnels and sewer systems beneath the city of Jarmunpek.

Meduz and Graxilius had long shared the ability to communicate between their minds and this was how they were able to keep their secret safe from many of the dragons they ruled over. If just one broke away and informed Voldestus of this treachery, then the men, women and children hidden below Jarmunpek would be dragged out into the streets and put to death.

The news was ominous. Voldestus himself and a large number of other dragons were approaching Jarmunpek at speed, and panic began to spread across the city.

Graxilius had called many of the Eastern Realms' most powerful dragons back to the palace in preparation for the dragon king's arrival, but Voldestus and his escorts were approaching at astonishing speed and it was unlikely that the bulk of the defending forces would arrive in time.

Meduz closed her eyes and dropped into a deep mana-driven trance as she reached out to the depths of Jarmunpek, amongst the dimly lit tunnels where the refugees were living in silence and connected with the elven cleric Hitara.

"The dragon king is coming," Meduz-Larr said and Hitara froze in fear. When she regained her composure, she set about alerting others with the immediacy required.

With the message safely delivered, Meduz-Larr opened her eyes once more to the sound of beating wings. Seconds later, a series of shadows fell over the palace and the empress glanced at her emperor.

They did not communicate for nothing needed to be said. The two elder dragons would fight Voldestus to the death if they had to.

The earth shook and the sound of large footsteps reverberated around the palace grounds as Meduz, Graxilius and the other dragons awaited the inevitable. Eventually, a large golden claw reached around the edge of the hole in the ceiling of the palace and Voldestus' giant maul peered over the edge.

There was an almighty crunch and suddenly half the wall of the palace was pulled away and then tossed to the side as Voldestus made a space for his large body.

"Why do you surround yourselves with their structures?" He boomed. "This is not how we dragons are supposed to live, sister."

Meduz-Larr stayed calm but several of the surrounding dragons hissed loudly at Voldestus. He ignored them and a small dragon stepped to his side. It was like nothing Meduz-Larr had ever seen, bright orange in colour, with a long sharp snout. Above its eyes there was a large, glowing sphere of blue energy that pulsated as it floated in place, and there was a slight taint of magical essence about the dragon that Meduz-Larr found unnerving.

Voldestus flicked away another piece of the palace wall. "Hard to believe those tiny little creatures achieved anything at all." he said.
"To what do we owe the pleasure of your presence, brother?" Graxilius asked, gripping the side of his throne tightly.
"Relax." Meduz-Larr instructed him through their mind link. But she too could hear the other dragons that had accompanied Voldestus circling above, perhaps looking for something, while others had landed and were skulking around the outside of the palace menacingly.

"I will cut to the chase then. I had word that your scout has been spotted in the Great Glade. Curiously, it attacked some orcs that have been helping out with a little problem of mine," Voldestus said.
"Whatever happened within the Great Glade was nothing to do with us." replied Meduz-Larr.
"You are absolutely certain of this?" Voldestus asked, still absent-mindedly pulling chunks of the palace wall apart and tossing the pieces aside.
"Why would I lie to you, brother?" Meduz-Larr asked calmly, her steely gaze firmly in place.

The sphere atop the head of the small dragon next to Voldestus suddenly changed colour to green for a few seconds and then back to blue. It seemed as though Voldestus had also noticed the change. The small dragon, meanwhile, continued to stare at Meduz-Larr.

Voldestus sighed and thought for a second or two before asking his next question.

"There are rumours that a very large crimson-coloured Dragon, an effective killer so I have heard, has been attacking my orc friends, and in the Great Glade, no less," Voldestus stated.

Meduz-Larr considered her response carefully as the tensions between herself and Voldestus grew. She knew of whom Voldestus spoke, but she could not allow his identity to be revealed. "That is news to me, brother. I have heard of no such reports."

The sphere flickered to red, and Voldestus clearly noticed it. "Curious," he said before continuing. "You know, I've lost a fair number of my dragons to this beast over quite some years. He appears, thwarts a raid here, a hunt there, and then vanishes, like a coward."

Voldestus stepped away from the smaller dragon, casually examining the inside of the palace as he did so. "You know how I feel about aiding the lesser beings of this world, sister. Do answer me one more question, for time is short and I'm tired from my journey."

Voldestus glared at his small sister, his pure black eyes piercing deep into her very soul. "Do you know where I can find those little elves?"

Meduz-Larr knew what was coming next. She connected with the weave, drawing mana to her from the surroundings. Her eyes glowed blue and her form became surrounded in powerful energies that electrified the air. Voldestus stared at Meduz-Larr in surprise, suddenly aware that Meduz was able to wield mana.

Without uttering another word, he let out a deafening roar that sent tremors throughout the palace of Jarmunpek. The air was filled with the sound of beating wings as Voldestus's dragons descended upon the palace, their scales gleaming in the light.

Meduz-Larr and Graxilius knew they faced a dire challenge. Meduz-Larr possessed powerful magic but was flightless, smaller than the other dragons, and unable to breathe fire. Graxilius, on the other hand, lacked magic and was similarly flightless, but this was two elder dragons against one and they would give everything that they had to defeat him.

The palace guards and loyal dragons rallied to Meduz-Larr's side as they prepared to defend Jarmunpek against Voldestus's onslaught. Meduz-Larr channelled her magical abilities, weaving intricate spells that created protective barriers around herself and Graxilius. Then she thrust her claws forward, and bolts of energy crackled from them, striking Voldestus with precision as Graxilius leapt onto his back and unleashed a burst of his energy breath into the giant golden dragon, who roared in frustration.

But Voldestus was a formidable opponent. His sheer size and strength made him a force to be reckoned with, and his tail swung with devastating power, shattering the walls and raining debris down upon the combatants. The clash of titans shook the very foundations of Jarmunpek as Voldestus's allies began their attacks outside.

"You choose death!" Voldestus growled and he leapt backwards, deliberately slamming his back against the palace wall so that he and Graxilius disappeared from sight, through dust, debris and flame.

Meduz-Larr attempted to follow them but a Lava Tooth landed onto the ground before her and ignited its inner fire. She just managed to sidestep its attack and destroyed the dragon with an almighty blast of ice that cut straight through its throat and sent it flying backwards.

Meduz-Larr leapt from the ground in a mana-fueled rage and hovered above the battlefield. Palace guards and allied dragons fought valiantly and their bodies littered the ground.

Outside in the palace grounds, Voldestus and Graxilius continued to fight. A huge blast of energy erupted from Graxilius's eyes and deflected off Voldestus's chest armour as he backed away from the golden dragon.

Meduz-Larr blasted forth with a series of powerful spells, mana twisting around her, forming first a shower of ice spikes, which shattered across Vodlestus's back, then a pummeling of stones which she threw up from the floor and hammered into the back of Voldestus' head and a barrage of light shards, which led to Voldestus spinning to glare at the empress in fury.

Meduz-Larr had no time to react. Voldestus spat a glob of yellow flame through the air towards her. What happened next was over in just a flash.

Graxilius had leapt from the stone floor, directly in front of the flame and took the hit directly into his body. He roared in agony, his form faltering as he crumpled back to the ground with a resounding thud. Voldestus stepped forward and bit down on Graxilius before he could react. There was a sickening crunch and Meduz-Larr watched in horror as her beloved emperor fell silent for the last time.

Grief and rage fueled Meduz-Larr's magic, and she unleashed a devastating spell that created a blinding explosion of energy, temporarily scattering Voldestus and his dragons. Seizing the opportunity, she made a fateful decision. With a final, mournful glance at the fallen Graxilius, she teleported away from the palace, her immense power carrying her far from the battlefield.

Voldestus roared and released an enormous jet of golden flame into the sky. The empress had escaped him, her betrayal rattling him to the very core.

The battle for Jarmunpek continued to rage on, but Meduz-Larr was gone, leaving behind a city in ruins and a devastated alliance. Her escape had come at a great cost, and she knew that the Eastern Realms would never be the same.

As the dust settled and the remaining dragons of Jarmunpek regrouped, the memory of the epic battle would forever be etched into their hearts. The empress had fled, the emperor was dead, and the fate of the Eastern Realms hung in the balance, uncertain and precarious.

Companions

Eastern Valleys - present day

Drakarim soared gracefully over the world as it passed by far below, with Nia hugging Giggles close to her chest on his back. The child had become accustomed to flight and the elves had fashioned a saddle and harness that allowed Nia and Giggles to sit comfortably and safely in position. Even if they both fell asleep or unconscious, they would be safely strapped to the elder dragon's back, along with their supplies. Though this did not stop Nia from holding onto the child throughout their time in flight, especially when she was asleep.

They had witnessed incredible views, from ancient ruined cities and civilisations to great natural wonders full of the most awe-inspiring beauty. The eastern valleys, over which they currently travelled, were an almost never ending series of valleys carved into the rock, upon which an incredible variety of fauna had evolved, vibrant reds and greens that reached as far as the eye could see.

Once they passed the valleys, it would be a short trip to reach the city of Jarmunpek, which was nestled alongside, and ran down until it met the banks of the Ardune Sea. Supposedly the home of the greatest sea beast ever discovered.

Nia looked at the child before her, whose face was full of the calm innocence of youth, nestled into the warmth of Nia's body and wrapped in furs. She had grown to love this little girl, and she suspected that Drakarim had as well. She was their anchor, a symbol of what they were both fighting for.

It was a serene moment of peace, but it was shattered when a sharp crack whipped the air around them and there was a flash of light some twenty feet ahead. Nia barely had time to regain her composure as Giggles awoke with a start, her eyes wide with surprise.

But Drakarim rolled almost immediately and tucked his wings tight to his side as he went into a steep dive, causing the winds around them to clash across their faces and the passengers to struggle for breath. Nia clutched Giggles tightly, holding her close. She tried to speak but the air caught in her throat and all she could do was hold on, as Drakarim stayed silent.

It felt as though time had slowed, but just as suddenly as they had entered the dive, they levelled out. Nia took the reprieve to take a note of their surroundings and was amazed to see trees, bushes and dense foliage passing them just below Drakarim's underbelly, and thankfully they landed in a small clearing on the edge of one of the valleys.

"Help me Nia." Drakarim said and Nia quickly dismounted and came around to the front of the dragon, clearly concerned that he had been wounded somehow.

To her surprise, she noticed that he was clutching a smaller dragon in both his claws. Its body was limp, but it appeared to be alive. The dragon's scales were almost crystal-like in appearance and it was a wingless breed. Drakarim looked shocked, and deeply concerned as he gently lay the dragon down on the long grass before him.

He then drew back, his eyes widened and he said with a shaking voice, "Meduz?"

Nia's breath caught in her throat and she moved closer. The creature was utterly beautiful, its scales catching every aspect of the light around them and reflecting the greens of the trees and the blues of the clear sky above. There were no visible cuts, but it did appear that the Dragon had taken some fire damage, and its entire body occasionally created blue sparks, perhaps due to some kind of mana cooldown.

"This is Meduz-Larr?" Nia asked, her voice deep with wonder. Drakarim looked at her for a moment and nodded, before gently prodding the dragon before him, hopeful for a response.

"My sister. But I do not know how she arrived before us. Perhaps she used magic?" Drakarim asked.

"Yes, most likely," Nia responded, "but why, and look." Nia pointed to a large scorch mark that ran along the side of Meduz-Larr's body. Drakarim let out a low growl, glancing to the sky above them as he did so.

"She has no wings, why would she.. How would she?" Nia whispered as Giggles climbed off of Drakarim's back and came to stand next to Nia, reaching out for her hand as she did so.

Drakarim's senses remained on high alert, and he scanned the surroundings, wary of any potential threats that might have followed Meduz-Larr. Giggles, sensing the tension in the air, clung tightly to Nia's hand, her wide eyes taking in the unusual scene before her.

Nia gently knelt beside the injured dragon, her fingers cautiously brushing against the shimmering scales. "Meduz-Larr, can you hear me?" she murmured softly, her voice filled with concern.

Nia closed her eyes and reached out, walking with the wind and embracing the forest around them. It answered almost immediately. A warmth came across all within the clearing and Nia focused this towards the fallen dragon before her.

Moments passed and then Nia opened her eyes and glanced up at the concerned face of Drakarim.

"Do not fear, for we are safe here. We can't start a fire as it will draw attention but the forest has agreed to keep us warm," Nia said. She stood and placed a hand onto Drakarim's snout, calming him further. "I will bless her with a shroud of calm until she awakens."

With that, Nia moved back to Meduz-Larr's side and knelt down. She closed her eyes and fell silent.

Drakarim had no option but to wait, so he circled his companions, wrapping around them like a barrier and settled down, his tail swishing absent mindedly as he continued to watch the skies.

Hours passed and as day turned to night, Nia remained in a deep trance, while Giggles fell into a peaceful sleep where she had settled on Drakarim's claw. Finally, as the trees rustled in the breeze and a distant owl welcomed the night with its song, Drakarim drifted into a wonderful sleep.

The following morning Giggles awoke Drakarim by prodding his nose impatiently. He blinked the sleep away and swiftly checked on Nia, who was now awake and had foraged a bag of berries and other woodland treats from the surrounding countryside.

"She will need to eat when she awakes." Nia said, referring to Meduz-Larr. "It won't be long now."

Sure enough, Meduz-Larr's eyes flickered open, revealing deep, intelligent orbs that gazed at Nia with a mixture of confusion and gratitude. She sat up slowly, and as her eyes adjusted she took in her surroundings, her gaze finally settled on Drakarim, who was staring at her in amazement.

"Sister?" Drakarim stammered. Nia saw Drakarim was shaking.
"It.. it can not be?" Meduz-Larr regarded Drakarim with astonishment. "Surexx? Is it really you?"
"I am here," Drakarim replied. Meduz-Larr sat up more, and examined Drakarim carefully.
"Where is your glow?" she asked, Drakarim looked confused. "Your fire body?"
Drakarim suddenly understood and he shrugged his shoulders, "I do not know."
Meduz-Larr nodded and she struggled to her feet. "Where am I?"
"Relax, you are not in danger here," Nia replied, her voice full of a calming peace. "You teleported in front of us as we flew towards Jarmunpek."

This seemed like it made sense to Meduz-Larr and she said, "I have yet to master that spell. The arrivals seem to be what is required in my minds-eye, but they are erratic to say the least. I had no choice."

She stepped unsteadily towards Drakarim and reached out to touch his large crimson face while he watched her calmly.

"We must get you to Jarmunpek," Nia said as she made ready to break camp and continue their journey, but Meduz-Larr sighed loudly and raised a claw.
"There is nothing but death and sorrow in Jarmunpek," Meduz-Larr stated, a large tear formed in her eye and she looked directly at Drakarim, "Voldestus murdered Graxilius. He saved my life and died for it."
This news rocked Drakarim to his core. "It cannot be?" He asked, but he already knew the answer. "I remember him well. He was a fine warrior and a wise friend."
"He loved you as a brother," Meduz-Larr said, her voice shaking with emotion.

The group fell to silence as the weight of the loss became obvious on both dragons' faces. It was Meduz-Larr who finally broke the silence.

"You must tell me everything that you have learnt," she said at last and Drakarim relayed the struggle that they had endured so far. His years of exile, with a fractured mind but a drive to do good where he was still able. He told her of the draklings who nurtured him back to health high up in the safety of the mountains, and of his journey to the great elven city of Thalindor, where he met the Ancients and more specifically, her friend Elunara.

As the two dragons talked, Nia listened, adding pieces of the story here and there where she could, and she realised just how incredible their journey had been so far, but the stark realisation that, with Jarmunpek and the Eastern Realms on the retreat, she was perhaps standing with the only two dragons able to confront Voldestus in the whole of the known world.

That their daunting task had now become an almost impossible situation to overcome. It felt as though their path ahead was now clouded, but Meduz-Larr seemed to suggest otherwise.

"In order to destroy Voldestus, we need to understand why Drakarim is not able to ignite his flame fully. He is a shadow of his former self and would be no match for the king," she said. "We must consult with Alacatus, his guidance and uncanny knowledge for the workings of this world could reveal the information that we need."

"The seer?" Drakarim asked, confused with this new information. "I understood that he perished during the purge?"

"Alacatus was disgusted at the actions of our fellow dragons, and he placed himself into a deep exile. He may not grant us an audience, but we must try," Meduz-Larr replied.

She pulled her cloak around her and stood up. "Alacatus left a gateway of sorts, just a few hours flight from here. Come, we do not have much time," Meduz-Larr instructed, and with that her eyes crackled to life and she hovered above the ground for a moment before taking off into the sky.

Drakarim glanced at Nia and shrugged. She returned the gesture and she and Giggles climbed aboard. Moments later they were airbourne, flying at speed towards the southern marshlands and the void portal.

An audience granted

Southern Marshes - present day

Drakarim landed some distance from the portal, using the thick fog of the marshes to hide their movement. Meduz-Larr, meanwhile, used her magical abilities to summon a distortion field, providing them with more cover both visually and audibly, thus allowing the companions to move undetected.

The Wise Ones located here would not be a challenge in combat, but they were protected by Iron Legion dragon troops, covered in dragon-scale armour, their flaming red eyes providing a stark contrast to the grey haze of the fog ridden marshes.

Beyond the Wise Ones and their guards was the imposing visage of the void portal, which hummed loudly and crackled and spat as it shone a myriad of colours onto the surrounding mirk of the marshes. It seemed that the portal had noticed the companions' presence, and was watching their every move.

As they carefully crept closer to it, Drakarim and the others noticed several large stakes around the portal, and on them were many human and dwarf corpses, as well as corpses of Wise Ones. Perhaps they had not done as instructed, or had fallen from favour with the king and were now warning others not putting their entire efforts into discovering the purpose of the portal.

Nia was concerned about how to proceed further, as any conflict here could be deadly for Giggles. Meduz-Larr stopped suddenly and stared at the portal with her bright, wide eyes.

"We must get closer. The distortion spell will keep us concealed but it won't last forever," she whispered.

"I could draw them away as you pass through," Drakarim offered, but Meduzz-Larr was not so sure about the approach.
"It is too risky. If Alacatus does not allow us to pass through to his realm, we risk being attacked here." she said. "Continue towards the portal and do not speak a word."

The companions continued on their way, edging cautiously past the various dragon-kin and their overseers, who were oblivious to the intruders, continuing their observations of the void portal from a safe distance.

Nia grew more anxious as they continued past human slave pens, where miserable captives cowered in the shadows, awaiting their fate and along rows of varying tools that lay on benches, dotted around the marshlands. Drakarim could not shake that feeling that the portal was watching them until eventually they crossed an unseen line, where the Wise Ones preferred not to venture.

The portal crackled and shifted between its colours as it hovered perfectly in place, its hum was near deafening now and Giggles placed her hands over her ears to try to block out the noise.

Drakarim turned his great head, anxiously watching the Wise Ones and the Iron Legion dragons to make sure they were still concealed. Everything appeared fine - the Wise Ones were deep in discussions, and examining large parchments in detail. However, moments later one broke away and stood watching the portal with a look of interest on its face. Then it turned to call for its companions.

"I think we.." Drakarim began, but before he could finish several huge sparks of energy launched forth from the void portal, enveloping the companions and lashing around at the air surrounding its surface.
"The distortion field has dropped!" Nia shouted and she released a volley of arrows towards several dragons now alerted to the party's presence.

However, just as it appeared they would need to fight their way out of the area, the void portal made an incredible sound and vivid colours flashed across its surface, before it lashed out with several long tendrils of magical energy that struck Drakarim and his companions. Seconds later they disappeared from sight with an almighty flash of the brightest white light, leaving the confused dragons behind.

Drakarim, Meduz-Larr, Nia and Giggles found themselves standing on a barren landscape. Above them, angry purple clouds rolled across a troubled sky, while red lightning crackled and flashed between them. It was a desolate world made from nothing but rock.

Drakarim had never seen this place before, but Meduz-Larr had. She stood now, patiently waiting, as if in any moment the silence would be broken.

"Is it.. always like this here?" Nia asked awkwardly.
"Alacatus prefers it this way." Meduz-Larr replied. Nia held Giggles's hand, the little girl clearly fearful of this strange new world upon which they had found themselves. There was, at first, only silence. The winds tumbled across the dusty terrain and whipped across their ears, whistling through the surrounding environment as they awaited a sign.

Eventually, Meduz-Larr spoke. "I know you are here, Alacatus, and I know you can see us. Stop your nonsense and welcome us." She circled around the area impatiently before speaking again. "Why do you wait?"

However, only silence followed. The wait was troubling and Drakarim grew uneasy. What if they were somehow trapped in this hellish place? However, eventually a loud, booming voice echoed out across the barren land. It was a voice that Drakarim immediately recognised from years past. It was the voice of the seer himself.

"It has been a long time since I last saw you, Meduz-Larr, and you have brought with you such important guests," the voice said. Meduzz-Larr sighed loudly. "Show yourself, Alacatus, we need to talk," she said.

Moments later, there was a loud beating of wings and a large shadow fell across the surrounding land and a massive red and dark green dragon that landed before them. It was perhaps even larger than

Drakarim, but this creature was like no other. For it sported one single large eye that peered between the new guests in wonder.

Giggles pulled Nia down to her level and she whispered. "That Dragon only has one eye Nee."
Nia smiled and nodded. "Do not fear Giggles, this one is a friend."
Alacatus looked at the little girl and said, "I may only have one eye, little one, but I see everything," and he smiled. It was a smile of warmth, and almost immediately the little girl felt comfortable standing before the mighty elder dragon.

Drakarim had not yet spoken, and he stepped forward and bowed his head to Alacatus. "It is an honour to see you again, my old friend. It has been many years since we last met."
"Indeed, it has." Alacatus turned and looked directly at Drakarim. "The road ahead will be long and dangerous, Drakarim, but you will not face it alone."
"Alacatus, we come to you for guidance. Our path ahead has become clouded." Meduz-Larr said. Alacatus nodded his understanding immediately.
"Ah, yes, Jarmunpek lies in ruins. The eastern dragon alliance that once lived as one proud nation, are scattered, and in disarray. Their emperor has fallen, and their empress is missing, but they will fight back for what they believe in. Even if it means they perish in the process," he said. Alacatus looked at Drakarim as he continued. "Your path ahead is not clouded. I see exactly where you need to be, and it is there that I shall place you. However there is one more piece to this puzzle, and without that, you will be unable to face Voldestus."

Drakarim could not help but wonder if Alacatus was referring to him. It didn't take long for this to be confirmed.

"Drakarim, you are not yet back to your full potential. You must seek out the catalyst to re-ignite your flame form," Alacatus instructed. Drakarim frowned, confusion written across his face. Alacatus approached Drakarim until they were standing directly in front of one another.
"You must seek out the bloodborne. It is only with their help that you can defeat Voldestus," he said.

Drakarim and Meduz-Larr exchanged looks, for the bloodborne had been destroyed during the purge. Some had attempted to side with the dragons, but found that once their usefulness expired, so did their lives, for the dragons were fearful of the power of the tether. Other bloodborne attempted to fight back against the dragons until they too were finally overcome.

Meduz-Larr was the first to respond. "Alacatus, there are no bloodborne left in the world. They perished during the purge."
Alacatus laughed briefly and smiled at his old friends. "Ah, but there are. The Bri-Tisa warlocks believed that they had made it impossible for bloodborne to create life with one another, however, a small number did have offspring," he said. "And their descendants live to this day."

Meduz-Larr and Drakarim exchanged surprised looks.

"Even if the bloodborne survive, I fail to see how this will help us," Meduz-Larr sighed.
"That is for Drakarim to discover. I shall watch the moment with much amusement," Alacatus replied with a wry smile and Drakarim was even more puzzled.
"Where would we find this.. bloodborne?" Nia asked. The seer's eye turned to regard her with interest.
"Ah, **Nialandra Kalin'tor**. The banished elf and friend of dragons. You are pure of heart and your spirit is strong. Your determination to bring those of my kind who would do evil to justice is an inspiration to many, and I am thankful for it," Alacatus said.
Nia shrugged her shoulders, "I am just one Elf, my offering is only small."
"That is where you are mistaken. You have many allies in the world, and your skills will only grow as you face more challenges. I hope that one day you too will be welcomed to Thalindor as an Ancient amongst the Great Council," Alacatus said with a smile, and then he paused thoughtfully for a moment, his one eye darting around as if searching for something out in the cosmos, before he then continued.

"Nialandra you are to introduce Drakarim and Meduz-Larr to the Grand Mage **Lorias Kwin** at the Tower of Light. It is here that you shall discover your path forward."

Meduz-Larr stepped forward and addressed the seer directly. "Alacatus, please return with us to the world. With your aid, we stand a better chance of defeating Voldestus." she asked, but the great elder dragon shook his head.
"I shall not, and I dare not, for Voldestus will wish to use my abilities to aid him and I would become the greatest threat of all," he replied. Drakarim reached out to his old friend with hope in his eyes. "Voldestus cannot control you, you would have nothing to fear," he said reassuringly, but Alacatus shook his head again.
"Alas, I have everything to fear. We all understand the feeling of being controlled, without a will of your own. The hopelessness that envelopes you like a thick fog that you cannot navigate," the seer sighed loudly, puffing out a small amount of smoke from his snout as he did so. "I will not allow any further harm to come to that beautiful world, nor do I deserve to walk there."

Meduz-Larr nodded. As much as she wanted Alacatus to end his exile and rejoin her, his words were final.

"Then we must part ways once again, brother. But we shall return when the time is right." she said and bowed her head to Alacatus, which he reciprocated.
"I am sorry to see Graxilius fall to the tyrant. Be warned, I believe that Voldestus will now plan to assault the Great Glade, with the help of an orc warlord named Grimwolf," the seer announced.
"Then it is true, they are in grave danger. We must warn them!" Nia said with urgency in her voice. The confirmation that Thalindor was indeed a target for the dragon horde was more than she could bear. Every ounce of her soul wanted to leave this place and warn her people.
"You will, but first you must visit the Tower of Light. From there your path will become clear." Alacatus concluded.

Before Nia could respond, there was a blinding flash of light and a loud crack like thunder, then colours phased around them, shifting from the deepest greens, to a pearl white and then a sky blue, whizzing at tremendous speed. Then, as quickly as the light hit them, it faded away, and the cold chill of the frozen wastes struck like a sledgehammer. Nia quickly pulled Giggles close to her chest, unfastened her cloak and pulled it around them both to keep the little girl warm. Drakarim lowered himself to the ground so that Nia could reach her supplies pack and she pulled out several blankets.

"We must reach the tower," Meduz-Larr called out over the winds, her voice nearly lost amidst the snow storm that whipped around the party, dulling their hearing as well as their sight.
"How do we know which way to go?" Drakarim asked but Nia was able to see the way thanks to her keen Elven eyesight combined with her spiritwalking abilities. She raised a shaking hand and pointed out to the distance.
"Climb on, my inner fire will keep you warmer." Drakarim instructed.

The walk would have been hard, if not impossible had Nia been on foot with Giggles, rather than on the back of the Dragon. Thanks to his size, Drakarim made easy progress through the thick snow and his warming inner fire gave him almost complete resistance to the surrounding weather. The companions pushed on, until around an hour later they found themselves just a short distance from the base of the Tower of Light. Its peak glistened high above, cutting through the dense clouds around it, torch lights emanated from various windows that adorned its exterior. It was a mighty, yet majestic sight to behold, and it almost appeared as though the tower didn't belong here somehow.

Nia spotted the gathering at the base of the tower before the two dragons did. "They are aware of our approach." she announced. Drakarim squinted. He could barely make out a wall of blue light that shimmered across the base of the tower, perhaps there were figures beyond that.
"Should we turn back?" he asked.
"No, I will speak for us, and make sure they know we mean them no harm," Nia replied and so Drakarim continued onwards.

As the companions approached, more of the scene became clear.

A large archway was located at the base of the tower, which led to an inner gate where two lines of archer windows overlooked any who approached. Below the archway, a platform extended outwards, with two immense stairways curving down from each side until they disappeared into the snowy grounds surrounding the tower.

A line of mages, mostly human, stood shoulder to shoulder and were dressed in white robes, their arms alight with shimmering magical energy. This in turn powered the glittering wall of blue light that surrounded them, while at their rear were even more magi, each standing ready to cast should they be needed. At their centre, an elderly human female stood dressed in similar white robes, but more ornate with golden lining and a high-reaching collar that arched around the back of her neck. She had a look of power about her and her eyes were cold and calculating.

Nia signalled for Drakarim and Meduz-Larr to stop. She dismounted, ensured that her bow and short sword remained strapped to the saddle upon Drakarim's back, then approached the tower with Giggles by her side, her arms outstretched in a show of peace.

The mages watched her approach with a mixture of amusement and concern, and the energy barrier remained in place before them.

"Two elder dragons, an elf and a human child arrive on the doorstep of the great Tower of Light. This is most curious indeed." the elderly mage said. Her voice was oddly present, despite the high winds that whipped around them. "I am Grand Mage **Lorias Kwin**. Please visitor, do introduce yourself."

Nia glanced back at Drakarim and Meduz-Larr and then to the grand mage who stood before her.

"I am Nialandra **Kalin'tor** of the eastern isles, spiritwalker and daughter of Queen Lorranis Kalin'tor. We travel to you from our mutual friend,

Alacatus, perhaps known to you as the elder dragon who sees all," she announced.

The high mage looked even more amused, and she exchanged glances, first with the mages by her side and then with Drakarim and Meduz-Larr.

"Please, tell me about the dragons who travel with you." she said plainly. Nia held a hand out towards Meduz-Larr. "This is Empress Meduz-Larr of the Eastern Dragon Alliance, ruler of Jarmunpek and defender of the Allied Realms. She has been instrumental in helping your people to the east in their continued survival, providing them with food, supplies and a place to call home. She has battled against King Voldestus one to one, barely escaping with her life. She has sacrificed much to be here," Nia said, then she gestured to Drakarim.

"You may have heard of a great elder dragon who once walked the world, defended the allied realms and tried to stop Voldestus from taking his rule. He was once known as Surexx the kind, survivor and hero of the people of the Allied Realms. Now he walks with a different name, free of the restraints forced upon him. This is the dragon elder Drakarim," Nia turned her gaze back towards the mages.

"We come to you in peace, to seek aid in the battle against Voldestus and his dragon horde. We wish to end his reign of terror and bring balance back to our world. A world in which the dragons can be free, and the Allied Realms can rebuild," she concluded.

There was silence from the assembled mages as Lorias Kwin spoke to her advisors with hushed voices, before she straightened up and addressed those present.

"Perhaps we can talk some more. You will need to stay under guard, and please understand that there are many people here who neither want to see nor trust a dragon. Keep your distance, or we will retaliate," she said, then she turned to lead the way into the tower without another word.

"If I may," Meduz-Larr said, and Lorias turned. "I have a magical skill of my own, if I may weave, I can reduce Drakarim's size so that he may accompany us within."

The grand mage glanced at a tall elven mage who stood beside her. The look on her face was a mixture of intrigue and horror.

"You can master the weave? How many dragons are able to do so?" she asked.

If Meduz-Larr wasn't mistaken, she was sensing a touch of fear in the old mage's voice.

"As far as I'm aware, I'm the only one," she answered, her gaze locked with the cold eyes of the grand mage. There was an awkward silence between the two, as Lorias Kwin's eyes bored deep into Meduz-Larr's soul as she searched for the truth.

"Good." she said finally. "Proceed with the spell."

Drakarim gave Meduz-Larr a disapproving look. He didn't like this suggestion at all, but she continued regardless. Mana fused around her, igniting her eyes and she focused her energy towards Drakarim.

Almost immediately, he felt his body reduce in size. The world around him seemed to grow and the tower became more imposing as it rose high above. Moments passed by and those who were watching were astonished to see he was now waist height to Meduz-Larr and still getting smaller.

"Enough!" He growled uncomfortably and Meduz-Larr seemed to realise suddenly that she needed to stop the spell.
"My apologies, I'm still new to this one." she said as the mana faded from her eyes. Drakarim looked around, a somewhat panicked expression on his face, while some of the other magi, and particularly Nia and Giggles were openly amused.

Giggles ran forward and threw her arms around Drakarim, who was shocked to find he was now only slightly taller than the little human girl.

"So cute!" she squealed with joy. Drakarim huffed, a small puff of smoke erupted from his snout.
"Oops." Meduz-Larr chuckled and she walked towards the tower without another word.
"How long will this last?!" Drakarim growled as he made his way inside the tower along with Nia and Giggles.
"Oh, a couple of days," Meduz-Larr replied with a smile and a wink. Giggles laughed cheekily.

The grand mage led the companions into the confines of the tower through the gateway, through its great hallways, and into the main meeting chamber beyond. As they wandered onwards, Nia was surprised to see so many people within, not just mages, but it appeared that other survivors from the Allied Realms had travelled to the tower and found refuge within its walls.

Meduz-Larr, meanwhile, was equally in awe. She had heard many tales of this great tower of magic users, who trained so diligently, and of the many mysteries that were hidden within its ancient walls.

Nia had noticed that Drakarim was unsettled, constantly scanning the area as if feeling threatened, so she moved closer as they proceeded along the hallway.

"Are you OK?" she asked. Drakarim shook his head.
"I do not feel safe inside another of these towers, surrounded by magic users. Something here disturbs me." Drakarim replied.
"I understand, but these people are here to help us. There is nothing to fear from them. Just say if you need to leave, I am sure Meduz-Larr will understand," Nia said. Drakarim was thankful for the advice and tried his best to overcome his uneasiness.

Nia sped up until she was alongside Lorias and Meduz-Larr.

"There are other survivors here?" She asked as the group began to ascend a large flight of marble stairs.

"They have been here for almost two weeks. We were strictly a magic-only community but a small city known as Fort Valian was attacked. They would have perished, so we offered them refuge here." Lorias replied.

"I see, it is lucky that the Tower of Light was able to assist." Nia said, as they passed a large group of exhausted looking dwarves.

"Indeed." Lorias replied.

A few moments later, they reached the top of the stairs, where it opened into a gigantic hall, full of the hustle and bustle of life within the tower. The spellcasting on display was incredible to witness, as mages of many arcane paths came together to better their skills. However, for Drakarim, it was nothing short of nauseating. Several of the mages turned in astonishment as Meduz-Larr and the tiny Drakarim walked past, and the mood in the hall began to change rather rapidly.

"These dragons are our guests!" Lorias called out, her voice echoing around the walls, "Spread the word that we have allies in dragon kind. They shall be treated with respect."

Eventually she came to a halt before two mages deep in discussion. One was tall and dark skinned, with runic scars upon his face and a shaved head, and the other was a kind-looking elderly man, with a twisted oak staff imbued with a bluish gem at its tip. Drakarim and Meduz-Larr both felt a touch of unease at the staff, exchanging a brief glance before the men were introduced. Both of them wore the white robes of the tower, but the tall mage with the runic scars robes were slightly more detailed, indicating perhaps a higher rank.

"Ah, here you are, let me introduce you to apprentice mage Galen and high mage Plagar. I am sure there is much to discuss including the events at Fort Valian, but first we must cover the most important aspects of your presence here." Lorias said.

Both Galen and Plagar bowed their heads to the newcomers as they were introduced to the group one by one, and both men eyed the dragons with caution.

"We have much to cover, but briefly, Galen here was sent to us in a similar manner to yourselves. Via Alacatus." Lorias stated, this news intriguing Meduz-Larr.
"You visited his mind realm? How is that possible?" She asked.

Galen relayed his story to the group and they listened in fascinated silence, but Meduz-Larr's eyes were drawn to the gem imbued within the end of Galen's staff.

"That gem. It feels familiar," she said and Drakarim nodded in agreement.
"It is an Armonis gemstone. After piecing together some of the puzzle, we believe that a version of this gem was used to create you, many years ago." Galen informed them. Drakarim felt a strange aura around the old mage, but it wasn't so much him that appeared to be emanating the aura, as it was his gem. There was a familiarity about that feeling that made Drakarim even more uneasy. He was about to turn and leave when Galen looked upon him with interest.

"Oh, and who is this young dragon?" Galen asked, walking towards Drakarim and reaching out as if to stroke his head, but Drakarim stepped back and gave a little growl.
"I am no baby." he said angrily. Meduz-Larr could not help but laugh as did Nia and Giggles.
"He is usually much larger than this. He is under an enchantment so as to fit within the tower," Nia explained, "courtesy of Meduz-Larr."

Plagar's eyes widened and he briefly exchanged a concerned look with Lorias.

Galen, now slightly embarrassed at his faux pas, said "Oh, my apologies." He looked up at Meduz-Larr in astonishment. "So you are able to weave? That is fascinating!"

Plagar too was impressed. "Transmutation magic is extremely advanced. How could you possibly achieve this without additional training?" Plagar asked, but Meduz-Larr did not look impressed with the question.

She sighed and took a moment before answering, and as the conversation continued, Drakarim skulked from the room towards the exit.

"Young mage. I have been present in this wonderful world for nearly 800 years. I have had plenty of time to discover and better my talents. Perhaps I could teach you a thing or two" Meduz-Larr said with a wink. Plagar appeared taken aback. "My apologies Empress, I have spoken out of turn."
Meduz-Larr waved it away, "I have much to learn, and am eager to explore the possibilities."
"I would be more than happy to assist in teaching you," Plager replied, but Lorias snapped a disapproving look towards him at that comment.

She raised her hands in a call for attention.

"It is most important that we are all in agreement," she began "that Valdestus's rule cannot continue. We must bring him to an end and destroy those dragons who are of the same mind." there were mutterings of agreement and nodding of heads amongst the crowd.

"On some of that, we can agree," Meduz-Larr replied. "However, you must all understand that there are many dragons who serve Voldestus out of fear and there are many in the Eastern Realms who wish to live in peace with the Allied Realms. I will not offer my aid in this cause if we do not have an understanding and a commitment to long-term peace between our peoples."

"These dragons are to be respected, not hunted." She said with a finality that reverberated around the hall.

An awkward silence fell over the room and there were many exchanged glances. Many of the mages looked to Lorias for a response, but it was Nia who spoke next.

"The elves of Thalindor wish for nothing more than a lasting peace across the world. Despite their understandable distrust of the dragons, they are in agreement that we must allow them a chance to live in harmony, once Voldestus is removed from power."

Lorias raised her hand. "Then it would appear that we are all in agreement. We work together to destroy the tyrant king, and that work continues after his end, to bring a respectable peace to the known world, where the Allied Realms may live as one alongside the dragons."

"Voldestus will come to us. He plans to strike against the Great Glade, where he will lay siege to Thalindor," Nia said.

"I agree, this is likely his next move," Meduz-Larr added.

"How can this be?" Plagar asked. "Surely he does not know Thalindor's location?"

"Alacatus informed us that Voldestus plans to drive the elves from the city, with the assistance of an orc warlord he has forged an alliance with. These orcs are able to travel within the Great Glade without harm. We are unsure how this is possible." Nia informed those present.

"The orc tribes are more fractured than they have ever been. Surely they would be unable to gather the numbers for such an attack." Lorias said, but Nia disagreed.

"We met some of the forces that will push against Thalindor. The clans have united under one banner and are a very real threat." she said and Drakarim confirmed to the group that what Nia had described was accurate.

"So the orcs siege Thalindor and either drive the elves out to be slaughtered by Voldestus and his dragons, or they force Thalindor to be revealed and thus it is destroyed," Plagar said. "Then we have much to prepare. We are a great distance from the glade and they need to be warned immediately."

He addressed Lorias directly. "We require a suitable plan for us to reach Thalindor in time. I would suggest a joint portal spell. Perhaps with enough mages concentrating their efforts we could cover a greater distance and reach Thalindor in time."

Lorias nodded her agreement but she had concerns, "it would take a great deal of effort. Our most talented mages would need to stay here to keep the portal open should we need to retreat. Thus our aid to the city would be limited."

Galen raised his hand this time. "I believe that there is another arcane tower somewhere within the Great Glade, possibly even Thalindor itself. If this is the case and we could get someone with an Armonis stone into that portal room, we would have a gateway in and out of the glade."

He went on to describe the portal room and the various gateways across the world that might be possible with its use.

Nia's surprise was evident. She had never seen or heard of an arcane tower within the glade, and certainly not Thalindor itself. However, if there was one, she had no choice but to locate it.

"Show me this portal room," she requested with a determination in her eyes. She could not fail her people, no matter what.

Rise, bloodborne

The Tower of Light - present day

Drakarim stood patiently outside the tower as heavy snow continued to fall quietly around him. He had returned to his original size which was a mighty relief, but in addition, he felt more at ease out here in the open, away from the smell of mana that seemed so encompassing within the tower. It now loomed above him, its fabled orbs slowly circling, illuminating the tower with their golden light and never-ending protection.

During an assault, those orbs would become powerful weapons, blasting incredible energy towards any who dared to attack. Thankfully it was a defence that the mages of the Tower of Light had never had to witness, but it was reassuring knowing it was there all the same.

Although the cold was not affecting him, Drakarim was growing increasingly impatient and his mind wandered to the thought of one day having to come face to face with Voldestus once again. Drakarim was defeated at their last encounter, but he tried to reassure himself that this time it would be different. Voldestus was a dangerous foe, but perhaps, with the aid of his new found allies, Drakarim could emerge victorious.

Either way, he had to try, no matter the odds against him.

After several hours, a figure emerged from beneath the tower and Drakarim watched as the silhouette moved through the torchlight. The figure was male. A young human with athletic build and an aura about him that felt immediately familiar to Drakarim.

The figure paused, and then walked forward until he was leaning on the edge of the overhanging balcony. He hadn't yet noticed the Dragon, who was partly concealed by the darkness of night.

The man looked sadly out across the frozen landscape. His posture and body language seemed like that of a defeated soul and he appeared to be deep in thought until, eventually, the young man turned and finally noticed Drakarim's presence.

Drakarim expected him to be surprised, perhaps even fearful at the sight of a dragon. However, the man was far from startled and instead of stepping away or reacting with overwhelming fear like most humans would, he just regarded Drakarim with a steely gaze.

The young man did not say a word as the snow continued to fall around them and the winds howled. There was an awkward silence that broke out between dragon and human. After several minutes, Drakarim finally decided it would be polite for him to speak.

"Greetings," he said.
"Hello." the young man replied as their eyes finally met, and a faint purple glint appeared in his eyes.

Drakarim's breath caught in his throat. There was something about the young man's voice, how he carried himself, and his facial features that seemed so familiar. Drakarim suddenly recalled a distant memory, on the day of the battle of the Black Marshes, when Talon Bloodborne removed his dragon helm, revealing his face for the first time, and the two friends looked at each other with such joy. This young man could only be a bloodborne.

In that very moment something incredible happened. A connection of sorts between man and dragon, a deep and hidden link re-established. It appeared as though the young man felt the same connection, and he stood startled, eyes wide as he watched Drakarim.

"I.." Drakarim started but as he tried to speak, the connection only grew stronger, the man's eyes grew brighter, blazing purple now, and Drakarim felt his body react, and his inner fire began to burn with a new invigoration. He had not felt this for many years.

"I knew it would be special." Alacatus' voice chuckled within Drakarim's mind.

The young man's face was now one of utter shock and he took a few steps back as he looked up at the giant flaming dragon that now stood before him. That dragon, was now somehow even larger, and burning brightly, lighting up the surrounding snow covered lands as his flames whipped around him with tremendous fury.

Drakarim's mind was racing through a series of memories of the young bloodborne that Drakarim once knew all those years ago, and Talon's face flashed across his mind's eye. The young man staggered back, his hand against his head as he too appeared to be overwhelmed with invasive memories and emotions.

"Yes Drakarim." Alacatas' voice echoed once more. "Talon Bloodborne had a child, he passed his Armonis imbuement down the bloodline." Drakarim didn't know what to say. He just stared, wide eyed at the young man standing before him.

"I.. know you?" The man stammered. "How do I know you?"

The voice of Drakarim's old friend was echoing through his mind.

"You are bloodborne." Drakarim managed. The young man was not sure how to react.
"Bloodborne?" he asked at last, and Drakarim nodded weakly. He could hear Talon's voice in his head. See his face. Feel his presence.
"Talon?" Drakarim asked. The man shook his head.
"Arwin. My name is Arwin."

The two stood bewildered as the snow continued to fall. The silence was palpable.
Arwin leant against the stone railing and let out a great sigh, his breath freezing as it hit the air. He stood motionless for a time, as thoughts

washed over him. Memories of his parents. Tales of their own time growing up in this dangerous and hostile world.

"I'm just a scavenger. An orphan," he said, his voice tinged with sadness but before they could continue their conversation, the tower's huge doors opened and Meduz-Larr stepped outside, closely followed by the others.

Many of them stopped in their tracks when they witnessed the giant flaming dragon that now stood before them.

"Your light has returned!" Meduz-Larr exclaimed in wonder, and then she saw Arwin's eyes and she blinked in disbelief. "A bloodborne?! How can this be?"
"I have much to explain. Where is Nialandra?" Drakarim replied.

Nia stood before the portals in silence, as Galen and Plagar explained their discoveries so far.

As they continued their discussion, she wandered slowly forwards and approached the portal to what was believed to be the Tower of Vine, knelt before it, and examined the intricate works at its base. The frame, she sensed, was made from the Nedai tree, a tree that only grew within the Great Glade.

Something within the artwork caught her eye and she examined it closely, sure enough, there, amongst the etched carvings were tiny elven figures, their houses and what could have been a small village surrounding a giant tree that ran all the way up the side of the frame.

"Thalindor," she whispered in awe. Plagar turned to Galen in surprise.
"Are you sure?" He asked. Nia glanced back at him and nodded.
"If there is a portal there," she said, "we must open it."
Galen shook his head. "Sadly, that is not possible unless we can get an Armonis gem into the chamber at the other side."

"The Ancient known as Oranlire holds an Armonis gem, and has kept the secret of the portal's existence for many years," the voice of Alacatus echoed into Galen, Plagar and Nia's minds all at once.

The three companions exchanged excited glances.

"Please tell me you heard that," Plagar exclaimed.
"Alacatus? Yes, he does that from time to time," Galen grinned.

Nia pondered their predicament, but something else was troubling her.

She turned to the others with excitement.

"The echo orbs, of course!" she exclaimed, and pulled open her pack. Galen was fascinated to see the orb, which glistened as Nia held it before her.
"I placed an echo orb within a cave, not far from Thalindor. I shall portal there and head to the city. If I am swift, I may be able to open the portal and allow the mages of the Tower of Light through."

Galen and Plagar agreed with the suggestion, hopeful that they might have a chance to save Thalindor after all. Nia turned to Giggles, who had been watching the conversation closely.

"I must go and save Thalindor and our friends there. It isn't safe for you my child, so you must stay here until I return," Nia said. "I know that I promised I would not leave you little one, but many will die if I do not go now."

Tears ran from Giggles's eyes, but she tried her best to be brave, squeezing Nia's hand before giving her a huge hug. "Love you Nee," she said through her tears.
"I love you too." Nia replied, "I'll see you soon. Tell that grumpy dragon to make sure you eat something today, OK?"

Giggles nodded, wiped tears away from her eyes and she stepped back. Galen placed a calming hand upon her shoulder as Nia held the echo orb before her and stroked a hand across its surface. The air cracked and in a split second, she was gone.

Some time later, Galen, Lorias, Giggles and Plagar reconvened with the others outside the tower and each of them were brought up to speed on the developments with Drakarim and Arwin, while they each explained Nia's situation as best as they could. Giggles did not hesitate in approaching Drakarim, who dropped his flame form and allowed the child to come closer for warmth against the surrounding snows.

"It is incredible to witness an actual bloodborne standing alongside us. I have read so much about your species in the great archives," Galen exclaimed excitedly. Arwin was still in shock and to be truthful he was still doubtful that he could be a dragonrider.
"The link between bloodborne and dragon appears to have re-established Drakarim's true form and power. It is an incredible tool that we can now utilise against Voldestus," Lorias said. There was a newfound positivity amongst those present.

Meduz-Larr regarded Arwin for a few moments before she said "We still have the issue that Arwin will be unable to ride Drakarim without protective armour, or he will succumb to the flames."
"Perhaps we can solve it with some defensive magic?" Plagar asked but Lorias shook her head.
"It is too restrictive and if the spell drops at any time, Arwin would be dead within seconds," she replied.

However, Galen had been deep in thought and eventually he approached Meduz-Larr. "Empress, if I may, please would you come with me. I may have something of interest to you."
Meduz-Larr's eyebrows raised in curiosity. "Indeed," she said, and together they made their way back into the tower, leaving the others to continue their discussions and plans.

Galen led Meduz-Larr through the corridors of the Tower of Light, towards the great archive. As they walked together he took the opportunity to ask Meduz-Larr some questions that he had long wanted to ask.

"Empress, do you believe that Alacatus will never return to this world?" Meduz-Larr sighed before she replied. "I am afraid that Alacatus has made his peace. He does not believe that us dragons, in our current state, should walk amongst the other races of the world. He believes we are unnatural and therefore a danger to those around us. In some respects, I agree. I do not yet understand how the Allied Realms will be able to live alongside us dragons."

Galen was incredibly sad to hear that, but still he held out hope that he would see Alacatus once again. He was fond of the kind dragon that had hidden himself away from the world, but could offer it so much more.

"I agree that times will be tough as we pass into the new phase, but hope that once we rid the world of this king, we can forge a lasting peace between the Allied Realms and the dragons," he said.
Meduz-Larr nodded. "Then we are in agreement, apprentice mage."
Galen laughed. "It is so strange to hear those words when they are addressed to me. I am only a mage because of this staff."
Meduz-Larr smiled, "I think you know that isn't true. The staff chose you because you have an uncanny ability to wield its magic. I have to say though, there is something about your gem that feels familiar. Perhaps in time we can explore that further together."

Galen smiled and agreed.
"That would be most welcome. I am always keen to learn, and that, interestingly, is how I discovered what I'm about to show you." he said as he led Meduz-Larr into the great archive.

Meduz-Larr was impressed. "It certainly is an incredible collection." she stated as she examined the various items that surrounded them.
"Indeed it is." Galen exclaimed. "As I searched the archives, I discovered a section just through here."

Galen led Meduz-Larr into a large armoury, complete with various mannequins adorned with armours dotted around the room. Meduz-Larr immediately recognised some of the pieces, like the Eastern Marauders' dreadmail and the armour of the queen's own **16th Battalion** who fought at the battle of Ruyan's Pass against the shadelings seven hundred and sixty three years ago.

"It is indeed impressive," she mused. "Perhaps some of these armour pieces can be re-worked for our own purposes."
"Possibly yes," Galen replied, "but this is what I wanted to show you."

Meduz-Larr's mouth dropped open and her eyes widened as she recognised the **black darian** armour laid out before her. For there, upon the table, battered and aged but still recognisable, was a complete set of bloodborne armour.

Meanwhile within the great hall, preparations were being made for war. Survivors from Fort Valian gathered what weapons and armour they could muster. Most would likely not be joining the battle at Thalindor but were instead preparing the Tower of Light for defence, should the dragons seek it out.

Heg and Barn had been coordinating these efforts for the past few days, and the tower's own forge was now packed with dwarves, who were putting every effort into their craft as swords, axes and various pieces of armour were swiftly stacking up.

"I've never seen a forge like this Barn. It's like the damned thing is enchanted or some'n," Heg grinned.
"It is." came a deep voice from behind them. Heg and Barn turned and nearly fell over from shock as they regarded the opulent elder dragon now standing before them. Meduz-Larr looked down at them and winked.
"We erm, 'erd about you," Barn said, breaking the awkward silence.
"Well don't stare, I need help and I've been told you are the ones to do the work." Meduz-Larr said expectantly. Barn glanced at Heg and then back to Meduz-Larr.

"Who told ya that?" Heg asked.

"A nice young valian with some interesting vocal talents," Meduz-Larr replied as she reached into a bag that was larger than Heg. She pulled out a dark plate helmet that seemed to glint a strange red tint as it caught the light. It was like nothing that Heg or Barn had seen before. Meduz-Larr passed it down to Heg who took it and examined it closely.

"This metal. I ain't never seen it before, but 'erd about it," she said, passing it to Barn. "Black darian."

"I don't get it. What do ya need us for?" Barn asked as he tried the helm on, but it was too large for his head.

"It needs to fit your friend Arwin." Meduz-Larr said. "It once belonged to a dragonrider, and must do so again." She placed the bag down before them and Heg peered inside, where she found more pieces of the armour.

"Arwin?" Heg and Barn asked in unison, then they noticed the figure walking towards them from behind Meduz-Larr.

A tall, muscular looking man with blazing purple eyes.

"Arwin?!" Heg and Barn called in unison once again. They stood watching as Arwin drew closer, mouths gaping open.

"Hey guys." he said, shrugging his shoulders. "So I'm a bloodborne."

The siege of Thalindor

The Great Glade - present day

The Great Glade loomed before Voldestus. Alongside him, a vast and varied dragon army, had gathered ready to obey his every order. Many circled high above, their ominous shadows falling over the vast and magical woodland below.

The Great Glade spread for miles and miles, as far as the eye could see, and the Nedai trees that grew there were tall and broad. Voldestus felt a tinge of trepidation, for the glade had remained protected for millions of years. Its defences were legendary, but this knowledge did not stop him in his search for vengeance, spurred on by hatred formed almost one thousand years ago.

Voldestus had put much of his faith in **Fangs of Felondon, the orc and goblin warband** that he had driven towards Thalindor these past months, and his scouts had informed him that they had finally located an entrance to the city. If the orcs were to betray him now, it would mean all of his planning had gone to waste. The **Fangs of Felondon** numbered more than ten thousand, the biggest army they had ever mustered, strengthened by ogre back bearers, dire wolves and goblin witch hunters.

Voldestus was all too aware that the elves would be strong adversaries, with the might of the Ancients and the Great Glade itself on their side, but it was a carefully calculated risk that the dragon king was prepared to make. The elves numbered far less than the orcs and once the vail that hid Thalindor from the outside world was broken, dragon flame would do the rest of the work.

Voldestus gripped the black orb and raised it before him. Seconds later the gnarled face of Grimwolf appeared.

"Are you in position?" Voldestus asked.
"We are." Grimwolf replied. "Once inside, we will destroy the artefact that keeps the city hidden."
"Then begin your assault." Voldestus growled. The image faded and he tossed the black orb aside, where it shattered as it struck the ground and a wisp of black smoke floated away silently upon the breeze.

Voldestus glared into the deep forest that sprawled out before him, and he drew on his inner flame. The heat surrounded him, scorching the ground beneath his claws. His snout flared and sparks of golden fire spat forth as he drew more and more, until his eyes were filled with golden flames that cracked and burnt like searing hot embers on a blacksmith's furnace.

Then, he released his fury.

An almighty torrent of flames burst forth from his open jaws with an ear splitting thunder clap. The earth itself resonated from the impact, as the jet of flame ripped through the gigantic trees that stood before him, incinerating them for hundreds of metres.

Birds and other wildlife scrambled for cover or became ash, and the trees split, their burning remains crashing to the ground, sending splinters of wood and leaves falling in all directions.

The dragon horde followed their king's example, each releasing their onslaught into the glade with everything they had to offer, a variety of dragon flame, acid breath and lightning that decimated the trees and killed any living thing that happened to get in the way.

"Forward!" Voldestus yelled and the dragons moved as one, unleashing fire and fury as they waded through the scorching mass of damaged and destroyed ancient foliage. Those dragons that circled above also rained down hellfire as the scorched land spread further and further.

Deep within the glade itself, Warlord Grimwolf, along with the red orc shaman Yarnuk and his warband approached the gateway to Thalindor, which still sat as a bastion of peace amongst the carnage that was taking place along the glades edge.

"I smell the stench of elven magic," Yarnuk said to his master. "This is the place."
"Burn it." Warlord Grimwolf ordered.

The shaman stepped forward and stretched out his hands before him. They ignited in a sickly purple and green light that hissed and streaked its way around his body. As he chanted, the sound grew louder and louder and the light that surrounded Yarnuk grew stronger and stronger until it blinded the surrounding orcs, goblins and ogres.

With an almighty bang, the nearby orcs were flung to the ground, burns all across their bodies, and as the smoke cleared, Yarnuk staggered towards his master one last time.

"It is done." he barely managed to speak.
"Good enough." Grimwolf grunted and he pushed the shaman aside, his lifeless body slumped to the ground.

Grimwolf peered through the smoke and removed his massive two-handed battle axe from his back. The black blade hissed, ready for blood. A blaze of arrows sped towards the assembled orc warband, fine crafted elven arrows that sang as they pierced the air and sought out their targets with pinpoint precision.

As orcs and goblins fell around him, Grimwolf remained where he stood, raised his axe to the sky and ordered the charge. A chorus of roars followed behind him and the orcs, goblins and ogres raced forwards to battle, baying for blood.

Meanwhile, as the dragons moved through the glade, burning and incinerating the great ancient Nedai trees before them, there came an ear splitting shriek that gave even Voldestus a reason to pause his attack. He called a halt to the front line and the dragons prepared themselves. Sure enough, just seconds later, the glade came alive to defend itself, as the fables had always said it would.

Thick vines edged with vicious thorns exploded from the ground and surged up to strike at several of the dragons who flew above the glade. One of the vines pierced straight through a dragon's body and it dropped from the sky with a screech, blood pouring from the open wound in its chest.

Voldestus glanced to his right, just in time to witness the ground itself burst up, sending rock, mud and tree roots into the sky as an enormous earth golem emerged. It leapt towards the nearest dragon and grappled it to the ground as flame still poured from its jaws.

The golem was made of mud, stone, wood and bone, its long arms wrapped easily around the neck of the dragon, who fell backwards under the surprise onslaught. The golem then pounded boulder and fury into the dragon's head, spewing blood and flame across the forest floor.

Voldestus looked around the battlefield, but everywhere that he could see, the forest was coming alive and striking back at the invaders. Vines were shooting out of the ground and curling themselves around those dragons not quick enough to evade their grasp, dragging them towards the earth, while many more golems were bursting through the trees and battling in defence of the glade.

The onslaught from the dragon horde had truly angered the glade and awoken its defenders with unmatched ferocity.

Clouds of smoke began to cover the sun and dragon flame ignited around the battlefield, as Voldestus battled on against the forest beings stomping towards him in growing numbers. He unleashed a ferocious jet of golden flame, sweeping his large head from left to right as he did so and his unique fire incinerated any in its way, but as much as the vines tried to pull the great elder dragon down, he was able to fight on.

Voldestus gave the order to push forward as he threw a Golem to the side in anger, and the Dragons obeyed immediately, without question.

Meanwhile, within Thalindor, the **Fangs of Felondon's forces** were making progress. They had lost a large number, but they were fierce combatants and fearless in battle. Orc direwolf riders clashed against elven soulwalkers, and the ogre's launched boulder after boulder at the elven lines from large sacks slung across their broad shoulders. Crushing many of them and sending others flying in all directions, buying time for the orcs to approach even more swiftly.

Atop the council's platform, as Elunara and Oranlire watched the siege unfold, it swiftly became clear to them that the orcs had a specific target. For they were weaving their way towards the base of the Eldertree, where the Ethervail lay open to assault.

The Ethervail was a mysterious artefact created a millenia ago by elves long since passed. Its purpose was to hide the city of Thalindor away from the rest of the world, safely concealing it within its own magical realm. If the orcs were to reach and destroy the Ethervail, Thalindor would surely be lost to the attacking dragons.

Elunara knew that she had precious little time to think, so she threw a glance back at Seraphina, who was being fitted with beautiful white armour by two suitors and then to the other Ancients.

"We must protect the Ethervail," she said. **Oranlire** nodded and joined her immediately, while **Alaric stayed to protect the queen**.

Elunara and **Oranlire** turned, and **Oranlire** cast a spell that launched the two Ancients across the city, until they landed at the huge base of the Eldertree.

There, on the trunk of the tree, was the Ethervail, a large green gemstone encased within bands of silver that wrapped around its circumference and wove into the tree itself.

The Ancients had arrived just in time for Elunara to throw another shield up that deflected a volley of flaming arrows that would have ignited the area around the Ethervail.

She glanced back, the Ethervail still held in its place by its silver vines. It seemed so exposed now and it was clearly the target of the orcs' assault.

There was a flash of movement out the corner of Elunara's eye and she span to engage with whatever was heading for them, but it was Nia that landed nimbly before them, arcane bow in hand and enchanted black wings that folded in and vanished once she safely stopped in front of Elunara and Oranlire.

"What are you doing here?!" Elunara asked.
"The tree!" Nia shouted. "We need to activate the portals!"
"How did you…?" Elunara started but Nia waved her away.
"Never mind that! If we activate the portals, the Tower of Light will send their mages to aid us!" Nia instructed with urgency.

Elunara glanced at **Oranlire** who nodded instantly. They had no time to question Nia and instead they had to focus on their tasks ahead.

"I have the key, follow me!" Oranlire said and he ran swiftly towards the base of the Eldertree, Nia hot on his heels as more arrows and a few blasts of dark magic ripped across Elunara's shield.

Elunara closed her eyes and sent her voice to all soulwalkers in the area to defend the Ethervail. With their help, perhaps she would be able to hold off the attackers long enough for the mages to arrive. She said a silent prayer and went about her work.

Nia and **Oranlire** weaved their way between the massive roots of the Eldertree, until the sounds of battle were nothing but a distant echo. **Oranlire** slowed to a walk as he reached a seemingly inconspicuous area of the tree's base, except for a circle of runic drawings that were etched into the ground before him.

"There is a vast history that many elves are not aware of, Nialandra. A history that some amongst us have buried deep down in order to protect Thalindor and our way of life. These portals within the tree were once used by the Allied Realms, to keep a constant communication network in place," he explained as he stepped within the circle and motioned for Nia to do the same.

Oranlire then pulled out a glowing blue stone that hung from a silver chain around his neck.

"Elli encar 'tika." he commanded. Mana immediately surrounded the two elves and they vanished in a blinding flash of blue light.

A second later, Nia and **Oranlire** found themselves standing in a large wooden chamber made from twisted branches and vines that wove around the room, and spiralled upwards to create a dome of foliage. Faint rays of sunlight flickered through the gaps between the branches above, providing a small but effective light source.

Nia felt as though the chamber was located somewhere high above the siege, which continued to rage on in the distance. She was disorientated, but Oranlire moved on with urgency and Nia followed. Across the room there were six portal frames, much like the ones that Nia had seen at the Tower of Light. However these lay on their back, facing the ceiling, covered in dust and weeds.

"Listen to me closely." Oranlire said and he grabbed Nia's elbow. "We don't have much time to discuss, but there is a traitor amongst us."
Nia pulled her elbow free, and glared at the Ancient standing before her. "Surely you do not mean an elf is responsible for all of this?"
"Only elven hands could have made those pendants. Or at least the original," Oranlire explained. "Consider it. It has to be someone amongst us that helped the orcs gain access to Thalindor. How could they have known about the Ethervail?"

Oranlire turned and hurried on with the task at hand. There was an awkward silence that hung in the air between the two elves. Nia's thoughts were racing ahead of her.

"Are the portals damaged?" she asked as she ran forward and examined the fallen portal frames.
"No, they were decommissioned." Oranlire said. He approached the white portal which lay upon its back, covered in moss and dirt. "Help me lift this."

Nia stepped quickly to Oranlire's side and together they lifted the heavy white marble portal until it was upright once more. Once again, the portal's intricate carvings were a marvel to behold.

The rim of the portal frame was carefully chiselled to create puffy clouds, which arose elegantly from the base and the gem which sat atop the portal was encased in a carving of the sun. Oranlire wasted no time, placing his hand on the portal and holding the blue gem necklace once again. A moment later the portal sprang to life with a crack.

Nia felt a surge of relief, for there, within the shifting portal that now floated before them were the faces of Galen, Plagar and Lorias, clearly startled to see the portal activate.

Lorias stepped forward and bowed her head to Oranlire. "I take it you must be Ancient Oranlire of Thalindor? I am Grand Mage Lorias Kwin of the Tower of Light. It is an honour."
"If I may," Oranlire started, "Your father was a fool. As was his predecessor."
"I'm sorry?" Lorias stammered.
"It was the Grand Mage Brandis Kwin that ordered the portal links between the Pillars of Twilight to be shut down and their existence to remain a secret," Oranlire explained. "He feared that the link would put the Tower of Light at risk. It was an order that I valiantly fought against but alas what does an Ancient of Thalindor know that a grand mage who is less than half their age does not know?"
Lorias looked taken aback. "I.." she started but Oranlire interrupted her.

"No matter, the damage is done. Thalindor is under siege and as I understand from Nialandra you are prepared to offer aid. I suggest we move swiftly. We are heavily outnumbered here and the invaders are pushing towards the Ethervail"

Plagar cleared his throat. "How do we proceed?" He asked.

"It should be a simple task," Oranlire replied. "We deactivate the locking spell that Brandis Kwin put in place and the link will then remain open, even if a gem is not present at both locations."
"What is the process?" Plagar asked.
"It is a simple spell, all you need to do is reach out with the staff and connect with the gem located at the top of the portal. If your mind is open, you will detect the spell's presence. Then it is simply a case of dispelling it," Oranlire instructed.

Galen did as instructed. He closed his eyes and pushed out with his senses, searching his surroundings for a sign of the enchantment. Just a few moments later he detected the lock, an ageing magical spell that lingered within the gem itself.

Oranlire repeated the task at his end of the portal link. Moments later there was a loud humming noise that briefly filled the portal chamber at each end of the link and then it faded away.

"There, the portals are joined once again," Oranlire announced and then, "As it should have been."

He turned and pointed to an exit portal that had appeared at the rear of the room in which he and Nia stood. "Nialandra, you must go and aid the defence. I shall direct the mages through from here and then rejoin you on the battlefield."
"Yes, Ancient Oranlire," Nia said and immediately left through the exit portal, while Galen and Plagar gathered their forces together from within the Tower of Light.

Soon, the Tower of Light's long preparations would come to fruition, and the might of their magics would clash against that of the dragon horde.

The empress returns

Jarmunpek - present day

Wall Breaker was an ancient elder dragon, named for its one single task. It was built specifically to break down defences, to digest walls and to reveal secluded enemies in any fortification.

The massive dragon spent most of his life waiting for commands, and when Voldestus came to power, as city after city fell to his might, Wall Breaker was always there to devour anything that remained. The dragon was almost as tall as Voldestus and Drakarim, but its maul was wide, and its mouth capable of consuming even the largest structure. Wall Breaker could not breathe fire, but instead was able to launch its digested food at speed, making it a deadly boulder launcher. It didn't have claws like many of its brothers and sisters, instead each of its legs ended in massive, ground shattering hooves, grown specifically, for crushing fortifications.

Wall Breaker stood over the ruins of the once great eastern city of Jarmunpek, its blue stone and gold walls shattered and broken before the elder dragon.

"Consume it all." had been the instruction from Voldestus and consume it he would. However, even for a dragon of its size and abilities that would take some time.

The palace itself was mostly destroyed, as well as the ancient council meeting chambers and government buildings, however the outer walls and old city still remained. Wall Breaker was mostly alone here, though there were some dragon stragglers from each side following the battle, some of which were too wounded to travel and had remained in the ruins of Jarmunpek hoping to survive unnoticed until they were strong enough to fly once again.

However, a contingent of inquisitors had also remained here, hunting for those survivors too weak to defend themselves, but also under explicit instructions to locate any members of the Allied Realms that may still reside within the ruins and dispose of them.

Night was beginning to fall across Jarmunpek as Wall Breaker continued its work. A screech crossed the sky, followed by a small burst of arcana. A series of flashes lit up the evening sky. Wall Breaker peered up slowly, as it munched on a mouthful of stone, momentarily curious about the new arrival, and then returned to its feeding when it lost interest once again.

Elsewhere in the city, a clutch of inquisitors searched through ruins by the southern quarter, which once housed the city's famous docks and a trade hub for the Eastern Empire. They had wandered dangerously close to the southernmost sewer entrance, one of the hidden pathways that unbeknownst to them led to the last remnants of the eastern Allied Realms.

A small number of survivors cowered in the darkness below, surviving on little food and who would be easy prey for the Inquisitors should they be discovered.

One of the inquisitors stepped closer to the entrance, which was secluded behind a batch of crates and rubble, and sniffed at the air in curiosity. Its heightened senses detected something amiss and the dark-scaled creature turned to its allies and signalled for silence. Its fire eyes burnt almost out of control and flames gushed from open fissures on its body as it realised it may have located its enemy and the thrill of the hunt began.

The inquisitors skulked closer to the hidden doorway, unaware that a newly arrived figure stood behind them, watching in silence. The figure was taller than them and vastly more powerful.

"Get out of my city." the figure's voice commanded. The inquisitors turned and surprise spread across their faces as they recognised the newcomer.

"The empress," one of them hissed, raising his long jagged halberd ready to order the attack. However, before he could do so, his entire body erupted in electricity that seemed to spring from the floor and engulf him completely. The lightning ripped through the inquisitor's armour and illuminated its face in bright blue light as tendrils of electrical current sprang from its eyes and open mouth. Seconds later, the inquisitor sunk to the floor, lifeless but shaking from the current that still ripped through its body.

The other four inquisitors staggered back from the shock but before they could reach Meduz-Larr, another inquisitor erupted in electricity. Meduz-Larr remained completely motionless, her eyes flashing furiously with mana as the remaining three inquisitors got within striking range.

The first leapt forwards with a long-handled battle axe and swung it down in a huge arc that would have decimated a human or elf combatant, but instead of striking Meduz-Larr, the battle axe shattered across an invisible field of energy and the Inquisitor staggered back in shock, dropping what remained of its weapon onto the floor as the last two inquisitors attacked immediately, with the only other option available to them. Each of them breathed fire forwards, this time the flames simply rolling around the magic shield. Meduz-Larr stood calmly within it, her eyes were blazing brightly.

Eventually, the inquisitors stopped their attack and stood hissing at Meduz, unsure how they should proceed.

"You have one last chance to leave my city." she growled, but the inquisitors were too stupid to realise that they had no chance of winning. The first lept towards Meduz-Larr and attempted to attack with claws rather than a weapon. As soon as it struck the invisible shield its arm exploded in a fountain of blood and it screeched backwards, falling to the floor.

The inquisitors tried once again to attack with fire breath, but this time as the fire built around Meduz-Larr, it slowly transformed into lightning that whipped around her in a sphere, lighting up the entire area in blue and white, until finally, she blinked. The electricity shot out at the remaining inquisitors, utterly engulfing them within its deadly current.

Eventually, Meduz-Larr released the spell and the burnt bodies dropped to the floor in a smoking mess. She sighed, stepping past them to the hidden entrance of the sewer tunnels, then turned and leapt into the sky once again. Her next confrontation would not be so easy.

Across the city, Wall Breaker was deeply engrossed in devouring a large stone wall made of the same blue stone as the rest of the palace and much of Jarmunpek. As it munched down its meal, slowly crushing the remnants of the palace within its powerful jaws, Meduz-Larr landed before it.

Wall Breaker stopped chewing and glared at the newcomer. Emotionless, it blinked its huge green eyes and Meduz-Larr stared back. Eventually Wall Breaker let the contents of its mouth fall to the floor and began a slow, lumbering walk towards her, its huge feet cracking open the ground beneath it as it did so.

Meduz-Larr sighed. She fused with the mana around her, and glared at the approaching dragon.

"Stop!" She screamed, but the beast was too dumb to stop, only seeking to devour her and continue with its destruction of the city.

Eventually she had no choice. There was an almighty clash of thunder and the air around Wall Breaker electrified, tendrils of lightning whipped around it, stabbing at it from multiple directions.
It didn't seem to make much of an impact, so Meduz-Larr followed up her initial attack with a barrage of ice that shattered across Wall Breaker's hide. This time, several of the spikes did find their mark, piercing its thick armour. Wall Breaker opened its giant mouth and launched a barrage of stone that seemed never ending. Initially Meduz-

Larr's magical shield held back the attack, but over time she could feel it weakening. Just as it was about to break, she used a small spurt of magic to launch herself backwards out of harm's way.

"Please, my brother." She pleaded, "Why do you side with Voldestus?" But Wall Breaker simply regarded Meduz-Larr with an unwavering stare.

A second barrage of stone flew at her just seconds later. This time Meduz-Larr dodged and landed atop some ruins not far away. She attempted to connect to the creature's mind in a desperate attempt to talk the dragon down. She did manage to establish a connection where she tried to communicate, and her voice entered its mind.
"We can both walk away from here. I do not wish you harm," she said and then waited for a response.

But here was nothing but guttural grunts., while Wall Breaker walked slowly forwards.

Meduz-Larr wondered if her words had made an impact and she waited cautiously, but just a second later, the giant dragon charged forward and smashed the ruin upon which she had sought refuge. She fell awkwardly, slamming to the ground as Wall Breaker's huge hooves stomped down onto the ground where she lay, one after the other, pounding the stone, throwing up dust and dirt all around.

Eventually, Wall Breaker stopped, and it sniffed around the ground for signs of its opponent. However, as the dust cleared, Meduz-Larr was nowhere to be seen. Wall Breaker turned around and around, in search of the smaller dragon, but it found nothing but air, while Meduz-Larr watched from a safe distance.

In this moment, she realised that she had no choices remaining. If she left Wall Breaker to its work, it would soon discover the hidden colony below the sewers and they would surely perish.

Meduz-Larr took a breath. Opening her arms wide, she summoned all of her will. Her eyes flashed with the power of mana, and she drew upon the light, summoning a beam of energy from the skies above. The powerful ray shone down directly into Wall Breaker's back. Initially it had no effect, but she focused the beam, ensuring that it became more deadly until eventually it ripped into the mighty dragon's heart. Wall Breaker staggered forward on unsteady legs, gasping for air before it stumbled forward and collided with the ground with an almighty crash that resonated across Jarmunpek. With one final twist of its body, its green eyes settled upon Meduz-Larr and she watched in silence as its life drained away.

As the dust settled, Meduz-Larr wiped away tears from her face. She took a deep breath, turned and left the scene in search of any other enemies or indeed allies who may need help.

Below the abandoned city, in a large open sewer system that had become home to thousands of refugees, the concerned civilians gathered to discuss their options. The desperation had grown unbearable, with many scavenger parties lost over the past month and the grounds caving in as the damaged sewer system restricted the survivors movements even further.

The survivors had nominated an elven spokesperson, Hitara S'imoor, cleric of the order of the leaf and once faith advisor to the Grand Mosin of the Eastern Realms. She had witnessed both the very best of this fragile world, and the very worst. Her faith, placed within the empress and emperor had garnered a suitable life for the refugees but this faith was now facing its greatest threat of all.

Hitara was an elegant woman, dressed in the best blue robes she could find, given the circumstances, and a popular choice for spokesperson amongst the refugees of Jarmunpek. She regarded those before her, all of which looked weak from hunger and pale from the continued lack of sunlight. She had no solutions to offer those gathered here. All she could do was join them in their prayers that eventually something would free them from the unending torment that they had so far endured.

"May the light shine." Hitara concluded and those gathered repeated the phrase back to her.

One father, who had been stroking his young son's hair and hugging him close, stood and addressed the gathered crowd.

"Please, Hitara, we have no choice but to leave. We are doomed down here."

Hitara shook her head solemnly. "There is far more danger out there. Inquisitors are hunting for survivors. None of our scout groups ever returned. The city is nothing but ruins."

She addressed the other survivors present. "We must wait out the dragons. Eventually they will leave and when they are gone, scavenge for food and supplies."

"There is nothing left out there!" One civilian shouted angrily.

"If you want to take your family and leave, then go!" Another responded.

Hitara appealed for calm. "Please Balan, I will not stop you and neither will anyone else here. But I beg you, as I have said, outside of the sewer is certain death for you and your family. The empress will return. Of this I am sure, and then we will have the security that we need."

"The empress could be dead for all we know!" A woman shouted from the back of the group and many others nodded in agreement.

As the conversation continued, a familiar voice drifted into Hitara's mind.

"I have left food at the southern entrance." It was Meduz-Larr. "Hitara, it is still dangerous outside, but I am dealing with them. Caution your people to stay hidden."

"You abandoned us, where did you go?" Hitara responded, but there was silence.

Eventually Meduz-Larr replied. "Emperor Graxilius is dead. The golden dragon came. I would have been dead too had I not fled. I am sorry Hitara."

Hitara felt a pang of guilt as she heard this news. "I am sorry, empress, we are grateful for your return."

"Collect the food before it is seen, I have much to do," Meduz-Larr said and then her presence was gone.

Hitara took several guards and headed to the southern entrance where, sure enough, they opened the door to find a pile of freshly-slain deer. As the guards took the supplies inside, Hitara stood at the doorway, looking out into the night. Several inquisitor bodies lay close to the doorway, and the stench of death was in the air.
"May the light shine upon you, Empress," she sighed and pulled the door closed once again.

Meduz-Larr was exhausted now. Her magic weakened and her body ached from confrontation after confrontation, but she would not rest. She owed the city her best efforts, and would clear it of the threats that remained.

Unbeknown to the empress, as the sounds of battle reverberated across the city, those pockets of surviving eastern dragons began to return. Some pulled themselves from half-destroyed buildings where they had been resting until healed, while others had spotted the battles from afar and had returned by flight to lend their aid where they were able.

The gutterlings, small, brown, flightless dragon-kin who stood just four feet tall and had almost goblin-like qualities, scattered to the surrounding boroughs of Jarmunpek when Voldestus first attacked, but now fought against inquisitors using their numbers and speed to overcome them.

Eastern snaketails, long slim dragons with shiny black scales and a vicious poisonous bite, emerged from the rubble to strike where they could and Thunderhawks sailed overhead once more, raining down furious electrical breath upon the Lava Tooths, who skulked about the outside of the cities walls.

Meduz-Larr listened intently, as a chorus of shouts began to erupt across not only Jarmunpek but also the great lands of the east as the dragons returned to battle once more.

"The empress returns!"

A united defence

Thalindor - present day

Nia drove her blade deep into the orc warrior's chest. Its dark red blood spattered across her leather armour and it gurgled its last breath as it slumped before her. To her side, several mages were engaging with more orcs and goblins, attempting to keep them at a distance as best they could. However, their numbers were slowly overwhelming the spellcasters' defences.

Orcs were tough, far more resilient than humans or elves and they were unpredictable in battle. Up close, the mages would be no match so it was vital that their approach was controlled. They used a combination of earth magic, which pulled the ground upwards to create walls of mud and stone that hindered the invaders' movements and kept them pinned in suitable locations for the elven archers to pick off safely, and controlled air magic that threw dirt and dust across the orcs' path, causing confusion as they attempted to push forwards.

A second line of mages would then follow up with offensive spells with the aim of whittling down the confused orcs numbers as best they could. However the orcs had spellcasters of their own, who wove dark, chaotic magic to mask their movements as they weaved down the valley path and into the centre of Thalindor. There, they would be able to spread out and engage the defenders more freely through its many small, winding streets.

Nia battled on, her arms heavy with the continued effort but she knew that if the Ethervail fell, Thalindor would be vulnerable to the dragons who were currently locked in a fierce battle against the Great Glade. She leapt over several fallen allies and attempted to make her way closer to the Ethervail, but as she passed through a narrow alleyway, a cold chill passed up her spine. Before her, the elven casualties were heavy, with many soulwalkers scattered amongst the dead. There, battling alongside the remaining defenders were two of the most precious and powerful elves that Thalindor had ever been blessed with, but even they were struggling to hold back the tide of attackers.

It was not just the invaders that thundered towards the Ethervail, but the risen dead, lumbering corpses of all combatants, bloodied, burnt and broken, each surrounded by a swirling mass of dark purple gas that appeared to be controlled by a figure standing on the far side of the field of battle.

"Tell us what ya need." a female voice said from behind Nia. She turned to find both Heg and Barn standing in the alleyway, followed by other dwarves and humans, each armed with whatever they could find. They were surprisingly eager to head into battle and Nia was glad to see them. She pointed down into the mass of orcs, goblins, ogres and undead.

"Help the Ancients. I'll take care of that spellcaster!" she shouted.

As they ran towards battle, Nia meanwhile, called upon her powers to enchant her form. Large black feathered wings sprung from the centre of her back and she immediately leapt to the skies, launching herself towards the figure who was still weaving its dark magic onto those below. Nia notched an explosive arrow mid-flight and launched it at the figure just before she landed. The resulting explosion threw the orc backwards and it briefly lost its concentration on its undead enchantment, slowing the advance of the undead.

Nia landed nimbly before the orc as it straightened up and glared at her with dark red eyes full of hatred. It Was much taller and broader than the other orcs she had seen. Its black cloak was adorned with bones and its large, long-nailed hands were covered in dried blood, while its face was a mass of piercings, tattoos and scars.

This orc was known as Veltish Karn, a shaman of the chaos guild, and was perhaps one of the most dangerous magic users to ally with the Fangs of Felondon. He scowled at Nia as she stood confidently before him, his blood curdled with rage and he raised his right hand. Nia noted with interest that the dark purple gas returned and re-established the link with the animated corpses below.

She wasted no time, dashing forward while drawing her short sword in one smooth motion and slashed Veltish directly across his stomach, as she spun past the large orc and settled into a defensive stance. Nia expected to turn and see him slumped on the floor, but instead he simply looked towards her and grinned a near toothless grin. Those few teeth he did have were sharpened into long spikes. Veltish appeared uninjured, and he simply raised his left hand and pointed at Nia.

Pain racked her body and she fell to her knees, making it almost impossible to fight back. Nia screamed in pain as Veltish closed his hand into a fist. She knew that every second she struggled against him was another second that the Ancients were vastly outnumbered below.

Heg and Barn lost sight of one another in the chaos that ensued. They were not used to fighting on a battlefield and the number of opponents was truly overwhelming. Barn wielded a one-handed axe that he swung with great strength, severing the head of a goblin who foolishly got too close and shoved the body back into its fellows to buy himself and others around him some time.
"Heg!?" He shouted, but he could not see the dwarf amongst the mass around them.

Heg meanwhile, threw herself forwards into a number of goblins who struggled to keep order against the marauding dwarf. Beside her was Arliff, an ageing farmer from the Bendarin region and Kol, the dwarf who had travelled with Heg and Barn in the mines below Fort Valian. Each of them fought valiantly against the surrounding mass.

"Look out!" Arliff yelled and threw himself in front of Heg, raising his shield before them in an attempt to block whatever was coming, but it shattered from the strike and he flew backwards with blood gushing from a head wound. Heg, shocked and dazed, glanced around and soon saw that what had attacked Arliff was an enormous, well-muscled ogre, armed with a bloodied warhammer.

Several arrows were embedded in the chest of the large beast, none of which had managed to slow nor take it down. Heg doubted her hammer would do the job but she readied herself all the same. The ogre swung at her and she dodged beneath the creature's swing, striking it in the knee with her hammer as she did so. It was a decent attempt but not good enough, and the ogre turned on Heg and continued its pursuit.

"Why me!?" she cursed, trying to make light of the situation as she narrowly avoided an overhead swing of the orgre's warhammer. It slammed into the ground just in front of her and the ogre growled in frustration. It tried to kick Heg with its huge feet, but as it did so, an arrow bounced off the side of its head and it turned to growl at the attacker.

"Now Heg!" Barn's voice shouted over the chaos, and Heg drew back before throwing her metal hammer at the ogre's head. It smashed into the beast's skull, cracking it open and knocking the ogre onto its back, still alive but not for long as Kol, Heg and Barn rained down blows until it stopped moving. The three friends stood breathing heavily for a moment and grinned at one another, before rejoining the fight once again.

Meanwhile, Nia struggled against the might of Veltish. The shaman was a powerful foe and the grip his magic had upon her was causing excruciating pain, but she would not give up. She pushed towards him in a vain attempt to swipe at his outstretched hand with her short sword. Just as Nia began to lose her strength, two gangly arms wrapped themselves around the shaman's head, covering his eyes and two legs wrapped around his waist. The face of Tobbin the gnome appeared over the shaman's shoulder as he rode the large orc like a horse.

"Crappin' orc!" Tobbin yelled at the top of his voice.

Veltish didn't take long to throw the gnome to the side, but it was enough for him to lose his concentration once again on his spellcasting. The undead below stopped in their tracks and Nia was freed once more. She notched an arrow and let loose. The arrow pierced deep into the shaman's forehead and he froze, before dark blood and a disgusting ooze bubbled from his face as he decomposed right in front of Tobbin and Nia.

"Crappin' dead." Nia gasped with a weary smile and she slumped to her knees.

The orc warlord Grimwolf had slain many elves, dwarves, humans, and even a few goblins as he had made his way through the filthy elven hideout. They were buried deep within the trees, cowering like little snakes who needed culling.

Grimwolf was an accomplished warlord, from a long line of famed warriors and this battle would be his crowning achievement, securing his right as the one true lord of the orc tribes. Tonight he would feast on the blood of the elven princess and spit upon her corpse as his minions watched with glee.

He stood now before the Ethervail, but two elves remained a thorn in his side. Elunara and Oranlire. They had slain many orcs and goblins and dropped three ogres who Grimwolf thought could do better, but now, as he engaged against these elves, he too had struggled to overcome them.

Now though, they were exhausted from battle, their mana drained and their morale dwindling. In Grimwolf's strong hands, he carried a weapon of fabled powers. It was known to his people as Bloodrend, an enchanted battle axe that would gain power as it slayed the warlord's enemies. This could then be released in a powerful burst of arcane energy.

Bloodrend had drunk well that day.

Elunara was the first to make a move, leaping towards Grimwolf and launching a flurry of throwing knives. She attacked with speed even a young elf would struggle to keep up with, as her dual daggers flashed and stung the warlord's armour, landing blow after blow. Grimwolf struggled to keep up his defence against her and backed away but Oranlire levelled his staff, the tip exploded in a barrage of sharpened fire blades at Grimwolf. Luckily for the orc, he still had soldiers around him, who rushed to provide a defensive wall against the second elves magical attacks, so he thrust Bloodrend forward and the flat of the blade struck Elunara in the face.

It was enough to stun her and also buy Grimwolf enough time to swing Bloodrend in a large arc that would have killed Elunara, had she not hastily erected a magical shield to save herself.

Grimwolf glanced to his right. The other elf was making short work of his soldiers and he would be a threat again soon, but he had enough energy stored in Bloodrend for one shot at the Ethervail. He knew it was now or never.

Grimwolf thrust the mighty battle axe forwards and the blade erupted in a blood red magical strike.

"No!" Elunara screamed and she leapt in front of the beam of energy and forced all of her mana into a protective shield that clashed with the incoming force from Bloodrend's attack.

For a long moment, neither of the magical forces seemed to be able to best the other, and on a different day, perhaps Elunara's magic would have held, but she was exhausted and was unable to hold up her shield. As soon as it dropped, the blast from Bloodrend sliced right through Elunara and into the heart of the Ethervail.

The Ethervail exploded into a million fragments, the blast knocking the surrounding survivors off of their feet. A huge, sharpened chunk of the Ethervail struck Grimwolf with a crunch, killing him instantly, and for the first time in more than seven hundred years, the ancient city of Thalindor revealed itself to the outside world.

The city was now vulnerable to attack.

A dragon falls

Thalindor - present day

Thalindor lay exposed some distance from the dragons and Voldestus grinned triumphantly. His eyes lit up with the thought of what would follow.

The Eldertree, which had been absent just moments ago, now loomed high above the rest of the Great Glade, its overhanging leaves casting a great shadow across the surrounding landscape and at its base. Spread out before it was the city of Thalindor itself, where thousands of elven dwellings were dotted across the forest, woven into trees with delicate pathways winding between them.

Voldestus urged the dragons onwards. "Destroy them all!"

The dragons collectively unleashed their inner flames and fire, ice, ash, poison, earth and lightning hammered down towards the city, blasting trees aside as they did so. The earth thundered with the fury of the attacking beasts and Thalindor vanished beneath the torrential assault as a cloud erupted across the landscape.

Voldestus stared into the distance as the surrounding dragons erupted into cheers of victory. Something told him that this was not yet over, and as the smoke cleared, he realised that he was correct.

Thalindor remained unharmed, a shimmering sphere rippled across the air around it, and hundreds of white robbed figures stood in an arch, glaring back at the surrounding dragons.

"Warlocks!" One nearby dragon yelled and the shocked cries echoed across the battlefield as Voldestus and the mages stared at one another, Plagar was with them.

Voldestus would make these mortals pay for this insolence with their lives. He drew upon his inner flame until it was utterly spent. The land around the golden dragon shook with his efforts and his eyes lit up in fury, but just as he was about to release his onslaught a large figure landed in the forest before him and spread its wings.

It took a moment for Voldestus to focus and truly take in the sight before him. A massive flame-covered dragon stood, wings outstretched and eyes wide open as they glared at the dragon king.

"You?!" Voldestus screamed "Impossible! I destroyed you!"

Drakarim simply glared.

Voldestus roared in furious anger. He unleashed his flame, but Drakarim was ready and released his own and as the dragons circled one another ready for combat, the Great Glade once again responded by assaulting Voldestus's allies with whatever it could summon.

Voldestus glanced around, alert and ready. "Where is that traitor, Meduz-Larr, is she here too?" He growled, but Drakarim shook his head and laughed.
"You should not have left her kingdom. She is there now, rebuilding her army," he replied.

Voldestus roared, full of rage. He breathed another searing hot flame at Drakarim, but he dodged the blast.

"How dare you defy me!" Voldestus roared. He lunged forward, and tried to kill Drakarim with one bite to his neck, but he spun away from the blow and raked his flaming claw across Voldestus's armoured chest. "What dragon king has to resort to wearing armour?" Drakarim mused. His taunts were inciting Voldestus. Drakarim wanted him to be angry. To make mistakes in his arrogance.

The two dragons stood before one another as the conflict around them continued.

"I've been wrecking your plans for many years." Drakarim continued and Voldestus's eyes narrowed.
"You! You were the crimson dragon!" He yelled.
"We could have had peace. We could have been free!" Drakarim shouted.

Voldestus drew in a deep breath, his enormous frame glowing from the effort and he then let forth a beam of golden fire that Drakarim barely managed to avoid. The swift blast glanced past him and Drakarim could feel the power of his opponent. He unleashed several bursts of his own, before a full inferno engulfed them both.

The two dragons' flames collided. Neither of them was able to gain any ground and the surrounding trees became nothing but cinders and ash as they continued their torrents of fire towards one another. Through the flames, Drakarim noticed Voldestus's eyes glance to the skies briefly, and he instantly reacted, managing to avoid an ice blast that shattered down across the earth.

It was the ice twins, Frostfang and Shatterclaw once again, attempting to repeat the surprise attack that they had pulled on Drakarim all those years ago.

Voldestus looked on in shock as Arwin Bloodborne leapt from Drakarim's back and plunged his twin blades into Icefang's side as he dropped within range. At the same time, Drakarim spun and extended his spiked tail, connecting with Shatterclaw. The blow launched him backwards through the trees, sending foliage and falling branches in all directions as the ice dragon screamed in pain.

"A bloodborne?!" Voldestus screamed in shock. "It cannot be?!"
"Oh, but it is!" Drakarim replied with a smirk.

Drakarim had no time to be concerned about Arwin, so instead he focused on the task at hand. Voldestus lunged forwards once more. This time his great golden maul made contact with Drakarim's armoured hide, piercing through the fire and gripping him tightly as searing hot pain exploded in Drakarim's side and he screamed in agony.

Drakarim pushed forwards into Voldestus and used his wings to give himself space to break free and more momentum to put Voldestus off balance and, but just as he pulled away, an icy blast struck his head, shattering on impact and stunning him momentarily. As Shatterclaw approached, Drakarim responded with an explosion of flame, fire ripping outwards in all directions with such force that the ice dragon staggered backwards, his face completely covered in flame.

Drakarim growled at Voldestus. "Really? You cannot face me alone?" He asked.

Voldestus did not respond, but instead leapt into the air to face Drakarim in an aerial battle. Drakarim responded, launching himself to meet the great golden dragon in the smoke filled skies above the battlefield.

Drakarim did not trust that Shatterclaw would stay out of the conflict for long. He knew he had to make this kill swiftly or he would once again become outnumbered.

The two dragons came together as they rose into the air, raking claws and teeth, splitting scales and digging deep into thick hide. Several times both Voldestus and Drakarim tried to land the final blow with a bite to the throat, but both the dragons were experienced, and neither of them were able to finish the fight.

Voldestus spotted a chance, and, using his larger bulk to spin the two dragons through the air, he released his grip and pushed with his hind legs, his claws cutting deep into Drakarim's flesh as he launched him towards the ground at furious speed.

A second later, Drakarim collided with the trunk of a Nedai tree, breaking its thick trunk in two with an ear splitting crunch and he roared in agony as he lay stunned before Voldestus.

Elsewhere, above the battlefield, Arwin sailed through the air, his blades still stuck deep within Icefang's chest, and the flames from the twin blades burning through his frozen hide.

Icefang tried to rid himself of the bloodborne by barrel rolling and diving through the air as he grimaced in agony, but Arwin was relentless, and he used the twin blades to climb up the dragon's neck.

Icefang yelled and dove towards the ground at great speed, plunging them both through the clouds towards the Great Glade below. Just before they struck the ground, Icefang tried to pull out of the dive. Arwin seized the moment and stabbed the base of the dragon's left wing with one of his blades, causing them both to thunder into the trees, where they rolled over and over into an open patch of ash and burning forest remnants.

There was a moment of silence across the scorched clearing as the confrontation continued some distance away. Smoke rolled across the area, as the roars of dragons met with the determined calls of the defenders. Thalindor was burning, but it had not yet fallen.

When Arwin came to, his head was pounding and he was concerned that he had lost sight of Icefang. He reached out briefly with the tether and found Drakarim's essence nearby. He breathed a sigh of relief and tried to focus on the task at hand.
The surrounding ground was utterly destroyed and a mix of earth golems, charred woodland animals and dragon corpses littered the area and burning ash lay underfoot. Eventually Arwin found Icefang's body a short distance away, so he pulled himself up with a pained grunt. He was exhausted and his body ached from head to foot.

He retrieved his blades from the ground and cautiously approached the area where Icefang had come to rest. The earth was churned up where the dragon had rolled across it and his blue blood was everywhere.

Arwin staggered on until he was close enough to touch Icefang. The dragon appeared to have died in the crash - his eyes were closed and he was still.

Arwin sighed in relief and turned away but just as he did so, Icefang's eyes opened and he immediately lunged for Arwin, but the young man was fast to react. He ducked to the side and plunged one of his blades into the side of the ice dragon's head, killing him instantly. Icefang's huge head slumped back onto the ash covered ground, finally silenced.

Arwin stood back and took a moment to gather his bearings. He had no time to celebrate the kill - he knew that Drakarim still needed him. He used the tether to guide him towards Drakarim's location, where Arwin hoped he would find him standing over the dead body of the dragon king.

Drakarim struggled to get back to his feet. He had endured a number of blows and the pain was ripping through his chest. Before he was able to get his focus back, he was once again under the onslaught of Shatterclaw's ice blast. Drakarim tried to ignite his flame, closing his eyes and giving it all the power that he possibly could, but he was seriously weakened and Shatterclaw had caught him by surprise.

As Drakarim threw everything that he had into pushing back the attack, the Great Glade around them thundered in response. The freezing blast was relentless and just as all seemed lost and Drakarim's body began to freeze, an earth golem burst forth from the ground and grappled with Shatterclaw. At the same time, vines sprouted forth from the earth, gripping the ice dragon in place and whipping around his neck to strangle him. Shatterclaw expelled a large gust of ice into the air as he attempted to fight back against these new combatants. He twisted and turned, snapping at the vines in a desperate attempt to free himself but the earth golem slammed both rocky fists into his head time and time again.

Eventually, he moved no more.

Voldestus knew that he had little time; he could not let the moment go. He drew upwards onto his hind legs and spread his wings wide as he took in a deep breath and his body began to ignite, one scale at a time until the golden dragon was a towering inferno.

Voldestus regarded Drakarim one last time before opening his huge mouth in preparation to unleash the final blow. Just as he was about to breathe the flame, a purple shaft of energy whizzed through the trees, blasting his armour plate from his chest with a resounding crack. Voldestus turned to address the new assailant, but the purple energy gripped him in a state of severe pain, excruciating, and all encompassing.

He was in shock, he hadn't felt this pain for many long years and fear gripped him.

Drakarim struggled to his feet as the ice melted away from his body and his flame slowly returned. He glanced towards Voldestus, who screamed in agony, eyes wide with terror. Drakarim sought the source of the purple energy to find the mage, Galen chanting with his staff outstretched, his eyes focused on the dragon.

"Now Drakarim! Finish this!" Arwin yelled, as he approached through the surrounding smoke.

Drakraim ignited his inner flame, his entire body pulsing behind the most powerful blast he had ever mastered. He thrust his head forward and an immense fire shot straight into the open wound on Voldestus's chest, pushing the great dragon backwards until eventually the flame turned blue, and it became focused, like a laser cutting through metal.

Voldestus's eyes, mouth and nose lit up as the blue flame destroyed him from the inside, and then, with one almighty explosion that rocked the entire Great Glade, Voldestus was launched backwards, bursting through Nedai tree after Nedai tree, until his body slumped into a smoking heap.

Drakarim fell to the ground and Arwin approached Galen, who still stood with his staff outstretched before him.
"Are you okay?" Arwin asked of the old mage. Galen seemed confused and dazed, but managed to nod weakly.

Drakarim staggered towards where Voldestus lay, his own wounds clearly visible and his whole body ached from the exertion. Voldestus seemed so much smaller now, his body broken and motionless. Drakarim noted that he was still breathing, and he moved forward, then slumped aside Voldestus's huge head. His breathing was laboured and blood was seeping from open wounds on his heavily charred face.

"It didn't have to be this way, brother." Drakarim said. "We could have had so much more. A life of peace."
Voldestus opened one eye weakly and sighed heavily, coughing up blood as he did so. "They will betray you…"
Voldestus's eyes then rolled up into his head, and they closed one final time as he expelled his last breath.

Drakarim sat motionless, his body wracked with pain. In that moment, as he lay next to the silent body of Voldestus, he felt so alone. Until he felt a hand upon his shoulder, and he turned to see Arwin, who had removed his helm. His face was full of sweat and his eyes glowed brightly.

"I am sorry," he said. "You had no choice."

Arwin knelt beside Drakarim and the two sat in silence while elsewhere on the battlefield, the remaining dragons had noted the king's death and many were withdrawing from the fight, fleeing to the skies while they still had the chance. Those that did stay were no longer fighting, but were bowing their heads low in a sign of submission and in mourning for their fallen king.

Within Thalindor, Nia moved between the bodies of the defenders as the orc hordes desperately retreated from battle. She hoped to find survivors to which she could administer healing but for most, it was just too late. The defenders had been victorious, but their losses had been significant.

Each and every elf who perished would be unable to help guide the forest into the night, and protect her for many years to come.

That honour had been ripped from them.

Nia found herself wandering through the streets of Thalindor, where survivors were still at work putting out fires and caring for the wounded. The civilians, some of whom had escaped through the portal to the Tower of Light, were slowly returning and stepping from the base of the Eldertree, bleary eyed and shocked at the sight that was before them.

Small elven children hugged their mothers close as they surveyed the scene. Thalindor was burning, and it lay vulnerable before the world for the first time in thousands of years. And as loved ones lay dead or were missing amongst the remains, the people of Thalindor were all too aware of the trials that still awaited them.

Nia made her way to where the Ethervail once stood. Before it lay the bodies of several ogres and tens of dozens of orcs and goblins. The fight here had been ferocious, and she stepped past the fallen defenders, feeling tears begin to stream down her cheeks, and she knew what was coming.

A few moments later, she discovered the body of Elunara, broken and blooded. She knelt and cradled her mentor's head in her arms, sobbing. Elunara's hand fell limply to the side and a silver coin rolled across the floor, where Oranlire collected it and joined Nia's side. He too was heavily wounded, and his face drawn from the efforts of battle.

"Mourn the loss, my child. She was the greatest of us," he said, then handed Nia the coin of Elunara. "Keep it close and she will always be with you. She was so proud of you, and rightly so."

Elsewhere, Heg and Barn celebrated the victory. Each of them had accumulated some wounds that would eventually scar and make a great campfire story. Meanwhile the Fort Valian defenders cheered as they came together to celebrate.

"Couldn't have done it without you." Barn said to Heg, who grinned and replied, "Of course you couldn't."

She knelt down at Grimwolf's body, and pried the warlord's battleaxe from his dead hands, whilst throwing aside her old metal hammer.

Barn laughed and said "Another upgrade Heg?"
Heg nodded and laughed, "Of course it is!"

Peace and freedom

Present day

Thalindor

At the base of the Eldertree, Drakarim stood before the high council of Thalindor, and the two remaining Ancients, Oranlire of Oakland and **Alaric Stormblade**. The city's residents had gathered for a grand ceremony, where those who had stood against the dragon horde were remembered and honoured. At the base of the Eldertree, there were thousands of garlands, one for each brave defender who fell protecting Thalindor and the tree was lit up with tiny enchanted lights for each and every lost soul.

Nialandra and Giggles watched with pride as Princess **Seraphina** addressed the gathered crowd.

"Arwin Bloodborne and Drakarim the kind. For your incredible bravery and valiant protection of this last great city of the elven peoples, I do declare that you shall hereby be named as 'Defenders of the Glade" the princess said. "You shall forever be welcome within Thalindor, and as well as our gratitude, you will always have our aid if ever you request it."

The princess held out a hand to **Oranlire**, and he approached as she continued. "This great enchantment, gifted upon you by Ancient **Oranlire**, shall give you the ability to return here, in the blink of an eye. For you shall always have refuge amongst us, and we thank you for your devotion to our city's protection and our peoples continued freedoms!"

The gathered crowd cheered loudly as **Oranlire** placed the enchantments on Drakarim and Arwin, many of them throwing flowers across the scene in celebration. Drakarim, full of emotion, glanced down at Arwin, who was beaming with pride, his dragon helm tucked under his arm, polished and cleaned by Tobbin.

Nia and Giggles approached Drakarim, each of them with a huge grin on their face.
"Well done." they said together and Giggles gave Drakarim's claw a huge hug.
"Thank you." he replied with a gentle smile.
"It's been requested that I meet with the council. I will speak to you shortly," Nia explained, and then she left.

As Nia approached Princess Seraphina and the council members, they greeted her with friendly smiles, and a warm welcome.

"Nialandra, you have done the city an extraordinary justice. We doubted your ambitions, but ultimately you have proven that we were in the wrong. Ancient Elunara had faith in you and now, as a result, we have many strong allies within dragon kind, and a chance at a new stable beginning for the known world." The princess approached Nia and placed her hands on her shoulders. "It has been agreed with those at the Tower of Light and the various settlements that Thalindor will stand as a new capital city for the Allied Realms. We would like to offer you a place with us upon the council, and as the Sentinel of the Eldertree."

Nia was taken aback. At first, she didn't know what to say in response. The other council members smiled at her, awaiting her answer.

"Allow me to explain what this title would entail. You would be charged with keeping the Eldertree's secrets from falling into the wrong hands. The tree is everything to our people, but its true value has remained untapped for an eternity. Perhaps there are areas of knowledge within it that we should be seeking and utilising. We may unlock further information about the true reason for our own creation, for we are beings of the Eldertree, and we have much yet to discover about ourselves."

Nia nodded her understanding and considered her answer for a moment. This was indeed a great honour, one that would allow her to stand amongst the council. To explore ways to open communication with the other Pillars of Twilight and of course keep Thalindor safe from further harm, more specifically from the traitor that Oranlire and Elunara had indicated.

"I accept." she said proudly. Princess Seraphina and the others smiled and clapped in response and Oranlire winked.
"Then it is done!" Princess Seraphina said. Nia thought for a moment - she did have one last request.
"I do need to ask you for one thing Princess, if I may?"
Seraphina nodded, "of course, go ahead."
"I do not believe that this has never been done in our history, but it is imperative that I request this all the same." The princess was intrigued. She raised an eyebrow and asked Nia to continue.

"For months now, I have been the carer for the small human child who we named Giggles. As I understand it, an elf has never parented a human child, but Giggles and I are not to be separated. I would very much like to adopt her as my own, and raise her here within Thalindor, amongst us elves, and with the guidance of an elven upbringing. This is the request I make."

The princess smiled and she said happily "This request does not need any thought, Nialandra Kalin'tor. I will see to it that you are officially named the parent to Giggles, now known as Kalin'tor."
The princess then lent forward, and whispered jokingly "Although could we look at a different first name for the child?"
Nia laughed, along with the others present, "We could," she said. "However, that would be a decision for Giggles. She does like it!"

Elsewhere in Thalindor, Arwin laughed as he watched Heg, Barn, and the other dwarves attempt to reconstruct a badly damaged elven home. The dwarves and humans did not understand how the homes were constructed, but they did their best to help.

"I just don't see how this gate even works." Heg said with frustration as she examined a piece of twisted wood in her hands.
"That's not a gate Heg, that's a latrine." Barn replied with a smirk, Heg dropped it to the floor, a look of disgust crossing her face as the others fell about laughing at her misfortune.

Arlestra watched silently from nearby. The valian had always been distant from the rest of the group, but perhaps been even more so after her time at the Tower of Light. Arwin noticed her watching, so he approached her with a friendly smile and a nod.

"Are you okay?" he asked.
"Yes. I am fine." her voice echoed through Arwin's mind. He sat down next to her and they watched the dwarves in silence for a moment.
"I think that we are going to stay in Thalindor for a while. I need to be close to Drakarim, and help protect the glade," Arwin said, "would you stay here as well?"

Arlestra regarded the others for a moment in silence, thoughtfully considering her answer.

Finally, she turned to Arwin and said "You have your family now Arwin. Heg, Barn and Drakarim included. You're the last of the dragon riders and your place is here."

"However, I do not have a place. As the last of my people, I feel it is my duty to perhaps try to return to Nerfanu and maybe, in time, return the holy city to its former glory."

Arlestra's words resonated with Arwin and he recalled that fateful day when Joselle and so many others died in the attack at Fort Valian.

"I understand," he said. "Perhaps if you can activate the portal from the other end, we would not be so distant."
He placed a hand on Arlestra's shoulder and said "On the matter of family, you have all of us here, Arlestra. Always."

Arlestra appreciated that. They watched the dwarves some more and then Arwin turned to her.

"Be careful. For if those spirits still linger, it will not be possible to take the city back."
Arlestra smiled. "Understood, Arwin Bloodborne." she said. Arwin's purple eyes briefly flared up and the two friends hugged one another.

Reidekaan Hills

The Reidekaan Hills were home to a small tribe of ancient hill giants, who had remained hidden within their homeland during the reign of the dragon king. The giants were pacifists, and their peaceful demeanour was deemed to be the perfect choice for the important task ahead. To bury the body of Voldestus and keep its location a secret from the outside world.

The hill giants were essentially a mass of rocks, which somehow held together and were capable of movement, though slow and cumbersome.

The Giants drove a tomb into the rocks, big enough to hold the body of the golden dragon and ensure that was where it stayed.

Drakarim and Meduz-Larr stood alongside one another, watching silently as two huge hill giants carried the broken body into the entrance of the great tomb. Their bodies rumbled as the stones ground against one another, reverberating across the landscape.

This day was a solemn occasion for Drakarim, but it was also the final chapter in a period of terror and injustice. The end of the reign of Voldestus and the Allied Realms rebirth.

Drakarim and Meduz-Larr bowed their heads one final time as the hill giants stood back. The hill appeared to come alive, rock upon rock rolled over one another until there was no sign of the tomb at all from the surface. The giants turned to the two dragons and then they too collapsed into the hillside, completely hidden from view once again.

"Let us hope it remains a secret." Meduz-Larr said at last. Drakarim nodded.
"Now we must part ways, Meduz. I have pledged to return to defend the Great Glade."
Meduz-Larr smiled and placed a claw upon Drakarim.
"As it should be, Drakarim the kind. As it should be," she then turned, her eyes ignited with the fusing of mana and she launched herself into the skies.

Drakarim took one last look at the entrance to Voldestus's tomb and allowed himself a smile.
"Sleep now brother. For you are free," he said, and he too, took to the skies and headed home.

Epilogue

Galen awoke with a start within his chambers at the Tower of Light, and for just a brief second, he thought he saw the figure of an elderly man, dressed in long dark robes, standing over him. He shook his head to clear it, and sat up on his bunk, before standing and moving to the side table, upon which a small bowl was set with water and a flannel.

Galen washed his face, letting the cold water seep into his skin. The feeling was refreshing and he sighed happily. Then he placed the flannel over his eyes and wiped away the sleep from the night before.
"You did well to kill the golden dragon," a man's voice said from somewhere within the room. Galen spun around with a start, but his chambers were empty.

Galen shook his head to try to fight back against the voice and it fell silent once again.

He was alone, with only the staff for company. He collected it from against the wall by his bunk and he stood for a moment examining the gem imbued within. For a moment the light was as it always had been, a bright blue, shimmering gently. But in a second, a flash of light so quick that he may have missed it, the blue switched to a dark purple and Galen was sure he saw the face of the elderly man once again, peering out from within.

At that moment, there was a knock at the door to Galen's chambers, and he opened it to find Plagar standing outside, waiting patiently. Plagar noticed the strain upon his friend's face almost immediately.

"Are you feeling OK?" He asked.
"I think we need to talk," Galen replied.

A darkness rises

Mordire was an elder dragon that had been all but forgotten.

She was ancient. She was powerful, and twisted beyond imagination. For when Mordire first hatched in the early days of the warlock's experiments, they felt as though they had achieved a triumphant victory.

This dragon was far more intelligent than any of her predecessors, and she was larger and stronger too.

Mordire was a completely black dragon, her matte appearance and rough scales, combined with white eyes and long, pointed snout gave her a terrifying visage. In addition, Mordire had the unique ability to not only breathe fire, but also spit poisonous acid that would burn her victims through to the bone. What the warlocks did not realise was that Mordire had been marred by darkness.

The Spire of the Wyvern stood upon ancient grounds. It was common knowledge that the area around the spire used to be civilised, and there were many ruins that backed up these theories. The ancient peoples of the black marshes were no longer there, and their deep history was largely unknown.

Feyrites, as they were once known, were deeply secretive and not technologically advanced. As such, their histories were not well documented, but feyrites did have a deep understanding of magic, though not in a sense that common mages would understand today, unless they were practising the black magic art of necromancy or dark spiritualism, as this magic used the death of a living being to create powerful and extensive spells.

As such suffering was used to create the magic, the spells themselves were unavoidably tainted by darkness. It was these magics that eventually were the undoing of the feyrite people, and as the Spire of the

Wyvern was surrounded by lands tainted by dark magic, so too was the tower, distorted and twisted by an unseen, powerful force.

As the warlocks continued their experiments, it was unavoidable that such a taint would interfere with their experiments and Mordire was a result of this. The black dragon's heart and mind were driven primarily by hatred and chaos. A dangerous and terrifying concoction for the birth of a new breed of dragon.

In the months after her creation, the warlocks became acutely aware that she would be a clear and present danger if she were allowed to continue to grow. As such, she was marked to be destroyed and it was completed with urgency.

Following her death, Mordire's body was disposed of along with many other failed experiments in the large, bottomless pit known to the dragons as 'The Deeps'.

It was here, in the darkness, many thousands of feet below the surface of the world that Mordire's final incredible ability came to fruition. For Mordire did not die. The black dragon was blessed with the power of eternal regeneration, and she arose once again.

At the time of her death, Mordire was only partially formed, with one wing much smaller than the other, and standing at a height of just five metres, she was killed long before her prime. But breathe again Mordire did, and weeks after her body had been disposed of, she was reanimated.

Her half-rotten frame, riddled with maggots, pulled itself through deep piles of dead and forgotten dragon corpses. It was here, in the dark, surrounded by the corpses of her brothers and sisters, that Mordire learnt of her place in the world, discarded, and unwanted, deemed a failure by those who created her. As the rains fell high above, slowly pouring to the bottom of The Deeps, the undying dragon would slowly gain her strength.

For Mordire did not need sustenance. She did not feed, but she did slumber, and it was during her infested rest that the taint within would grip her in its icy embrace, and wrack her mind with the musings of one driven by chaos and nothing but the black.

"Tie to me the minds of those who have expired."

And when Mordire opened her eyes, their white fire burning in the dark of the deep, she found her new purpose.

She reached out and touched the bodies of her fallen kin. She nurtured their bones in her embrace.

She gave them a new life. Her life.

They writhed and pulled and clawed their way free, moaning and crying to their new mistress, and step by painful step, the undead dragons clawed their way to the surface…

Printed in Great Britain
by Amazon